A CHARLIE & SIMM MYSTERY

THE
OTHER
SIDE

A.J. McCARTHY

Black Rose Writing | Texas

©2022 by A.J. McCarthy

All rights reserved. No part of this book may be reproduced, stored in a retrieval system or transmitted in any form or by any means without the prior written permission of the publishers, except by a reviewer who may quote brief passages in a review to be printed in a newspaper, magazine or journal.

The author grants the final approval for this literary material.

First printing

This is a work of fiction. Names, characters, businesses, places, events, and incidents are either the products of the author's imagination or used in a fictitious manner. Any resemblance to actual persons, living or dead, or actual events is purely coincidental.

ISBN: 978-1-68513-042-8
PUBLISHED BY BLACK ROSE WRITING
www.blackrosewriting.com

Printed in the United States of America
Suggested Retail Price (SRP) $19.95

The Other Side is printed in Adobe Garamond Pro

*As a planet-friendly publisher, Black Rose Writing does its best to eliminate unnecessary waste to reduce paper usage and energy costs, while never compromising the reading experience. As a result, the final word count vs. page count may not meet common expectations.

To good friends and good times
Rodney, Margaret, Kenny, and Luce:
Do you remember that weekend?

THE
OTHER
SIDE

CHAPTER 1

Some days, she longed for something different; an event, a catalyst, excitement splashed upon her existence. Other days, she wished time stood still and nothing changed.

Charlie sighed as she polished glasses and lined them up on the counter. Frank worked by her side, preparing drink orders for the few people scattered throughout the pub. Monday mid-afternoons were not known for a rush of clientele, even in downtown Montreal. The meagre lunch crowd had cleared out, and it was too early for after-work patrons.

"What's up?" Frank's movements didn't slow as he flicked a glance toward his business partner and best friend. At six-foot four, the twenty-five-year-old was a full foot taller than Charlie. Even with her long brown hair tied into a topknot, his height and muscular frame made him look twice her size.

"I don't know. I guess it's just one of those days." Charlie set the towel on the counter and faced her friend. "Do you realize I've worked in this bar since I was sixteen? That's twelve years. It's like I've done nothing else."

"Are you unhappy about that?"

"Sometimes I feel like I missed something."

"You went to university. You got a degree. You inherited this bar." He tapped his index finger on her forearm. "And you got a husband last year. You should be grateful."

Charlie resumed her polishing. "I'm not complaining. It's just... something."

Frank's raised brow held meaning. The 'something' was no secret.

Charlie grimaced. "Yeah, I know. But I'm also worried about Simm. I think he's unhappy." She raised a hand to forestall Frank's rebuttal. "I know. I say that a lot lately. It could be my imagination."

A fierce wind sent a torrent of raindrops against the window, threatening to wipe away the words "Butler's Pub". Pedestrians on Drummond Street clasped coat collars under their chins. A middle-aged couple huddled under the dark green awning as they battled with umbrellas.

Charlie's frown deepened. If April showers brought May flowers, she wondered what this May rain would deliver. The foul weather certainly didn't boost business.

To contradict her, a man stumbled into the pub, as if a large hand shoved him over the threshold. A drenched jacket did little to protect his hunched shoulders, and the hood cast a shadow over his face. The newcomer straightened, caught sight of the bar, and shuffled the remaining ten feet to drag himself onto a heavy barstool. He thrust back his hood and leaned his elbows on the dark mahogany counter.

Charlie's eyes narrowed as her gaze zeroed in on him. "Craig Reeve? Is that you?"

The man focused on her. "You don't recognize me?"

"Yeah, sure. It must be the light," she said, forcing a reassuring smile onto her face.

Craig was a long-time customer of Butler's, often visiting with his wife Holly and, sometimes, with friends. He was a cheerful, slap-you-on-the-back guy, always ready for a joke and a laugh. Charlie remembered him as tall and broad, his head held high as he surveyed the bar, on the lookout for excitement.

Craig's current look was a sharp contrast to her memory of him, as if he had shriveled into a caricature of himself. In his early thirties, he looked at least ten years older. Forty pounds lighter, too. His energy and joie de vivre seemed to have taken a hike. She searched her mind to recall the last time she'd seen him.

Charlie cast a concerned glance toward Frank before she smiled at her customer. "What can I get you to drink?"

"I'll have a beer. Whatever you have on tap."

"Kilkenny, wasn't that your drink?" From the corner of her eye, she saw Frank's ebony hand expertly filling a tall glass from the spout. "It's been a while since we've seen you. Were you away? Sick?"

Charlie danced around the subject, but she wanted to understand what had happened to him.

Craig's head slumped, and he muttered a few words Charlie strained to hear.

"What was that?" She leaned forward and tilted her head toward him.

"Almost a year," the man said. "A horrible, lousy year."

The emotional pain in his voice made Charlie's breath catch. "What happened? Tell me."

Craig raised his head and met her gaze. "You remember Damon? Tall guy. In good shape. Used to come here with us."

An image of a handsome man with a mischievous grin flashed through her mind. "Yeah, I remember him." An ominous feeling washed over her.

"He's gone." Craig scrubbed his hands over his face.

Charlie's wide-eyed gaze flickered to Frank before she reached over and laid a hand on Craig's forearm. "He died?"

He shrugged. "We assume he did. They never found him. It's been terrible. It tore us apart. I lost my job as a restaurant manager. Now I knead dough at a pizzeria. Holly left me." His voice broke on his last words.

A chill crept up Charlie's spine and eased into her heart. "He disappeared?" Her voice was barely above a whisper, as if they were children telling stories around a campfire.

Craig focused on the amber liquid in his glass and nodded. "The police, search dogs, volunteers; no one found anything. They finally gave up. He could've drowned or got carried off by someone or something. Either way, he's probably dead."

Charlie slid out from behind the bar and onto the barstool next to Craig, her attention focused on him. "Tell me everything. Where did this happen?"

"Near Wakefield."

The name meant nothing to her. "Where is that?"

"The Gatineau Valley. On the other side of the Ontario border, across from Ottawa. We rented a cottage for the 1st of July long weekend. Just to hang out and have fun." He snorted without humor. "A hell of a lot of fun it was."

Craig frowned and extracted his phone from his pocket. He squinted at the screen. "Damn. Gotta go."

"Wait." Charlie clutched his sleeve, her eyes bright. "I want to know what happened."

"I don't have time now. I'll come back."

"Come tomorrow. I have someone I'd like you to talk to."

Craig nodded, his gaze unfocused, as he zipped up his jacket. "Yeah, okay. I'll see you then."

Charlie's forehead was creased in thought as she watched him amble out the door. She turned toward Frank. His brawny frame was rigid, and he stared at her through dark, narrowed eyes. They had known each other for years; Frank was her best friend. She needed to justify herself.

"Craig needs help." Charlie reclaimed her seat on the barstool and crossed her arms on the counter. "Look what happened to him. He's not even the same guy."

"I'm not arguing with you."

"Why are you staring?"

"He won't like it." Frank shook his head as he picked up the rag and wiped the counter again.

"I think he will. Eventually he will."

"He didn't want to go back."

"He won't. He'll be helping a friend of mine. There's a big difference." Charlie's serious gaze pleaded for her friend's understanding. A slender finger pointed toward the door. "Did you see the change in Craig? He's gone through hell. Can you imagine how Damon's wife feels? They need closure." She paused. "Besides, I think Simm needs this too. It's a win-win."

"You're probably right." Frank grinned at her. "Despite your many charms, I think the man is suffering from a slight case of boredom."

"I hope that's it." Charlie stared outside at the teeming rain. She slid off the stool and headed to the back of the pub. "I can fix boredom."

CHAPTER 2

Charlie burst through the door at the top of the stairs, sidestepped around a plastic case of power tools, and entered the office. A year earlier, she gave up her apartment on Bishop Street, and they renovated the rental above the pub to accommodate an office and their living quarters. It was still a work-in-progress; functional but in perpetual construction.

Two heads lifted and pivoted in her direction. One of them belonged to a handsome, dark-haired man with chocolate-brown eyes, a straight patrician nose, and a welcoming smile on his full lips.

The other was also handsome, with the same shade of brown eyes. He wore a soulful expression, and his nose was barely visible. He rose to his feet, stretched his round, squat body, and padded over to Charlie. She bent and gathered him in her arms, planting a kiss on his dark pug nose before switching her attention to the man at the desk.

"I hope you're not planning to kiss me after kissing him," he said with a wry expression.

"C'mon, he's your son."

"He's a dog. And a smelly one, too. He needs a bath."

The animal cast a concerned look at his mistress.

"Don't worry, Harley. He's just grumpy because he's paying bills." Charlie planted another kiss on the dog's head.

"I'm always paying bills. It never ends." The man ran his hands through his thick hair.

"Now you understand how I used to feel. You don't know how glad I am that you took on the job."

The pub had originally belonged to a close family friend. Charlie worked in the business part-time as a student, evolving to a full-time manager after graduating from university. When the owner, Jim O'Reilly, died nine years earlier, he left the establishment to Charlie, and she altered the name from O'Reilly's to Butler's. Last year, her new husband and her old friend Frank came on as partners to help her run and expand the business.

Charlie circled the desk, swiveled the man's chair to the side, and settled onto his lap, the dog still in her arms. "I've got news for you, Simm."

"Good news or bad news?" Strong arms circled her waist.

"Hmm. Some of both, actually."

"I sense a mystery."

The pug snuggled between them and snorted a few times before closing his eyes and settling in for a nap.

"Did you ever meet Craig?" Charlie asked.

"Can't say I recall him." Simm stretched to kiss her cheek. The dog grumbled in disagreement.

"I haven't seen him in ages, almost a year."

"All right. What about him?"

"He was here earlier. He started to tell a terrible story about a trip to a cottage in the Gatineau area for a long weekend last summer. One of his friends disappeared. Vanished. They never got over it. Craig lost his job, and he and his wife broke up."

"I'm guessing this is the bad news. How did it happen?" Simm's brow creased.

"I didn't find out. He had to leave. But he'll be back tomorrow. I thought you could…"

"Oh no, you don't." He hoisted her off his lap and stood, looking down at her from his height of six feet. The disgruntled dog slid to the floor between them. "I'm a businessman now, remember? Your partner. No more private investigating for me."

Charlie faced her husband. "But Simm…"

"No. I've moved on. I'm not going back. We agreed this is what we wanted."

Charlie braced her feet apart and put her fists on her hips. "Winston..."

The man advanced toward her, his brows lowered, and his finger pointed threateningly at her. "Don't call me that, Charlene," he said with a sneer. "How many times have I told you?"

Charlie bent and snatched the pug off the floor. She held the animal to her chest, his flat snout facing the ominous-looking man who bore down on them. Wide, worried eyes dominated the dog's face.

"Frank!" Charlie's shout for help reverberated through the room as she backed toward the door, her gaze never leaving Simm's. Footsteps pounded up the stairs, and a draft of air surged through the door as it burst open.

"I don't believe this." Frank huffed out a breath. "Not again. How many times do I have to rescue you?" He snatched the dog from Charlie's grasp. "You don't need to see this, Harley."

As soon as the animal was clear of Charlie's arms, Simm sprang forward and nabbed her by the waist. High-pitched squeals and laughter overpowered Frank's mumbled 'Get a room' before he stomped down the stairs.

CHAPTER 3

Just before noon the next day, Simm slid onto a barstool, unable to hold back a dejected sigh. Frank's smirk didn't go unnoticed.

Simm fended him off with a raised hand. "Don't say a word."

"I didn't say anything. I wasn't going to." Frank wiped down the counter. "I feel for you, Bud." Customers wandered in and took seats in front of the television that hung over the bar. Others opted for a table. Frank signaled Sarah, the new server, to take orders.

Frank was indispensable to Charlie and Simm. Last year, they expanded their business by acquiring another pub a few blocks over on Peel Street, and Frank leapt at the chance to become a full partner and support them in running the two establishments. Melissa, a longtime server, helped handle the managerial tasks, and the two made an excellent team.

Frank had suffered through his own struggles in the past year, the worst of which involved a breakup with his longtime partner, Paul. Heartbroken, he soldiered on, with Charlie and Simm's encouragement. A strong relationship developed between the two men in Charlie's life, and the bartender was their anchor.

"I know what you're thinking," Simm said. "I lost another battle. But I'll just hear the guy's story. Nothing more. I'm doing it for Charlie."

"I understand." Frank's shaved head reflected the soft overhead lighting as he nodded in agreement.

"I won't take on a case. Nothing like that."

"Of course not."

"I gave up my license, and my hands are full with everything here."

"They sure are."

A hand settled on Simm's shoulder and gave it a light squeeze. He twisted his head to see his wife smiling sweetly at him. He was a sucker for that smile. "Are you finished with your meet-and-greet?" he asked her.

"Yep. We're both happy." She looked at Harley, who stood by her side, his curly tail wagging. Three times a day, Charlie and the dog paraded around the block. Harley refused to deviate from the ritual. The shopkeepers and regular customers routinely had a treat ready for him as he passed. Often Charlie heard a "*Bonjour*, Harley" before anyone took the time to greet her. She didn't mind. It offered her a chance to mingle with the locals and catch up on the neighborhood news.

"Let's take a booth," she said, nodding toward a quiet corner. "Do you want to join us, Frank?"

"I'd love to, but I'd rather not leave Sarah on her own. The nice weather is drawing a crowd."

Simm recognized that as the excuse it was. Frank had no intention of getting drawn into his wife's plan.

"Can Harley hang out with you?" Charlie said.

Frank swung the gate wide, and the pug circled behind the bar and settled into his bed underneath the counter, content to watch his friend work.

Charlie and Simm retreated to a private booth after Frank assured them he'd direct Craig to their table. He made good on his promise. Their visitor arrived a few minutes later and settled into the seat opposite them.

Simm studied Craig as they exchanged greetings.

"Yeah, I think we met a while back," Simm said. He didn't mention he wouldn't have recognized the other man. He'd use the word 'emaciated' to describe the husky man he recollected. And the jovial gleam in his eye had vanished.

"Almost a year ago, before it happened."

"We want to hear your story," Charlie said. "Simm's a private investigator. He's…"

Simm held up his hand, hoping to stave off any further explanations from Charlie. He already had enough damage control to do. "I used to be a private investigator. Until I married Charlie and became a partner in the bar. We bought another pub, and it's more than enough work to manage."

Simm didn't get into the details of his past life. He had embarked on a career as a cop before taking on the business of private investigating. He'd met Charlie as a PI. A little over a year ago, she hired him to track down the person responsible for sending her anonymous letters and packages. He quickly fell for the pretty pub owner and pitched himself into a new line of business. He was content with that role. Almost.

Charlie interrupted his thoughts, "I really wanted to hear your story, and Simm is interested, too. He may have insights to offer."

"Any help would be great." Craig spoke in a dull monotone. "Honestly, in the past year, no one's come up with anything. The cops assume he drowned."

Charlie reached over and squeezed the man's hand. "Why don't you tell us how it happened?"

"It's kind of a long story."

"We've got all afternoon. We'll order food, and you can take your time." Charlie raised a hand to signal a server before focusing her attention on the man opposite her.

Craig sighed before he spoke. "We wanted to have an enjoyable weekend. Get out of the city, just adults, change our minds. Holly's parents were happy to keep the kids for us. Bryan and Megan found someone to take care of theirs for a couple of days. We really looked forward to it."

"Where was it?" Simm asked.

"In the Gatineau Valley, close to Wakefield. We found the place online. It had everything we wanted. It was the right size for six. On a quiet section of the Gatineau River. The perfect spot."

******

"This is perfect. Even better than in the pictures." Megan roamed the kitchen, opening drawers and peeking into cupboards. "It has everything we need." A bright smile lit her face. Her long blond ponytail flipped from one shoulder to the other as she spun around and flung open the fridge. "This'll soon be full."

The three couples had travelled in two cars, and both trunks were full of their bags, groceries, and enough wine and beer to keep them going for a couple of days, they hoped.

"It's open and bright. I like that." Holly admired the windows that filled one wall and afforded them a prime view of the trees with the river in the background. "Beautiful," she said.

Craig wrapped his arms around her from behind. "Just like you." He tucked her shoulder-length brown hair behind her ear and kissed her neck.

"Cut it out, guys. We still have to unload the cars. There'll be time for the horizontal mambo later." Damon swept past them and deposited a box of food on the long wooden table. A man with energy to spare, he chafed his hands together and addressed the group. "There's more where that came from."

Bryan shot a look at Damon. "Yeah, we'll be right there." He pointed outside. "There's a fire pit in front."

"The owner mentioned he had firewood for us," Craig said. "Hopefully, enough for the weekend."

"If not, I'll get more. There's gotta be a store nearby."

"Leave it to Bryan," Damon said with a laugh as he set another box on the table. "Always looking for a store. I bet you can't wait to go off on your own, snooping around."

The unassuming man shrugged his shoulders. Bryan was used to Damon's teasing, and like most things, it slid off his back. Of medium height, with brown, closely cropped hair and a stocky build, he resembled a teddy bear and had a personality to match.

"Pete seemed nice." Megan said, deflecting the ribbing aimed at her husband. "We can contact him if we need something."

When they had arrived, the owner climbed from a pickup truck and greeted them. Pete Dunn, a tall, heavily built man in his late forties, handed them the key and showed the group around the outdoor area before wishing them a pleasant weekend.

"Is there room in the fridge for the beer?" Damon heaved two cases of beer onto the kitchen counter.

"Food gets priority. You guys can put your beer in coolers if you have to." His wife, Alanna, flashed a sharp, brown-eyed glance at him and handed Holly perishables to fill the shelves of the refrigerator.

"Let's check out the bedrooms and decide who goes where. We can dump our stuff." Bryan headed toward the stairwell, bags weighing down each arm. A few seconds later, he coaxed the others up. "You should see the view. We have dibs on the first room on the left."

Bodies scrambled up the stairs, followed by a room-to-room scurry. The bedrooms were similar, but the views varied. Craig and Holly reaped the second-best view. Damon, the last one up the stairs, grudgingly settled for the last room.

"It's bigger than the others." Alanna's tone was conciliatory. "I like it."

Damon raised his voice. "If I wasn't alone to unload the cars, I wouldn't have been last."

"Quit your grumbling. How much time will you spend in your room, anyway?" Craig said.

"I don't know. It depends how eager my wife is." A wolfish grin lit Damon's face, and his blue eyes glimmered with mischief. Alanna nudged her elbow into his ribs, and he doubled over in fake pain amid the laughter of his friends.

Backpacks, overnight bags, and duffel bags were tossed onto beds before the six set off to explore the outdoors.

"There's the path that leads to the river." Damon sprinted ahead. "Last one there is a rotten egg."

The others, accustomed to their friend's antics, maintained their lazy pace. In their early thirties, they lived in a western suburb of Montreal and craved the quiet and beauty of nature.

Large, leafy trees surrounded the property. Despite houses within walking distance, they had the illusion of complete privacy and isolation. Huge globes of white hydrangea blooms, bright orange daylilies, and purple irises sprouting from mounds of skinny green leaves filled the gardens and encased the well-trimmed lawn. Purple and pink clematis climbed the south wall of the house.

The approaching dusk of Friday evening made the path difficult to navigate, but the verdant hostas on either side served as a guide. Several exclamations and a few ripe swear words filled the air as they made their way over small rocks and roots that poked through the hard-packed earth. The laments turned to awed cries of joy when the group faced the expanse of water. The gold and orange of the sunset reflected off the river in a postcard-perfect picture.

Cell phones captured the moment.

The discovery of two overturned canoes to the left of them, partly screened by shrubs, broke the serenity. "Look at this." Damon leapt into the greenery, oblivious to the damage the damp, muddy ground inflicted on his shoes. He tugged on a canoe. "Where are the paddles?"

"Must be at the house." Bryan pointed to the other side. "There's a pedal boat over there."

"Let's go out." Damon labored to turn the canoe upright.

Alanna cast a nervous glance at the river. "It's almost dark. We can wait 'til tomorrow."

"It's time to get the barbeque going and uncork a bottle of wine."

Shouts of agreement from four people greeted Holly's suggestion.

Craig pivoted toward the path. "I'll check for wood. We can sit by the fire."

******

"Keep in mind we were from the suburbs of a large city. We were familiar with barbeques, but rivers and fire pits were from our days of camping with our families years before." Craig's gaze strayed to the window beside him.

People crowded the now-sunny downtown streets of Montreal, eager to be out of the office buildings and into the burgeoning spring warmth. Many selected Butler's for their lunch break, and the din of conversation rose. Charlie glanced over her shoulder to see if everything was under control, but Frank had called in extra help. Confident they had time to listen to the rest of his story, she urged Craig to continue.

"We were like teenagers, let out of the house by our parents. Man, it felt good. That first night, we cooked up hamburgers and relaxed around the fire, drinking beer and wine. We laughed and told stories until midnight. At that point, we called it a night. We wanted to get up early and enjoy Saturday to its fullest."

Craig stared blankly at his hands clasped in front of him.

******

Damon shuffled down the stairs and stretched long and hard. "Boy, that smells good. My timing's perfect."

"When the work is done, as usual." Craig accompanied his remark with a wide smile. He eyed the heavily laden table.

Damon sauntered into the kitchen and cackled. He snatched a piece of bacon off a platter and his eyes brightened. "Oh, muffins. Who made those? If I knew they were here, I'd have been up long ago. They'd all be gone, and I'd be nice and fat." He patted his flat stomach. A grin like that of a well-satisfied Cheshire cat spread over his face.

"That'll be the day. You eat like a horse and never gain a pound." Bryan set a thermal pot of coffee on the table.

"It's because I lead a good life, my friend," Damon said as he patted Bryan's belly. "You should follow my example." His arm waved toward Alanna with a flourish. "I take excellent care of my beautiful wife. I'm quiet. I never swear or talk bad about people." His eyes widened, and he gazed at his friends with an innocent expression, pretending to be surprised by the guffaws of laughter. He raised a long finger in the air. "And I never lie or invent stories."

Chuckling, Bryan took a seat at the table and smiled as the others followed suit. "I can't wait to jump into that river."

"How cold do you think it is?" A frown marred Megan's smooth forehead.

Damon talked while he chewed on a muffin. "I tell you what. I'll get in first. Then I'll tell you if it's warm. You trust me, don't you?"

"Not for a second. I'll dip my toe in and find out for myself."

"Smart move, Megan." Alanna's remark earned an exaggerated hiking of her husband's eyebrows. She swung her gaze to Craig. "You talked to the owner. Did you ask how safe it is to swim in the river? What about the current?"

Craig swallowed a bite of bacon. "He said it's perfectly safe and calm in this area, all the way up to Wakefield. Like swimming in a lake."

Equipped with a cooler and folding chairs, the group headed to the small private beach on the riverbank. Bryan dropped the paddles beside the dock and helped Craig and Damon haul the canoes out of the overgrowth. The women set up the chairs on the dock, facing the sun that promised a warm day ahead.

"This is beautiful," Holly said. "There are hardly any other cottages. None on the other side. It's so peaceful."

Megan murmured a contented response as she settled into a lounge chair and raised her face to the sun.

Alanna was bent over the cooler as the sound of stampeding feet hammered on the wooden dock. Strong arms seized her waist and swept her into the water. The river swallowed her screech, but Damon's laughter echoed through the air as he surfaced first.

"You asshole!" Alanna pelted a furious glance at her husband before she swam to the ladder.

"Ah, c'mon. You said you wanted to swim."

"Yes. On my own terms and once I took off my cover-up." She squeezed water from her dark-brown ponytail before doing the same with the black crocheted garment concealing her bathing suit.

Damon kept himself afloat beside the dock and flashed her a grin. "Take it off and come in. You can take it all off. Nobody'll look, will they?"

Normally, someone may have responded to his joke, but everyone remained silent under the cloud of Alanna's fury. The friends were accustomed to the occasional spat between the couple and knew it would blow over, but they weren't willing to stoke the fire.

Damon wisely distanced himself. With powerful strokes, he propelled his body through the water.

"Sorry, guys," Alanna mumbled, as she dried herself with her towel. "I hate when he does that."

"I don't blame you. Craig knows better than to do it to me." Holly glanced over her shoulder at her husband, who nodded his head in sharp consent.

"Same here." Bryan directed a smile at Megan.

By the time Damon returned from his swim, Alanna had cooled off and she accepted his whispered apology. The chatter and joking banter picked up as everyone lounged in the chairs or spread out on the dock.

After a few minutes spent relaxing, Damon raised his head and surveyed the group. "Who wants to go in the canoe?"

Craig was the first to speak up. "I'll go, but not with you."

"Why not?" Damon said, affronted.

"You'll dump me in the water."

Damon's eyes widened in fabricated shock. "I wouldn't do that."

His friends tossed out various snorts and expressions of disbelief.

"I swear on my mother's grave I won't dump you in the water."

"Your mother's not dead," Holly said, not moving her head as she soaked up the sun.

"My grandmother then."

Bryan shoved himself out of his chair. "All right, I'll go."

As the two men pushed off, Megan shook her head. "Bryan is so gullible. He falls for it every time."

"Maybe this time it won't happen."

Alanna laughed. "Holly, you're just as gullible as Bryan if you think that."

A shout and a loud splash caught their attention. Bryan floundered in the water as Damon floated beside him, a maniacal laugh echoing over the river.

CHAPTER 4

"Never again."

"You always say that," Damon said with a grin. "And you always do it again."

"Well, that's the last time, I swear." Bryan wrung out his t-shirt and draped it over the back of his chair.

"You always say that, too. Nothing wrong with a little swim." Damon nudged his wife with his toe. She lounged in the chair next to him, her eyes shut, her face directed toward the sun. "Right, honey?"

"The water's freezing," Bryan grumbled.

Damon shrugged. "Wimp."

"Nutcase."

"Are you kids getting grumpy? You want something to eat?"

Holly's suggestion received an enthusiastic response. They unpacked and devoured sandwiches and snacks, after which Damon dived into the water for another swim.

"My God, that man has energy. He can't sit still." Holly sat on the dock and dangled her feet in the water.

"You're telling me." Alanna shook her head as she settled beside Holly, cautiously lowering her feet into the chill of the river.

"I'm going in with him this time," Craig said as he dragged off his shirt and dive-bombed into the water. "Whoa! That *is* cold," he said as he surfaced. He swam toward Damon, his strokes neither as strong nor smooth as his friend's.

"I feel like having a little nap," Bryan said. "Hon, you want to have a nap with me?"

"Sure, why not?" Megan raised herself from her chair. Her husband slung his arm over her shoulder as they strolled side-by-side up the path to the house.

Holly laughed. "Those two. They're like rabbits. It's a wonder they don't have a dozen kids running around the house instead of just two."

"I'd be happy with two. Or even one."

"I'm sorry. I didn't mean…"

Alanna waved her hand. "Don't worry about it."

"You still can't convince him to have kids?"

"No. He worries his father passed his genes down to him, and he thinks he'll be a lousy father." Alanna rolled her eyes.

"Damon's great with kids. He loves them."

"I know. I've seen him with your kids and Megan's. But he's not convinced." Alanna's gaze shifted to the men fooling around and laughing in the water. "Besides, I'm not so sure it's a good idea anymore."

"What do you mean?"

Alanna shrugged a slender shoulder. "Nothing. I'm just being silly, I guess."

Holly missed her chance to probe further when Craig climbed onto the dock. The floating structure rocked as he plucked his towel from a chair. Damon followed behind, thrashed like a dog and sprayed water on the women. He crowed at their shrieks of protest.

"Let's get that pedal boat going. The four of us can go out." Enthusiasm brightened Damon's face.

"If you promise to behave." Alanna's eyes held a stern warning.

Damon grinned and bent over to wrap his arms around her for a long hug. "I'd never do that twice in one day. I value my life too much."

"Let's do it." Craig headed to the well-used boat. Damon followed close behind. After much tugging and grunting, it floated beside the dock and the four of them swiped dead branches and leaves from the bottom.

Holly cocked her head and looked at it with suspicion. "Do you think it's made for four people?"

"Sure, it is," Craig said. "We'll pedal. You girls sit on the back."

Alanna stepped onto the small boat. Holly followed. It rocked dangerously when the men climbed in, and the women squealed and grasped the sides of the boat. Once everyone was positioned in their seats, it stabilized.

"This is great," Holly said. She shuttered her eyes and tilted her head back, resting it against the seat. Alanna murmured her agreement and did the same. They sat back-to-back to the men and dangled their feet in the water as the boat surged across the river. The men argued about who put more effort into pedaling. According to Damon, it was him.

"I think we're taking on water." There was a note of concern in Holly's voice.

"We're fine." Craig spoke with the confidence of a man who sat in a dry seat.

"Holly's right. The back end is sinking." Alanna directed her words over her shoulder to the two men.

"There's nothing to worry about. These things don't sink." Damon's gaze remained front and center.

Alanna pointed to a sign between her and Holly and aimed a wide-eyed gaze at her friend.

MAXIMUM WEIGHT—600 LBS

Holly's brows furrowed as she did some quick math. "How much do you guys weigh?"

"I don't know," Craig said. "Between us, maybe close to 400."

Holly and Alanna exchanged another worried look when the back end sank lower into the water.

"I think we should turn around," Alanna said. "We're going to be swimming back to shore soon and lugging this thing."

Craig twisted and stretched his neck to get a good look. "You have a point. We're going down."

Damon peeked behind him. "I have a better plan. We're about thirty feet from the opposite shore. I'll get out and wait there. Craig will take you girls to the dock and come back for me."

"What'll you do by yourself?" Craig eyed the deserted shoreline ahead of them.

"I'll hang around. It's going to take half an hour, tops, for you to make a return trip. I'll be fine." Damon pointed ahead. "See that rock? We'll slide it in there. It'll be easy for me to get out."

Craig steered the tiller toward a huge rock nestled on the riverbank, and, at the women's urging, the men increased the speed of their pedaling.

They got the boat as close to shore as possible to let Damon wade over rocks and under protruding branches to reach dry land. Holly moved to the front seat and took control of a set of pedals. They headed back to their home dock as Alanna used her hands to scoop water from the boat.

The ascent out of the rocking vessel proved awkward once again. Standing on the dock, Alanna shaded her eyes and peered across the river. "I don't see him."

"He's there," Craig said. "He may have gone to explore or take a leak. I'll go get him."

"Do you want me to go with you?" Holly said. "I can help."

"I'm fine. I'll be right back." He pedaled backward to reverse the boat and swung it toward the opposite side of the river.

"What's up? Where's Damon? And where's Craig going?"

The women turned as Megan stepped onto the dock.

"We weighed down the pedal boat, and Damon got out on the other side. Craig's gone back to get him. Bryan still asleep?"

"No. When I woke up, he was gone. And so is the car. He must've gone to get beer or something."

"Or to snoop around." Holly laughed.

"Craig's on the other side." Alanna riveted her gaze to the trees where she had last seen Damon.

The women watched Craig climb out and wade toward land, tugging the pedal boat behind him.

"I hope he ties it well." Holly chuckled. "It'd be pretty funny if the boat got away, and they had to swim after it."

"That would make a cool story." Megan laughed, but Alanna remained silent.

The girls helped themselves to drinks from the cooler and settled into the lounge chairs. Alanna kept a concerned gaze on the action, or lack thereof, on the other riverbank. After several minutes, she interrupted the girls' chatter. "What's taking so long?"

"You know them," Holly said. "They've found something interesting to explore."

"I suppose." She didn't appear comforted.

A half-hour later, Craig emerged from the trees and climbed into the boat, heading back toward the women.

"What the... where's Damon?" Alanna leapt to her feet, panic creeping into her voice.

"Craig'll be here soon. We'll find out what's up. I'm sure it's okay." Megan spoke in a reassuring tone, but her gaze was fixed on Craig.

The three women stood on the dock and willed Craig to move faster. His expression as he neared them wasn't reassuring. He was still thirty feet away when Alanna yelled out to him. "Where's Damon?"

"I don't know. I couldn't find him."

"What? He's got to be there. Are you sure you went to the right spot?" Alanna's gaze slid to the opposite shore.

"Yes, I recognized the big rock. It's the only place with a rock that size."

"He must be pulling a prank on you." The tinge of worry that laced her words marred Holly's attempt to remain calm.

"Dammit. I yelled and hunted everywhere. When he comes back, I'll strangle him."

"Not if I get to him first," Alanna said as she wrung her hands.

"Where's Bryan?" Craig asked. "We'll go back together."

"We'll all go. We can take a canoe," Holly said. "But we'll have to wait for Bryan. Call him and get him back here."

"I'm on it." Megan tapped her phone and let it ring. A breathless Bryan finally answered.

"Where are you?" Megan said.

"I'm on my way. Almost there."

"Hurry. We need help."

"What's up?"

"We'll explain when you get here." Megan disconnected the call and bent to haul the canoe closer to the dock.

"Take your phones. We'll keep in touch over there." Craig dug into the waterproof bag and removed the cell phones. He looked at the extra one in his hand. "This is Damon's. So much for calling him." He stared into a distressed Alanna's eyes. "Holly and I will head over with the pedal boat. The rest of you can take the canoes with Bryan."

"No way. I'm coming with you guys. I'll pedal. Holly, you get on the back." Alanna lowered herself into the right-hand seat of the boat and waved her arm for the others to follow. They all turned when the sound of thrashing branches and pounding feet reached their ears. Bryan burst into the opening and barreled onto the dock.

"What's going on?"

"What happened to you?" Megan asked as she seized her husband's arm. His t-shirt was torn on the right shoulder and blackened with dirt, as were his shorts.

"I tripped, running down the path. I knew something bad happened. What is it?"

"Damon's disappeared." Alanna's voice caught on the words.

"What? How?" Bryan's wide-eyed gaze moved from one to the other.

Megan explained the story to him as Craig, Alanna, and Holly shoved off from the dock. Bryan and Megan readied the canoe and followed behind.

Their faces grim and determined, the group disembarked beside the big rock Craig used as a landmark. They waded to shore and attached the watercraft to a sturdy tree.

"Follow me," Craig said. He used rocks, trees, and branches to heave himself upward. His sneakers made it easier for him. The sandals and flip-flops of the others made grasping a foothold almost impossible.

After six feet of scaling, the land leveled out, but it was thick with trees and shrubs.

"Oh my God, where could he be?" Alanna's voice trembled. "He must've gotten lost in here."

"That's what I thought," Craig said. "I almost got lost looking for him. I yelled and yelled."

"We'll have to spread out." Bryan spoke with authority. "But not alone. One set of two. Another of three. We can't lose anyone else."

Alanna stayed with Craig and Holly as they headed to the left, muscling through the trees.

"Did you find tracks to follow?" Holly spoke to her husband's back as she traipsed through the undergrowth behind him. Alanna took up the rear.

"I didn't notice anything. I wasn't really looking. I thought he'd be nearby, and I expected him to leap out at me. I was on my guard for that. Then, I got worried, and it was too late to think about tracks."

"He has to be hurt, or he'd answer us." Tears trailed down Alanna's cheeks.

"I'm sure he's okay." Holly's tone was assured. "There's still a chance he's playing a trick on us. If he's in trouble, he's smart enough to get out of it." Her eyes lit up as an idea occurred to her. "You know what? He may be back at the cottage. Call him. He may have gone to the dock and found his cell phone. It's possible."

Holly stared at her husband for encouragement, but his expression said he didn't possess the same confidence she did. Alanna's shoulders drooped as she speed-dialed Damon's phone. It rang without an answer.

"Let's keep looking," Holly said. They trudged through the forest, shouting Damon's name incessantly.

The two groups swapped text messages, but they had no good news to share.

"Is that water up ahead?" Alanna drew her friends' attention. "Are we back at the river?"

"I doubt it," Craig said with a shake of his head. He gazed around and tried to get his bearings. "We'll check it out."

Several feet farther, they came upon a body of water and stood on the bank, taking in their surroundings. Trees and more trees encompassed them. Craig pulled up a map on his phone and located an icon that placed them on a stream flowing into the Gatineau River.

"Do you think he fell in?" Alanna, her face ashen, clenched her hands and peered into the water for a sign of her husband.

"He's a strong swimmer, and it doesn't look deep." Despite her words of comfort, Holly's worried gaze followed the fast-moving current.

Alanna raised a hand to her mouth and stifled a sob. "Maybe he slipped and smashed his head."

"We need to have faith. We'll find him." Craig gave Alanna's shoulder a quick squeeze.

Two hours later, along with the daylight, their faith slipped away. Using text messages, the sun's position, and the GPS on their phones, the five friends reunited beside the boats.

"We can't abandon him," Alanna said through her tears. "He's alone somewhere. He's hurt."

"We have to go back," Bryan said. "It's almost dark. If he isn't at the cottage, we'll call the police."

With a steady arm around Alanna, Craig led them to the boats. The sun set behind them as they headed to the cottage. All eyes were trained on the dock, hoping for a glimpse of a tall, laughing man. He'd be pleased with his joke and ready for a drink. The closer they got to their destination, the more certain they were he wouldn't materialize.

Forty-five minutes later, two police officers from the Sûreté du Québec, the provincial police force, huddled at the kitchen table with them. Craig recounted the story from the first trip across the river with four passengers to the last quest with five.

The two men asked questions and took notes, but when Alanna suggested they gather a team, complete with rescue dogs, to scour the woods, the cops presented another proposal.

"We'll wait until tomorrow. If he hasn't returned, we'll search then." A sensible tone accompanied the cop's statement, but it didn't soothe the wife of the missing man.

Alanna stiffened and sucked in a quick breath. "What? If he hasn't turned up? You think he'll just walk in the door? We hunted for hours. He's gone."

"I understand it's hard to accept, and it's normal to worry. But people often go somewhere and return when they're ready. He may be lost, and somebody will pick him up and bring him here. He could have stopped for a drink at a bar. There are plenty of possibilities."

Alanna's arm swept dramatically toward the river. "It's complete wilderness out there. I didn't see any bars in the forest."

"There is life over there. If you walk far enough, you'll arrive at Wakefield Heights Road, and that'll eventually take you to civilization. He could have crossed the covered bridge and ended up in the village of Wakefield. He may march in that door any minute."

"Where is this town?" Alanna stood. "I'm going to look for him."

The police officers glanced at each other before giving Alanna directions to Wakefield, along with a suggestion directed toward everyone to remain calm.

As soon as the police officers departed, Alanna grabbed her bag and rummaged for her car keys.

"I'll go with you," Bryan said. "You can't go alone."

"We should all go." Megan reached for her bag.

"No," Alanna said, her voice firm. "Bryan and I will check it out. If we need help, we'll call."

The others traded concerned glances but nodded glumly.

"I guess we should eat." Megan spoke first after Alanna and Bryan left. "It'll give me something to do, and we'll be hungry at some point."

Craig and Holly joined her to toss together a salad and some submarine sandwiches. No one's heart was in it, and they worked in silence.

They ate methodically, their cell phones on the table beside them, waiting for an urgent request for assistance or, better yet, an exclamation of joy because they'd found Damon.

Neither of those events occurred. Instead, forty minutes later, Alanna and Bryan arrived, their somber expressions revealing everything.

Alanna dropped her purse on the table and threw herself into a chair. "Nothing. It's a little town with a few bars and restaurants, and a couple of businesses. We went into each one. Nothing."

Her face crumpled, and her sobs filled the room. "I can't believe it. He disappeared. What'll I do?"

Holly put her arms around her friend. "Tomorrow, the police will step in, and we'll find him. Damon's tough. Whatever happened, he'll be okay until tomorrow. He may have a broken leg or something, but that's fixable. We have to stay positive."

"Holly's right. We gotta hang in there." Craig hoped his wife's prophecy held true.

CHAPTER 5

Sunday breakfast was far from the cheerful meal of the previous day. Dark circles underscored Alanna's red-rimmed eyes, and food remained untouched on plates.

"What do we do? Call the police or look on our own?" Holly asked.

There were two votes for each option. Alanna slumped in her chair, a dazed expression on her face, until she lifted her head. Her gaze shifted between her friends.

"Why can't we do both? We can all look for him."

"You're right," Craig said. "I have the cop's number. I'll contact him, and we'll get this started."

If they expected a manhunt within half an hour, they were disappointed. The police officer said he'd send a car over, but it arrived forty-five minutes later. The shift had changed, and two new officers knocked on their door. They had their own questions about the rundown of events. The frustration level of the friends inched upward as each minute passed.

"We understand your concern, but your husband has been missing for less than twenty-four hours," one cop said. "Normally, we don't begin a search at this point."

"I know. You think he's sitting in a bar somewhere, having a drink. They have all-night bars around here?" Heavy sarcasm coated Alanna's tone.

"There could be several explanations, and many of them don't involve injury." The cop held up his hand to forestall any further arguments.

"We'll make inquiries and do a preliminary exploration where he was last seen. If we see signs of foul play, we'll certainly move the search to another level."

A few heads nodded in satisfaction, and Alanna accepted the compromise. At least something would happen.

The preparation took longer than expected. The officers went to their car to use the radio and to spread a map on the hood of the vehicle. Half an hour later, two more officers arrived. The group stood beside the patrol cars, talking for several long minutes as the occupants of the house watched in anxious anticipation.

"What the hell are they doing?" Alanna ran her hands through her hair.

"Discussing strategy, maybe." Holly's suggestion was meant to be helpful but did nothing to allay Alanna's frustration.

Craig gazed at the police officers with narrowed eyes and a frown. "Trying to decide where they're going to eat lunch, more likely."

"They're wasting time. We have to get going. If they don't do something soon, I'll go on my own."

As if they'd heard Alanna's statement, the cops made their way toward the house. The five friends filed out onto the deck. Humidity added a heaviness to the surrounding air, and a fine sheen of sweat covered the faces of the men in uniforms and tactical vests.

"We've requested the boat. It should be here soon. We'd like you to show us where you last saw him." Officer Tremblay addressed his request to Craig.

"No problem. We'll go with you."

"No. Only you. We don't need many people."

"We can look too." Holly's voice rose in protest.

"If we need help, we'll let you know." The cop's voice was stern and didn't leave any room for argument.

"Oh God, they're going to make us wait here for news," Alanna said under her breath. "I'll go crazy."

Megan squeezed her friend's arm. No words would ease the stress.

Another long hour passed before a cube truck arrived with a zodiac boat in tow. Both the truck and the boat had the Sûreté du Québec's markings on the side. More discussions, map consultations, and radio transmissions followed before one cop approached the group to ask Craig to come with them. They had to launch the boat from another property.

Craig cast a glance at his friends before he climbed into the back of a patrol car. One cop remained behind, standing grimly beside a vehicle.

"He's guarding us, making sure we don't take off to look for Damon," Bryan said, a tremor of frustration in his tone.

"Damn." Alanna paced the floor. "That was my intention. If they think they can keep me caged up, waiting for news, they have another think coming."

******

A police vehicle was foreign to Craig. If he wasn't stressed over Damon and the search, he'd take an intense interest in it. Instead, his mind jumped to possible scenarios, and the pace of his breathing increased.

When they arrived at the public dock, the driver maneuvered the truck into position to lower the boat into the water. Interested neighbors and passersby paused to witness the undertaking, and Craig saw them talking among themselves, their faces animated and curious. Someone would soon approach the cops to ask what had happened.

Craig realized he looked like a criminal, sitting in the back of a police car. He was thankful no one knew him. His thankfulness ceased abruptly when Craig spotted Pete among the growing crowd of onlookers.

Craig disembarked eagerly when a police officer released the door for him. They lowered the boat into the water, and he took a seat in the vessel with Officer Tremblay and another one named Leclerc. He guided them to the spot on the other side by the big rock.

Craig led the way to the top of the bank, but before he moved forward, Tremblay gripped his elbow. The man's expression of dismay surprised him. "What's wrong?" Craig asked.

"How many people were over here?"

"Just the five of us."

"Five? You roamed all over the place?"

"Yes." Craig's stare was incredulous. "We looked for Damon. We couldn't just stand on the shore and yell, hoping he'd hear us."

"All of this," the police officer said, sweeping his arm to encompass the crushed leaves and broken branches, "makes our job a lot harder."

"We thought he was playing a joke on us. We couldn't desert our friend. We had to find him. And you guys wanted to wait twenty-four hours."

The cop held up his hand. "All right, I understand. I'm just stating it makes our job harder when we don't have a trail to follow, and evidence is destroyed."

"So, what do we do?"

"We're here now. We'll look around, but we'll need a different plan."

They covered the same territory the friends had walked, with no better results.

"We'll head back." Officer Leclerc's expression was tense. "I'll talk it over with my supervisor, and we'll put together a strategy. In the meantime, please stay away. Let's not make it any worse than it already is."

Craig nodded his acquiescence. As the boat returned to the launch site, he spotted four anxious people standing on the dock of the rental property, observing their progress. He sent them a half-hearted wave but didn't look forward to giving them a less-than-hopeful update. It wouldn't make them feel better.

******

"So, what are they going to do?" Holly asked.

Craig shrugged. "He didn't say. I guess they'll let us know."

They sat around the kitchen table. The police had left after issuing a stern warning not to go back to the other side of the river.

Alanna stood and paced to the window before swiveling and marching back. "We're supposed to sit and twiddle our thumbs while they think about what to do?"

"I don't know what else to tell you." Craig glanced toward Bryan for support, who tilted his head and gave him a sympathetic look.

A knock on the door drew their attention. Megan rushed to greet the police officers who stood on the deck with solemn expressions.

Officer Tremblay stepped into the room. "We wanted to let you know what'll happen over the next few hours."

"Great," Bryan said, sitting straight in his seat. "That's exactly what we hoped for."

"We'll relay a team with dogs to the area where Mr. Verne was last seen." He turned toward Alanna. "We'll need an article of your husband's clothing; a t-shirt or something he wore recently and hasn't been washed since."

"No problem. I'll get it right away."

"Not yet. I'll fill you in on the rest first." He swung to address the group. "We'll send another team to question the closest neighbors and people in the town. If you have a recent picture of Damon, we'll require that as well. Another team will question each of you. I know it feels as if you told us everything, but often there are things you don't realize you know until we ask the right questions."

"When will this happen?" Bryan asked. "I have to go home tomorrow. I work on Tuesday."

"We'll see how quickly we can do it, but we'd prefer you stay here as long as possible. At least until we have further developments on the case."

"I'm not leaving." Alanna was adamant. "I'm not going home without Damon."

"I'll stay too. I'll contact my boss. It'll be okay." Craig turned to his wife. "Holly, what about you?"

"I'm sure there'll be no problem. And I'll talk to my parents about the kids."

All eyes swiveled to Megan. She darted a look at her husband before answering. "I'll see what I can do. But I'm not sure my parents can keep the kids."

The police officer nodded. "Let us know. We're getting the teams together now."

******

"Did you stay? What happened?" Charlie rested her elbows on the table and leaned forward.

"We got in touch with the owner. The place was empty until the following weekend, so he said we could stay." Craig's mouth twisted into a grimace. "Pete's a bit of a busybody. He insisted on coming over to discuss it with us. Asked a lot of questions. The rumor had already spread about a missing person, but we didn't want to talk about it with a stranger. It upset Alanna."

"I'm sure it did." Charlie understood the other woman's pain. She threw a quick glance at Simm and tried to imagine her life without him.

"Don't get me wrong. Pete was a good guy. He felt bad, and he didn't charge us for the extra days we were there." Craig leaned back against the bench. "Bryan and Megan had to go home, but the cops questioned them first. Holly's parents offered to keep the kids as long as we wanted, and our bosses were really understanding. We stayed. And they questioned each of us separately. I don't think it helped much."

"They continued the search?" Simm asked.

"Yep. They didn't let us do anything. The cops insisted we keep our noses out of things. We stayed close to the cottage and waited for news. News that never arrived."

"They found nothing?" Simm tapped his fingers on the table as he spoke. Charlie knew his mind spun through all the possibilities.

"Absolutely nothing. Zilch. Of course, as they liked to remind us, we had destroyed the evidence in the forest. They questioned everyone close by and in the town. They sent divers into the river. There was nothing."

Charlie leaned back in her seat, her expression perplexed. "How long did they search?"

"Three days. We left on Thursday. There was nothing else to do. They told us they'd keep investigating, but there was no point in us being there." He shook his head wearily. "That was the worst drive home. Alanna cried all the way. Talked on the phone with Damon's mom. She was out of her mind with worry and grief. She's a widow, and he was her only child."

"A year ago." Simm's forehead was creased in thought.

"Almost. A little over ten months."

"No news."

"Nada. The official report is that he's presumed drowned. Since a body never turned up and there were no witnesses, the case is still open. We keep in contact with the local police. There's never anything new. I've even driven up a couple of times by myself, just to snoop around, ask questions. I never really have any hope, but at least it feels like I'm doing something."

Simm's voice held sympathy. "It's been a rough year."

"You're telling me." Craig took a long sip of his beer. "Holly left me about six months ago."

"Because of Damon?" Charlie asked. This had bothered her since she'd seen Craig the previous day. She didn't understand the connection between Damon's disappearance and Holly leaving Craig.

"It took a toll on us all. But, I guess, it changed me. I don't know. She claimed it did." He shrugged. "Or it changed the way she looked at me. Anyway, she said she needed space. I gave it to her. Then, not too long after, she didn't need space anymore. She moved in with someone else."

Charlie winced. The action didn't go unnoticed by Craig.

"Yeah, exactly. So now I'm alone every second week. The other week, I have the kids. In case you couldn't tell, this is my alone week." He raised his head and gazed at each of them. "That's my sad story. It's good to get it out. I realize you're being nice, Charlie, but I don't think there's much you can do that the cops haven't done."

"Why don't you give me your phone number, anyway? If I think of something, I'll call you."

After exchanging numbers, Craig thanked them for the meal and their time. He left, shoulders sagging, a shell of the man Charlie had known.

CHAPTER 6

"What do you think?"

"I think it sounds like the police did a thorough job. Search dogs and divers. They interviewed everyone. They did everything they could." Simm toyed with his coffee cup as he spoke.

"Don't you think it's weird someone would disappear like that, without a trace?" Charlie frowned, her gaze focused on her husband.

"It's strange, that's for sure. It's not the first time. It won't be the last."

They sipped their coffee refills while the lunch crowd thinned out.

"That poor woman, losing her husband like that. It must drive her crazy."

Simm tilted his head and pursed his lips. "Maybe she's the one behind his disappearance."

"Why do you say that?" Charlie couldn't hide her surprise.

"It's usually the spouse."

"I don't believe that."

"Think whatever you like. I'm the one that sleeps with one eye open." A wry smile curved Simm's lips.

Charlie swatted his arm; her burst of laughter drew amused glances from many of the patrons.

Moments later, her voice grew serious. "Is there anything we can do?"

"I already told you; the cops did a good job. What more is there?"

"Fresh eyes."

Simm sighed. "Charlie, I think it's great you want to support Craig, but there's nothing for us to do. And we've got a lot of stuff on our plate with the pubs."

"Exactly." Charlie wrapped her fingers around his wrist. "We never take a break. Why don't we book a weekend at this place? We can check it out, ask a few questions, do something different for once."

"You tired of this?" Simm raised his eyebrows as he nodded toward the bar.

"Not at all. It's my life. You know that. But we never take a day off." Charlie flung her hands in the air. "I can't remember when I last took time off. A weekend getaway is exciting. The crazy summer rush hasn't started yet. Frank and Melissa can easily handle things. We'll offer extra hours to Sarah."

Simm narrowed his eyes. "Who are you and what have you done to my wife?"

Charlie folded her arms over her chest. "I'm serious."

"I see that, and it worries me. When have you ever thought about taking a vacation?"

"Never. That's what I'm saying. It doesn't mean I can't evolve. It's time." Charlie leaned her head on his shoulder. "C'mon. Don't you look forward to a few days away from paying bills?"

******

"We'll have to pack fly dope."

Charlie's hands stilled. "What is that?"

"Bug repellent."

"Will there be bugs?" She clutched a t-shirt to her chest. Their bags were on the bed, and Charlie agonized over what she needed. Simm insisted a weekend trip warranted a weekend bag and not a large suitcase.

"There could be." Simm tossed a cap into his bag and zipped it shut. "It's cottage country. We'll be near water and trees. Most likely there'll be mosquitos and black flies."

Charlie grabbed her phone and tapped out a text to Craig.

"Have you never been outside the city?" Simm stared at her, budding astonishment on his face.

"Of course. We went to Dublin, remember?" She glued her gaze to the phone, waiting for a response.

"That's a city. I mean, have you ever been to the country? Camping? Hiking in the wilderness?"

"No," Charlie said, jamming her hands onto her hips. "Don't tell me you have, Mr. Trust Fund Baby."

Charlie liked to tease Simm about his origins as the son of a wealthy real estate tycoon. Because of his intense dislike of his late father, he had turned his back on those origins, and he shunned contact with his brother Walter, who he painted with the same moral brush. According to Simm, Walt had taken on the family business and the character that went along with it.

Simm took her teasing in stride. "First, I don't live off a trust fund. Second, I went to summer camp every year as a kid. I did a lot of hiking, camping, canoeing, all that stuff."

"So, you know all about mosquitos?"

"My fair share."

"Fine. You're officially in charge of fly drugs or whatever it is."

"I'll get some bear spray at the same time."

"What?"

"You never know. Better to be prepared."

Charlie typed another quick text to Craig.

******

"This looks nice." Charlie stretched her arms and shoulders after over two hours of sitting in the car.

"You sound surprised. Didn't you see the pictures on the website?" Simm heaved the bags out of the trunk as Charlie studied the wood-shingled cottage surrounded by trees and flower gardens that showed the promise of vibrant color in a few weeks. Harley scooted ahead and explored the bushes.

"I did. I'm usually skeptical of pictures on websites. I suspect they make things appear better than they actually are. But so far so good."

Charlie had lived her almost thirty years in a city apartment. Neighbors were a shout away. Conveniences were a walk away. A private cottage in what was an isolated area, by her standards, fell outside of her comfort zone. But, she reminded herself, you learned nothing new within your comfort zone. She'd try it. Besides, this had been her idea.

"I thought the owner was going to meet us here."

Tires crunched on gravel. A black pickup truck pulled into the driveway, a man in his late forties at the wheel. When he climbed out of the truck, Charlie saw he was at least as tall as Simm, with a husky build.

He sauntered toward them, a wide smile on his face. "You must be Charlie," he said as he gripped Simm's hand. "I'm Pete Dunn."

"Actually, she's Charlie and I'm Simm, but don't worry, you're not the first one to make that mistake."

Charlie held out her hand. "My real name is Charlene. My mother was the only one to use it."

Pete laughed. He had a pleasant, unremarkable face. Slightly crooked front teeth and light brown hair, trimmed close to his scalp in a military style, gave him a geeky look. "As you've probably guessed, I'm the owner. I'm happy to have you here no matter what they call you. I'll show you around the place."

They had what seemed like a ritualistic tour, but Pete spoke with obvious pride in his property. He pointed out where to find canoe paddles, life jackets, and wood for the fire pit. Charlie inquired about an odd-looking door placed at an angle between the ground and the cottage's foundation.

"Don't concern yourself with that," Pete said. "It leads to the basement, but there's nothing in there. And I keep it locked, so there're no worries about intruders."

Charlie noted the padlock on the door. It looked flimsy, but she berated herself for her paranoia. They weren't in Montreal. No one could see the building unless they were in the driveway. Tall leafy trees surrounded them, giving the impression of seclusion. Craig's description had been right on.

As Pete prepared to depart, Simm brought up the subject of Damon's disappearance. Dismay darkened the man's face.

"You heard about it on the news, I guess," he said.

"We knew Damon. We came here to look around."

"Simm was a private investigator," Charlie said, "We thought he could help get answers."

A speculative expression bloomed on Pete's face, and Simm rushed to tone down Charlie's statement. "We're not likely to uncover anything the cops couldn't find."

"I'd be surprised if you could. I'm not a cop, but they seemed to cover their bases," Pete said.

"What do you recall about what happened?" Simm asked.

Pete squinted his eyes and stared off toward the river. "I realized something was up when I saw police at the public boat launch. Imagine my surprise when I saw that guy in the cop car. He was one of my renters."

Charlie offered the name. "Craig."

"I guess that was him. I was worried I had a bunch of criminals in the place. He seemed like a shifty-looking character, so it didn't surprise me."

Charlie hastened to defend Craig. "He was assisting the police."

"I realized that afterward, but it still gave me a bit of a shock. This is a quiet area. We don't have crime here. I didn't like the idea of being the one to import it."

"Do you remember meeting Damon?" Simm asked.

"Yeah. A tall, slim guy. I saw him when they arrived, and I showed them around the place."

"You never saw him again after?"

"No." He shook his head. "That was the only time. Strangest thing, him disappearing like that. Terribly sad for the family, losing someone."

"It sure is," Simm said. "Do you live nearby?"

"As the crow flies, it's not far. Just downstream, on the river. By truck, I got to go up to Riverside Road, and it's a twisty drive. It's faster by boat."

"Are there a lot of houses and cottages nearby?" Charlie wasn't just making conversation. She wished to put her mind at ease.

"A fair amount. More and more new places going up. People getting out of the city."

"Must be a lot of rentals." Simm nodded toward the man's cottage.

"Oh, yeah. They're popular."

"Many people stay for just a weekend?"

Pete's eyes glinted. "I see where you're going. Yeah, it mighta been somebody like that."

Charlie spoke up. "Do you think Damon drowned? Or do you think something else happened?"

Pete folded his arms over his chest. "I can't say, really. There are a fair number of drownings. People get foolish when they're on vacation, and they don't realize how dangerous water can be. But his wife and friends didn't believe that was what happened, so maybe it was a crazy person who decided they wanted to kill somebody. It had to be a stranger. Nobody from around here would do that."

The three of them fell silent for a moment as they watched Harley happily explore the property.

"He won't do any damage, will he? I rarely allow pets. I don't like them." Pete's gaze moved between Charlie and Simm, looking for reassurance.

Charlie presented her most charming smile. "You don't have to worry about Harley. He's very well behaved. And I watch him like a hawk."

Simm drew Pete's attention away from the dog. "Do you have any other houses you rent?"

"Nope. Just this one. It's enough. I restore and sell old furniture, and I have my mother to take care of. I don't need anything else."

"Well, we really appreciate you taking the time to show us around." Simm clapped a hand on the man's shoulder, drawing the visit to a close.

"No problem." Pete moved toward his truck with a wave of his hand. "You need anything, just let me know."

Charlie and Simm watched him drive away before they climbed the steps to the deck of the cottage. It afforded them a partial view of the river and some rooftops over the expanse of trees.

Charlie unlocked the door and let Harley lead the way into their temporary home.

"This is really kind of nice, isn't it? A lot of wood, but it gives it a rustic feel." Charlie wandered through the main room until she spotted a windowed door. "Oh, what is this?"

She stepped into a small octagon-shaped room closed in by floor to ceiling windows. A skylight in the peaked ceiling added more sunlight to the room. A low round table squatted in the heart of the area with comfy-looking armchairs surrounding it. From where she stood, Charlie had a one-hundred-and-eighty-degree view of greenery, colorful flower beds, and a glimmer of the river in the distance.

Charlie sank into a chair and groaned. "Isn't this lovely? Imagine spending the day here, reading a book and drinking tea."

Simm leaned against the doorjamb, his hands in his pockets and a glimmer in his eyes. "Since when do you drink tea? And when do you take five minutes to read a book? You've always got a hundred things to do."

"Maybe someday I won't have a hundred things to do, and I could read a book. And I'd learn to love tea if I could do it here."

Simm took Charlie's hand and tugged her out of her seat long enough to take her place and pull her back onto his lap. "It's nice to see you relax a bit. If this is what it takes, we'll do it more often."

Charlie wrapped her arms around his neck. "That sounds like a good plan. Hopefully, we won't be looking for a missing person next time." She settled her head on his shoulder. "Maybe we can create a new person."

Simm twisted his head and gave her a narrow-eyed look. "We're not getting into this now, are we?"

"Why not? Now's a good time. We can create right away."

"I don't mind practicing, but you know how I feel about the creation part."

"I do. And you know I think your fear is… misplaced."

"You were going to say irrational."

"Yeah, but it sounded too harsh." Charlie shifted to have a full-on view of Simm's face. "Listen, honey. You can't throw away a chance to have a family because you think you carry some genetic predisposition for evil. You're not an evil person. Chances are your child will be perfectly normal."

"And if he or she isn't?"

Charlie sighed and positioned herself with her head nestled on Simm's chest. "Then we'll deal with it."

"I just don't know."

"Your father was twisted and mean, but I'm not afraid to have your child. I know you're not like him, and you'll teach our kids properly."

"Nurture overcomes nature?"

"That's what I believe."

Simm kissed the top of her head and held her a little tighter. "Let me think about it, okay? For now, let's just enjoy this."

CHAPTER 7

After the luxury of eating an immense breakfast in the sunroom, Charlie and Simm set out toward the river to work it off. The air still held the chill of early morning, but it promised warmth to come.

Charlie drew a deep breath as the river came into view. The water reflected the trees and sky like a mirror. Simm stepped onto the dock. It wobbled slightly under his weight, and ripples worked their way outward. Charlie stood on the grass, taking in the surrounding sights. To the left of the wooden structure, lily pads floated in the shallow water. She half-expected to see a frog sitting on one of them, warbling his song.

A trill of pleasure escaped Charlie's lips when, farther to the left, a mother duck led a train of ducklings to a quieter corner of the river. She glanced at Simm to see him smiling at her innocent display.

"How cute is that?" Charlie asked.

"Pretty darn cute."

With their layered clothing and a backpack filled with snacks, bug repellent, and bear spray (Charlie insisted), they climbed into the pedal boat and eased onto the river. Harley balanced himself between them, his little flat nose raised in the air, sniffing furiously.

Craig had filled them in on the landmarks, and the big rock stood out among the outcroppings like a headstone in a cemetery.

With the boat secured to a tree, Simm grasped Charlie's hand and pulled her up the slope to flat land. They stood side by side and absorbed the sight.

Freshly sprouted leaves adorned the tall trees. The sun snuck through where it could and brightened spots of the forest floor. The spring beginnings of undergrowth and moss provided an uneven carpet of green, seeking to smother the dry leaves and branches left over from the previous fall. Charlie shivered. The temperature was several degrees lower under the verdant canopy.

"We have to picture it as the cops first saw it," Simm said. "Nothing's trampled now. It probably looks similar to when Damon first came upon it."

"Before Craig and his friends destroyed the evidence," Charlie said wryly.

"Exactly."

"What's our plan?" Charlie glanced up at her husband's intense profile.

"We have to put ourselves in Damon's shoes. He may have stood here as we stand now. Where would he go to explore?"

"What if he didn't have time? What if someone ambushed him as soon as he got here?"

"It's possible. But we have to consider two things. According to Craig, Damon was tall and fit. The assailant would have to be strong."

"Or someone surprised him. Bashed him over the head and knocked him out."

"And how would this person carry a dead weight?"

Charlie shrugged. "Maybe there were two people. Or more."

"Something to think about."

"What was your other thing?"

"If someone assaulted Damon, it couldn't have been premeditated. How would someone know he would be here?"

Charlie thought about it for a moment. "Maybe Damon wandered farther inland, came upon someone, and that person attacked him."

"Excellent point. We're back to square one. Which direction?"

Charlie looked around her. "I'd go right."

"Why?"

"I have no idea."

"Sounds like a good reason. Let's go."

Charlie led the way as they shoved aside tree branches and shrubs, following the shoreline to the right of them. The musty smell of river water and decay hung in the air, and tiny insects buzzed in Charlie's ears as she negotiated her way over the boggy terrain. Her sneakers weren't new, but she liked them and didn't look forward to scrubbing off the mud.

"Be careful where you step. There could be bear poop in here."

Charlie's pulse ratcheted up, and she whirled to face her husband with wide eyes. "Please stop with the bears. That's all I'll think about now."

"Sorry," Simm said, but his grin made it clear he was anything but sorry.

It wasn't easy to resist his teasing smirk, but Charlie glared at him for good measure before sweeping her arm, giving him permission to lead the way. As they trampled through the forest, her gaze remained fixed on the ground. Charlie didn't know what bear poop looked like, but she guessed she'd figure it out if she saw it. And if she didn't, Harley would surely point it out to her.

"Do you hear that?" Simm asked.

Charlie halted in her tracks, ready to flee at the slightest sign of movement. "What is it?" Her voice trembled.

"Water. We must be close to the stream Craig mentioned."

Charlie strained her hearing and caught the faint sound of water flowing over rocks. They used it as a guide. Within minutes, they stood on the bank of another body of water, this one a twenty-foot-wide stream. The current carried leaves and branches toward the river.

Simm removed a map from the back pocket of his jeans and unfurled it. He ran a long finger over the trail of the waterway. "This comes from a northeastern lake. This is where the Gatineau River narrows, and the current gets stronger." He raised his head and gazed downstream.

Charlie studied the frown that marred her husband's expression. "What is it?"

"It took us all of fifteen minutes to cross the river. That means it took Craig thirty to take the girls to the house and return for Damon." He pointed to the map. "If he went left, he would've headed toward Wakefield, but it's far. Damon couldn't have gone that far in thirty minutes. But he could've made it here." Simm glanced at his watch. "It took us about twenty minutes to get here."

"You think he fell in this stream and was washed into the river? From what Craig said, he was a strong swimmer."

"Unless someone knocked him out and dumped him in."

"The divers didn't find him in the water. It doesn't seem that deep. You'd think he would have snagged on something along the way."

"Maybe. Maybe not." Simm looked downstream again. "We need a boat."

"You want to go down the river?" Charlie's heartbeat picked up. All this talk of drowning made her uncomfortable, and the idea of getting into a boat added to her anxiety.

"Yeah, I think we should. But I can go alone if you're scared."

Charlie brushed aside her concerns. "I'm not scared, and you're not going without me."

Back at the cottage, they contacted Pete and asked if he could refer them to a boat rental business. He had a better suggestion. He'd loan them his boat if they met him at the dock. Simm took him up on his offer.

Within an hour, Charlie perched at the helm of the boat with Harley on her knee, grasped in her clutches. She craned her neck to peer into the murky water on each side of her, uncertain what she looked for. Despite the bright orange lifejacket securely attached around her torso, she didn't want to topple into the flowing water.

Simm sat behind her at the midway mark. Pete manned the small outboard motor and guided them slowly downstream. He had insisted on coming along, claiming he could fill them in on the locals and anything else of interest. It seemed like a sensible solution.

Pete was a guide with an active curiosity. He pelted questions at Simm like bullets from a machine gun. They ranged from inquiries about their lives in Montreal to theories about Damon's disappearance. Charlie recognized Pete's offer to help them for what it was: an endeavor to ease his loneliness. He came across as a nerdy, awkward man, aiming to please everyone, but forgetting to please himself. Charlie guessed he had few friends.

Not all of Pete's chatter involved questions.

"This place on the left is mine," he said, pride clear in his tone. Charlie understood the pride. It was a lovely home. Old, but lovingly cared for, with a deck running along its length. Chairs gave an uninhibited view of the river and the lushness of the trees on the opposite bank. A rolling green lawn connected the house and the river; towering trees provided a privacy border on either side of the property; and an impressive boathouse nestled beside the dock.

"Do you have a large family?" Charlie asked, swiveling to face him.

Pete's face collapsed. "No. My brother passed away a few years ago and my wife not long after. Unfortunately, we didn't have any children. My mother requires a lot of care, so she moved in with me. It's just the two of us in that big house."

Charlie experienced a flash of sympathy. As she had suspected, he was lonely.

Pete's tone altered when they coasted past the neighboring house. "These guys are quite something. They're rolling in dough. Marcus Vaughn. He owns a big company in Montreal, and she comes from old real estate money. This is their little home away from home." His words dripped with sarcasm.

Charlie's eyes widened. She had considered Pete's home big, but this one took it to another level. It was a recent construction with a huge two-story wall of windows facing the water. The vast property, easily twice the size of Pete's, had a line of trees on each side, separating it from the neighbors. Heavy equipment, workers, and a partially completed stone wall occupied space on the lawn. Simm whistled behind her.

"Nice place," he said.

Pete scoffed. "It set them back a few bucks, but they probably didn't notice too much difference in their bank account."

"Lifestyles of the rich and famous," Charlie muttered.

"They're putting up that damn stone wall." Pete's normally subdued tone took on a harsh edge. Charlie glanced back. His nostrils flared, and his eyes were hard and flinty. "They had the nerve to tell me to hack down the trees between our lots, so they could put up their fancy wall. No way would I do that. What do they think? I'm going to crawl through the trees at night to admire their stupid house? I'm fighting them on it."

Charlie exchanged a look with Simm before she directed Pete's attention to the next home. It was pleasant but humble compared to the Vaughn residence. Several of the houses on their path appeared at least fifty years old.

These homeowners met Pete's standards. He knew their names and backgrounds and details that Charlie considered excessive. A few were full-time residents, while others had seasonal homes.

"The next guy stands out like a sore thumb. He's the local oddity, even more so than me." Pete's awkward laugh echoed over the water.

Pete slowed the boat as they neared the home. It was to their left, the first they'd seen on that side of the river. He lowered his voice while they glided by. "He's a hermit. Name's Noah Wolfe. Goes nowhere. Grows his own vegetables. Hunts his own food."

"Hunts?" Charlie said, her thoughts flashing to bears and large wild animals. "What's around here to hunt?"

"Rabbits. Deer and moose when they're in season. He has pigs and sheep. Fishes a lot."

"It's a way of life, I guess." Simm's voice remained matter-of-fact.

"Yeah, but you should see him. He's odd. Looks a lot like that big guy from Harry Potter."

"You mean Hagrid?" Charlie asked, recalling the looming bearded man from the books and movies.

Pete snapped his fingers. "That's him. Exactly."

Neither Charlie nor Simm commented as they stared at the ramshackle building, hoping to glimpse the so-called hermit. The most they saw was the snout of a pig poking around the house.

The river narrowed as they continued downstream. Pete took his time, letting the current do most of the work, the motor rumbling in a slow idle. The properties became more luxurious. They had larger boathouses. Some homes had boats of multiple sizes, along with Jet-Skis and other water toys.

"It seems odd for your neighbors to build where they did," Charlie said. "This looks like a place for people with their money."

Pete flapped a hand in dismissal. "They prefer their privacy, even if it means living next to us."

"Where does this river lead?" Simm asked, changing the subject.

"Eventually to the Ottawa River."

"And divers searched it looking for Damon?"

"I don't know how far they went, but they searched. I remember that much."

Charlie cast sidelong glances at the water. The idea of Damon's body in there radiated shivers along her spine.

Simm must have sensed her disquiet. "I think we've seen enough for now. We can head back."

CHAPTER 8

"I say we go see the hermit." Charlie deposited a grilled cheese sandwich on a plate and handed it to Simm.

"I say I go see the hermit, and you stay here." He pressed a glass of cold water into her hand. They made their way to the sunroom to enjoy their lunch with a view.

"No way. Why would I do that?"

"Because I'd feel better if you were safe here."

"And I'm going to let you go by yourself? What if you don't come back? Like Damon? Do you think I want to live like Alanna, never knowing what happened to my husband?"

"I can take care of myself," Simm said.

"You're not going anywhere without me." Charlie's tone made it clear she would stand firm.

Once again, they traversed in the pedal boat. A deep frown marred Simm's face. Charlie knew he'd get over his mad. He needed to understand she'd go insane if she stayed behind and worried about him. They had to go into it together and protect each other.

On the opposite side, Simm led them in the general direction of the home of Noah Wolfe, otherwise known as the hermit. They knew if they followed the riverbank, they would come upon it. According to Simm's GPS, it was a one kilometer walk from where they arrived ashore. The rough terrain made it seem farther.

As they approached the stream that flowed into the Gatineau River, anxiety formed in Charlie's chest. "He's on the other side of this. How do we pass?"

"Apparently, there's a bridge to cross by foot. We'll find it."

A trampled path led them to a wooden structure that spanned a narrow section of the stream. Charlie came to a full stop and studied the bridge. The wood was gray with age and dotted with empty spaces where planks of wood used to be.

"This is great," Simm said as he strode toward the bridge.

Charlie grabbed his elbow. "Wait. Do you think it's safe?"

"Of course. Just step over the holes. Besides, it isn't deep here."

Charlie's gaze drifted to the water flowing over the rocks underneath the bridge. Simm was right about the lack of depth. It still looked like a painful experience. Realizing she had little choice if she wanted to keep up with her husband, she gathered Harley into her arms and followed Simm across, gripping the wobbly railing.

Relief flowed through her when her feet hit solid ground on the other side.

They heard it before they saw it. The furious snapping of branches and the crunch of leaves underfoot heralded something large and unknown. Charlie and Simm stopped in their tracks. Out of necessity, so did Harley, but if it wasn't for the restraint of his leash, he would have hurled his small body toward the oncoming force. His ferocious bark either warned or enticed whatever barreled in their direction.

A creature the size of a small pony charged through the trees; its open mouth displayed gleaming white teeth and its jowls flapped with each stride. Powerful muscles exerted under a sleek brown pelt as they propelled the animal toward the couple at breakneck speed. A bark resounded from between his massive jaws.

The heart-stopping sight stunned them into silence, even the fearless Harley.

With a leap, the dog soared through the air and dived toward Charlie. She had the vague impression that Simm tried to reach her first, but he was no match for the speed of the enormous animal. His front paws landed on her shoulders before they both crashed to the ground.

Hot breath enveloped her face as he emitted another mind-numbing bark inches from her ears. Charlie's sole focus was the glimpse of enormous white teeth as she braced herself for the puncturing of her throat. Time suspended. Either that or the beast hadn't decided how to proceed with his strike. Instead, a dribble of drool spilled upon Charlie's cheek as he panted from above her.

Charlie dragged her gaze away from the dog's immense head to see her husband peering at her from over the animal's shoulder. His lack of concern at her imminent demise struck her as odd. She expected a frantic attempt to save her life. When the animal vaulted off her to frolic with an excited Harley, she understood.

Simm gripped her elbow and tugged her to her feet. He brushed branches and leaves from her back as she watched her pug try to sniff a behind that was at least a foot higher than his nose could reach.

"What is that?" Charlie's wide eyes took in the wonder of the magnificent animal.

"Some type of mastiff, I guess. He's big. Must be a hundred and fifty pounds." Simm looked her up and down. "You okay?"

Charlie moved her gaze to her husband's concerned expression. "I thought I was done for."

"So did I, but his butt was wagging like crazy. He just wanted to play."

The animal swung back toward Charlie, and in one bounding stride, was in front of her again. Before he could flatten her on the ground once more, she muttered to him and scratched him behind the ears. He rewarded her with rolling eyes and a doggy grin.

"Bosco."

They swiveled to face a man as oversized and imposing as his pet. His grooming, however, was not as neat. Long, shaggy hair fell onto the shoulders of a torn and dirty jacket. A salt-and-pepper beard brushed his breastbone. Charlie understood Pete's comparison to Hagrid.

"Come."

The dog responded instantly, racing to his master's side to squat beside him. But his backside continued to wiggle from side to side. Harley, as if sensing he should stay in his own camp, sniffed the man's legs, wagged his tail, and returned to settle beside Charlie.

Simm cleared his throat. "Nice dog. He's pretty big."

The other man grunted. His narrowed gaze remained pinned on the couple.

"Bosco's a nice name," Charlie offered, hoping to appease the large man.

"He's Italian," he stated, as if that explained everything.

"He seems friendly."

"He can be unfriendly too."

Charlie didn't want to be around when either of them was unfriendly. "You must be Mr. Wolfe. I'm Charlie, and this is my husband Simm." Charlie took a few steps forward and held out her hand. He stared at her outstretched appendage for a moment before his gaze slid away from the couple. Charlie snatched her hand back and shoved it into the back pockets of her jeans.

"How do you know my name?" His dark gaze returned to her face.

"Mr. Dunn told us." Charlie didn't see any harm in being upfront.

"Old gossip. Should mind his own business."

"He is nosy, but I think he's just lonely."

The big man snorted and turned away. He trudged through the trees with the dog on his heels.

Simm shouted after him. "Mr. Wolfe, we have questions about the man who disappeared last year."

Noah halted but didn't turn. He twisted his head to speak over his left shoulder. "He tell you I had something to do with it?"

Charlie spoke up. "No, Pete said nothing like that. Damon was a friend of ours, and we hoped to get answers."

"I already talked to the police. I don't want any more questions." He plodded farther into the enveloping trees.

"Damon's disappearance was really hard on his friends and family," Charlie raised her voice another notch. "It changed their lives in a lot of ways. Terrible ways. We promised we'd do our best to uncover what happened. It won't take long. I promise."

No one budged for several long seconds, including the disgruntled man. Charlie crossed her fingers.

When the word came, they barely heard it. "C'mon," Noah said with a jerk of his head before he set off toward his house.

Charlie flashed a triumphant smile at Simm as she hustled to catch up. For such a large man, he moved fast. An intimate knowledge of the surroundings likely worked to his advantage.

They approached a clearing and Charlie spotted the ramshackle house they had seen from the river. Its appearance didn't improve from this angle, but she had a better view of the animals. She also spotted a garden that grew to one side of the structure.

"You seem self-sufficient," she said.

He grumbled something in response. She didn't think it was a polite 'thank you'.

"Cute goats." It was one last try on Charlie's part to get into his good graces.

"Ask your questions. You got five minutes."

Charlie glanced at Simm, mentally passing him the torch.

"Did you see anything or anyone suspicious?" Simm narrowed his eyes.

"Nope."

"Do you fish? You have a boat? Do you go out on the river?"

"Yep. Saw nothing."

"What are the animals for?"

Both men swung their attention to Charlie. It was clear her question threw them off.

"The goats are for milk," Noah said with a frown.

"And the pig?"

The man's big shoulders shrugged. "The goats like him."

Simm shot his wife a perplexed glance before he brought the conversation back to what he considered important. "Have you met the neighbors? The ones with the big house?"

"We don't hang out together much." His mouth twisted into a brief sneer. "I don't think they like my style."

Simm pivoted to look over the river. "You have a pretty good view of their place. You ever see them outside?"

"Too much."

"They not good neighbors?"

"Make a lot of noise with their boats and Jet-Skis." Noah shook his head in disgust.

Simm persisted with his questioning. "They live there year-round?"

"They come and go. Probably have houses in a few places." He shifted on his feet, his impatience clear.

"I'm sorry," Charlie said. "Would you mind if I used your washroom?"

"I mind. Lots of trees around here," he said with a wave of a big arm. "Take your pick. I won't look."

Charlie strove to conceal her shock. She hadn't expected an outright refusal of her request, and she had no intention of pretending to pee behind a tree. She sent a helpless look in Simm's direction.

"I think we're done here anyway," her husband said. "We'll find a tree for Charlie on our way back. Thanks for your time."

Without a word, the man turned his back to them and lumbered toward his house.

Neither Charlie nor Simm spoke until they were well out of earshot.

"Do you see a tree you like?" Simm said.

"Funny. I wanted to look around his house."

"I know what you wanted, and so did he, apparently."

"So much for being a master detective, I guess."

"You did good." Simm whirled a curious gaze on her. "What was with the questions about the animals?"

"It's simple. He likes animals." Charlie shrugged. "That says a lot about a person. I don't trust anyone who doesn't like animals. Harley liked him, too. Says a lot."

CHAPTER 9

They waited ten minutes for a spot at the bar. Even for a Saturday night in May, the crowd impressed Charlie. Her practiced eye was accustomed to the hustle and bustle of a pub in downtown Montreal. She expected a different beat in a small town.

The beat was the same. It was the type of clientele that differed.

At Charlie's pub, a liberal smattering of low-key suits and preppies hung out among the more boisterous students. Here, the ambiance was rowdy and included all ages and career paths. This was vacation country, and everyone felt the vibe.

A young, friendly strawberry blond, who introduced herself as Ellie, led them to their seats, handling greetings, orders, and come-ons along the way. Charlie made a mental note to let her know a job was available in Montreal, if she wanted a change.

Recorded music provided background noise. In a corner, a raised platform big enough for a small band was set up for karaoke, and Charlie privately hoped they escaped before that happened. She wasn't against having a good time, but it was impossible to talk while someone screamed off-key into a microphone and called it singing.

Charlie suggested they eat their meal at the bar counter. If they wanted the local opinion of what happened, the best sources were the bartenders and the regulars. Charlie bided her time until the preliminary greetings were over before she launched into her questions.

"Did you hear about the guy who went missing last summer? He was an acquaintance."

"The one they never found?" The bartender, a guy in his early twenties, nodded his head as he deftly pulled a draft beer for a customer. "Yeah, there was talk."

"What kind of talk?"

He shrugged a shoulder. "Just speculation. Usually, the bodies surface downstream somewhere. He didn't, so you hear all kinds of theories."

"What do you think happened to him?" Simm asked.

"No idea, but chances are good that he drowned."

"Probably ran away from his wife. I think about doing it lots of times." Bursts of raucous laughter and a few comebacks followed the remark of the grizzly bearded man two seats down from Charlie. She smiled as if amused. God knew how many times she'd heard that joke.

"Same as the other guy," another man volunteered.

Simm's gaze swiveled toward him. "What other guy?"

"A few years back, a guy from Ottawa disappeared. They never found him, figured he drowned. Just like this guy."

"He disappeared from the same spot?" Simm asked.

"Around there. I'm sure it was a coincidence. I'm just saying it's not the first time."

Charlie shot Simm a glance and was certain the wheels spun in his brain. This could make a difference. "What was his name? Can you think back?"

Someone eventually came up with Seth Long as the victim's name, and Charlie filed it away in her mind.

"Don't forget the other one." This from a man with a heavily lined face, unruly gray hair, and a drooping moustache. "That Dunn fellow. Eddie was his name."

Charlie and Simm's heads pivoted in his direction.

"Dunn?" Simm said. "Any relation to Pete Dunn?"

The man nodded. "Yep. His brother. He drowned in the river."

Charlie's blood chilled. Pete had mentioned the death of his brother, but he said nothing about a drowning. "Did they locate his body?"

"No, they never did. He washed away."

Charlie slid a look at Simm and knew his thoughts were the same as hers.

"Your friend may still turn up." Ellie picked up the conversation.

"Damon's gone almost a year," Charlie said. "It hardly seems likely."

"Maybe he lost his memory and wandered off." The girl's remark earned a few nods, although Charlie suspected the men at the bar would accept anything she said.

"The cops must've questioned a lot of people." Charlie tried to snag the group's attention.

The bartender spoke up. "Yeah, sure. I think they wrote it off as a drowning from the get-go. Once they're washed downriver, they don't always turn up. It's been a few times they never discovered a body."

"Are there that many drownings?" The casual attitude of the locals surprised Charlie.

A forty-something woman sitting beside Simm spoke up. "There's a lot of people on the water, and a chunk of them don't know what they're doing."

Charlie wondered if Damon fell into that category. From what she understood, he was athletic and an excellent swimmer. He was also a daredevil and a bit of a show-off. Had his antics last summer caused his death? Was there something more at play here? Could someone be killing people and making it seem like they drowned?

The subject tilted to the current hot topic, the Stanley Cup hockey playoffs. Charlie tuned the others out as she ate her fish and chips and pondered what they'd heard. She was eager to leave the pub, an uncharacteristic move for her. She loved checking out other establishments to see how hers compared. But she wanted Simm's take on the idea of a serial killer.

Her spirits deflated when they were in the car, negotiating the dimly lit country roads, and Simm made clear his lack of interest in her theory.

"It's so unlikely. Do you realize how many drownings they have in the summer months? It's like they said, people don't know how to behave around water. If someone drowns in a river, they're washed downstream, and that's it. You can't argue with that."

"But two people in the same area within a few years. And Pete's brother, too."

"Yeah, it happens. And the more I think about it, the more convinced I am Damon suffered the same fate. I understand it's hard for family and friends to accept. They want answers. They want a body to give them closure. But that's the way it works out sometimes."

Charlie slumped into her seat. "I hate giving up."

"We're not giving up. We said we'd talk to the police, and that's what we'll do tomorrow. Then we'll go back to Montreal and tell Craig about our trip."

CHAPTER 10

"That sugar pie was delicious, but it may keep me awake all night." Simm rubbed his stomach as he climbed from the car.

They stepped over the threshold into the cottage, and Harley gave them an enthusiastic welcome. Charlie was accustomed to his happy greetings, but something more bothered the little dog. He streaked across the room, barked furiously at the wall, and raced back to pounce on Charlie's legs.

"What's up with him?" Simm asked.

Charlie laughed at her pup's antics. "I don't know. I guess he really missed us. Maybe because he was left in a strange house."

Simm shrugged before delving into the fridge for a cold drink.

"I'm glad we went to that pub tonight," Charlie said, leaning against the kitchen counter. "It presented us with another lead to follow. We'll have to look into Pete's brother more thoroughly."

"Don't get your hopes up. Just because someone else disappeared without a trace, it doesn't mean there's a direct connection to Damon."

"I know. I just have a good feeling." She grimaced. "Or a bad feeling, I guess, depending on how you look at it. Pete purposely deceived us about his brother. He should've mentioned he died in the same way as the others. There's a connection. We just have to find it."

"My little detective," Simm smiled and drew her into a hug. "Harley, quit barking," he said, over Charlie's shoulder. "We're home now, and there's nothing to worry about."

Charlie's mind dwelled on the other victim. "How will you find information about Seth Long?"

"We're going to visit the police detective tomorrow, aren't we? I'll ask him. And it won't be difficult to trace news reports from the time. If we're lucky, maybe we can track down the family and question them."

"Sounds like a good plan. At the same time, we'll ask about Eddie Dunn." Charlie glanced down at the pug who had settled on the floor between them, a low growl rumbling in his throat. "C'mon Harley, let's go relax in our calm spot for a few minutes."

Charlie cut over toward the sunroom. The dog followed on her heels, but halfway there, Harley took up his frantic barking again. Charlie stopped and swiveled toward Simm.

"Did you hear that? Was that you?"

Simm lowered the water bottle from his lips. "Hear what? All I hear is barking."

"There was a noise, like a bang. Or more like a thump."

"Harley! Stop." Charlie picked up the excited dog and cradled him in her arms. "We both heard it. There's something in the basement."

"How would something get in? The place is locked up tight."

"Maybe someone broke in. We have to call the police." Charlie's voice trembled, and her gaze was glued to the basement door. She was poised to run.

Simm raised his hands. "Whoa. Let me check it out. If I see anything suspicious, we'll let Pete know. He can decide if he wants to contact the police."

Charlie's heart pounded faster. "You can't go down there. What if he's still there?"

Simm gave her a steady look. "Charlie…"

"You don't believe me. I heard a noise and so did Harley."

"I believe you. But there's probably a simple explanation. Why would anyone be in the basement? Pete said there's nothing in there. To make you feel better, I'll check it out."

"I'm coming with you." Charlie knew Simm thought it was a waste of time, but she wouldn't relax until she was sure there was no intruder.

"Fine. Nothing I say will change your mind, anyway."

Simm snatched a flashlight from a kitchen cabinet and made his way down the stairs to the basement. Charlie followed close on his heels, the dog still clutched in her arms.

Neither of them had explored this space, and it was even creepier than Charlie expected. The steps were made from old wooden boards, narrow and uneven. The handrail wobbled under her grasp. She knew if she fell against it, she would tumble into the darkness below.

The flashlight parceled out a limited view, but the area seemed to be unoccupied. Simm patted the walls, exploring futilely for a light switch. When they reached the bottom and Simm swung the beam around the room, they spotted a string hanging from a bare bulb in the ceiling. The dim glow did little to improve Charlie's first impression.

The underground chamber was dark, damp, and dismal. It was also small, half the length of the cottage. The only other door was the trapdoor that led to the outside.

Charlie pointed a shaky finger toward it. "He must have gone through there."

"There's no sign of anyone having been here," Simm said. "Look. There's a box. It must've toppled over and made the noise."

Charlie gazed at the empty wooden crate lying on the pocked cement floor. "It wouldn't fall over on its own. Someone must've knocked it over."

"I'll check outside. We know no one's down here."

Charlie agreed with Simm, and even though she knew he'd scout the area to ease her mind and not because he believed there had been an intruder, the effort comforted her. At least to a certain extent.

They traipsed up the stairs and outside, circling the cottage to approach the trapdoor. Charlie's hand grasped the back of Simm's shirt as she followed him in the gloom, her gaze bouncing from side to side in search of a trespasser.

Simm shone the beam of the flashlight on the padlock. "It's still locked. It wasn't disturbed."

Charlie acknowledged the basement was empty, and the door was locked, but she wasn't convinced it was always the case. Harley wiggled his way out of her arms and carried out his own investigation of the area, starting with the trapdoor. From there, his squat little body sniffed its way past Simm and Charlie and whirled in circles several times before heading toward the water.

"No, Harley. Come back."

The dog regarded his mistress with a disappointed look. He cast a wistful glance toward the water before heading back to Charlie's waiting arms.

"What do you think of that?" she asked her husband.

"I think he caught a scent. It could be a mouse, a groundhog, or a stray cat."

Charlie conceded his point and followed Simm into the cottage, but not before casting a last probing gaze into the bushes by the river.

CHAPTER 11

The local building that housed the Sûreté de Québec wasn't large. It comprised a handful of rooms, one of which was a holding cell.

Simm had called ahead, hoping to schedule a meeting with the officer in charge of the investigation, and he was in luck.

Of average height, Lucien Marois had the physique of a man who could eat anything and never gain a pound. A full head of salt-and-pepper hair and wire-rimmed glasses gave him the air of a college professor. The badge clipped to his belt said otherwise.

He greeted the couple with a firm handshake and a courteous smile. Simm had briefed Marois about the purpose of their visit, and Charlie's gaze strayed to the thick file in the center of his desk. She was certain it related to Damon's case.

They both refused the detective's offer of coffee before Simm further explained their interest in the missing man. "He was a friend of someone we know. We promised we'd look into it."

"Let me guess. Craig Reeve?"

"You remember him?"

"I remember them all. Interesting group."

"What do you mean?"

The man leaned forward and folded his arms on his desk, the thick file like a chess piece between them, waiting for the next maneuver. "I can't discuss a case with you. But I checked you out. I know you're an ex-cop and an ex-PI. From what I heard, you're a good guy. I can share things that are more or less public knowledge, but that you may not be aware of. If you question the right people, you'll get the same answers."

The detective had piqued Charlie's curiosity. She leaned forward in her chair to catch every word the man said.

"Take your friend Craig, for example," Marois said. "Do you know what his wife asked me? If we thought Craig killed Damon."

Charlie's eyes widened. "Why would she say that?"

"That's what I said. But she buttoned up after that. Said she was in shock and blurted out something stupid. It's a question you could ask."

Marois flipped open the thick file and scanned the summary sheet on top. "Did you know about the other guy? Bryan? He was MIA for a while." His gaze lifted. When Simm nodded, he continued. "He and the wife went to the house for hanky-panky. When she took a nap, he left the property. Claimed he went to buy beer, but when he couldn't produce a receipt or tell me which store he went to, he backpedalled and said he couldn't find the store. He just drove around. There's a missing gap. But only Superman could cross to the other side, make someone disappear, and get back within that time frame."

Charlie glanced at Simm. He pressed his lips tightly together. She knew questions raced through his mind, but the detective wouldn't deliver the answers.

She turned to Marois. "Damon wouldn't just disappear."

"Some people do. He and the wife could've been having problems. Apparently, he was a prankster. He could've tried some stupid stunt and plunged in the river. End of story."

"What about the other guys that disappeared?"

Marois' forehead creased into a frown. "What other guys?"

"We heard about two other men who disappeared. One of them was Pete Dunn's brother."

A flicker of recognition crossed the cop's face, and he nodded. "What makes you think they're connected?"

"Someone mentioned them at the pub last night."

"Yeah, you're going to hear all kinds of theories there. Did they mention aliens, by any chance?"

Charlie grimaced. One local had chattered about creatures from outer space.

Marois unfolded his arms and placed his hands on the file. "You know I'd love nothing more than to find the bodies, even if it meant opening a murder investigation. But we have nothing except missing people. Unfortunately, in lake and cottage country, it's not unusual for someone to drown and never be found. Usually, we have no witnesses and no trace of evidence, so we have to presume they accidentally drowned."

Charlie balanced the sweep of disappointment at his statement with her curiosity about Craig and Bryan. They were either at a dead end or a fork in the road.

"If there's any more information, it'll come from the friends," the cop said with a meaningful look at Simm.

"I think you're right," Simm said. "We're heading to Montreal tomorrow. If we find anything, we'll let you know. I'd appreciate it if you did the same."

A nod and a handshake sealed the agreement as Marois wished them a safe trip.

CHAPTER 12

Charlie looked up from her book to see her husband standing in the sunroom's doorway. It had been two hours since they'd returned from the police station. Simm had logged onto his computer as soon as they walked in the door.

"Any luck?" she asked.

"Seth Long was a loner. Didn't have a wife or girlfriend. Nobody missed him for over a week. He was due back from vacation and didn't show up at work. Someone contacted his mother. It took a while before they tracked down where he'd gone, and by then, there was no sign of him."

"Did you talk to his mother?"

"I tried. No answer. I left a message. With any luck, she'll call me back."

"No clues, no nothing?"

"Nada."

"How sad. What about Pete's brother?"

"I haven't traced anything yet. I thought I might try to get the information from the horse's mouth if I could." Simm glanced toward the window. "It's a nice day, and I've spent enough time on the computer. How about a trip in the canoe?"

Charlie snagged the life jackets from the storage box, and she and Simm proceeded to the river. She pulled on the bright orange contraption, knowing she'd suffer from the heat, but it was better than drowning. She'd heard enough warnings.

As Simm knelt on the dock to untie the canoe, the sound of motors drew their attention. Two Jet-Skis emerged from around the curve in the river. The engines whined as they sped up and raced upstream with a rooster tail of water behind them and waves rippling in their wake.

Charlie held her breath as they swerved toward the opposite shore of the river at a blistering speed. At the last second, they spun to the left, creating an arc of spray that saturated the trees on the shoreline. The entire event lasted less than a minute, but it looked like a choreographed presentation.

The teenage boys—from this distance, that's what they appeared to be—conferred for a moment, seemingly pleased with their performance. Simm waved an arm in the air to catch their attention and motion them over.

His move worked. The boys had a brief discussion. One of them nodded his head and gunned the engine of the watercraft. The other followed behind, a little too close for Charlie's liking. Their behavior seemed dangerous to her untrained eye.

Charlie expected an unwanted shower as the boys headed in their direction, but they had the sense to slow their speed as they neared the dock.

They appeared to be in their late teens. Both had the current style of longish hair. That's where the resemblance ended. The one nearest to the dock had dark hair, almost black, and his cocky grin displayed white teeth perfected by expensive orthodontics. His shirtless torso showed signs of a love of sports or a personal trainer.

The other boy's light brown hair fell to scrawny shoulders above a caved-in chest. A forced smile and nervous glances overshadowed his attempt to copy his friend's cockiness.

"Nice machines." Simm added a note of man-to-man appreciation for anything motorized. The dark-haired boy's chest expanded, and he shot a grin toward his friend.

"If I'd known they allowed those on the river, I would've rented a couple," Simm said.

The boy shrugged a confident shoulder. "It's not allowed, but who's going to stop us?"

"Yeah, I guess. Not too many cops around here."

"They wouldn't say anything to me."

Charlie fought to suppress a cringe. This kid was the epitome of entitlement, the offspring of one of the wealthy cottagers.

Simm didn't bat an eye. "Who you connected to?"

"My old man's the one with connections, but they know me too." He raised a hand to sweep the hair out of his eyes.

"I bet. You from that big house down the river?"

"Yeah, opposite the creepy guy." He glanced toward his skinny friend, who answered his look with the requisite laugh. "That's just our summer spot."

"From Montreal?"

"Summit Park."

Simm whistled, showing appropriate respect for the wealthiest neighborhood in Montreal. "Nice spot. What's your old man do?"

"He's into lots of things. Bars, restaurants, casinos, all the fun stuff."

"We have a couple of pubs in Montreal. Maybe we know him. What's his name?"

The boy snorted a laugh, as if it was comical to imagine his father associated with someone as lowly as a pub owner. "Marcus Vaughn."

Simm responded with a raising of his brows. "I've heard of him, but we haven't met. Maybe someday." Simm took a step back, signaling an end to the encounter. "Anyway, we were going for a quiet canoe ride, but we'll wait until you're finished with your fun."

"You go ahead. We'll get out of your way. Wouldn't want to tip you over." The glint in the boy's eye said he wouldn't mind making that happen. He glanced at Harley, who sat on the dock, wearing his doggy life jacket and patiently waiting for his usual share of attention. "That's an ugly dog."

Charlie bristled, but Simm gripped her hand and tugged her back another pace when the boys roared downstream, water spraying in their wake.

"I thought you'd give them hell for acting like that on the river," Charlie said.

"I have no authority to say anything. And you catch more flies with honey."

His reasoning made sense. Giving them a piece of her mind would alienate the boys, but it still stuck in her gorge to let them get away with their behavior. "Flies like those two can stay where they are. I don't want to catch them."

CHAPTER 13

Pete's pickup truck was in the driveway when they arrived at the cottage. He shoved himself away from the truck and smiled as they pulled up beside him.

"Just wondered if you guys had decided when you were checking out."

"We plan to take off tomorrow after breakfast." Simm met the man halfway between the vehicles. "Is that okay with you?"

"Sure, no problem."

"I'm glad you stopped by. We were at a pub last night, and the subject of all these drownings came up." Simm didn't mention he was the person to raise the subject with the locals. "We were sorry to hear your brother was a drowning victim."

A pained expression crossed Pete's face, and his gaze swung to the trees that separated them from the river. "I... I don't like to talk about it."

Charlie's chest tightened, and she instinctively reached out a hand to him. She drew it back as it occurred to her Pete may not appreciate her pity. Instead, she sent Simm a look, and her eyes pleaded with him not to press the subject.

"I also wanted to ask about your neighbor. Marcus Vaughn, is it?" Simm said. "What do you know about him and where his money comes from?"

Pete trounced on the change of topic as his gaze returned to Simm. "Not an awful lot. Just that he has a few businesses and lives mostly in Montreal."

"We met his son with a buddy of his. They were riding Jet-Skis on the river."

Pete rolled his eyes. "Yeah, well, if you met him, you met the father. Two peas in a pod."

Simm grinned. "That's what I figured."

"So, you like this place then?" Pete turned to Charlie.

"It's a beautiful spot." Her remarks were sincere. For a quiet summer getaway, this place topped the list. "But I got a fright last night. I heard a noise in the basement."

Charlie expected concern, or at the very least, a frown from Pete. She didn't expect a snicker.

"You're in the country here. There're all kinds of animals moving around at night. It was probably a raccoon trying to get into the garbage bin."

Charlie was determined not to be brushed off so easily. "Who else has a key to the basement?"

Pete's head jerked back, his expression serious. "No one else. I don't take chances with my property."

She had annoyed him, but Charlie's remorse was short-lived.

Before going to bed last night, she had positioned a table and lamp in front of the basement door. She figured if anyone tried to come through, the lamp would shatter and alert them to an intruder. Simm hadn't argued with her, but she knew he didn't harbor the same fears.

The lamp survived the night, but Charlie had a restless sleep.

"I'll check everything out, but I can assure you I've had no trouble around here. Never."

Charlie guessed the mysterious disappearance of a tenant didn't fall into the definition of trouble.

"We know that, Pete," Simm said. "Still, we wondered if you had another weekend available, maybe in a couple of weeks." Simm shoved his hands in his pockets and avoided his wife's curious gaze.

Pete frowned. "That won't be easy. It's booked for the entire summer, and I need to take advantage of the downtime over the next few weeks to get work done on the grounds. The noise might bother you."

"If it's just outdoor work you're doing, it won't. We're early birds, and we can spend time on the water or do other things."

"I tell you what; I have your email address. I'll send you the dates, and you can let me know if you still want it." He climbed into his truck and lowered the window. "Leave the key in the box by the door. I'll come by after to clean up. Nice meeting you."

Charlie and Simm smiled and waved as Pete pulled out of the driveway. When he was out of sight, Charlie swung toward her husband. "We wondered about coming back?"

"I know. It just popped into my head. Something tells me we're not done here."

"With everything Marois told us, there's not much left to find."

"I get that, but I want to come back. If I'm wrong, we'll spend the weekend relaxing. That wouldn't be so bad, would it?"

Charlie tilted her head for a moment. "No, I guess it wouldn't be, but it'll shock Frank."

CHAPTER 14

"I'll be back in a few minutes. I'm going to run to the store. We don't have enough coffee and eggs for tomorrow."

Charlie set her glass of water on the table beside her and stood, rousing Harley from his nap at her feet. "I'll come with you."

Simm frowned. "I won't be long. It's five minutes away."

"I'm coming with you," Charlie said as she brushed past him. "You know the rules. We don't leave each other while we're here."

"I hardly think I'll be attacked and kidnapped in the middle of the day at a convenience store."

"I know that, but I don't want to take chances."

"You're still afraid someone's in the basement, aren't you?"

"That too."

Simm shrugged and headed for the door as Charlie hooked Harley's leash.

The store wasn't big. It was attached to a gas station and sold the bare necessities at a higher-than-normal price. But it was close, and it had eggs.

Charlie decided to pick up a couple of items they'd need for the next day. With a basket hanging on her forearm, she selected a loaf of bread and tried to remember if they had enough butter.

A loud male voice distracted her from her study of the shelf. "They don't have the brands I like here. We'll go to the grocery store in town."

"We don't have time to go that far. The Prestons will be here in an hour."

"We can't serve them no-name slop from this place."

"I stocked the fridge with excellent food. I just need a couple more things. Don't worry."

Charlie stiffened when she heard the conversation but tried to appear casual as she peeked over her shoulder at the couple who stood farther down the aisle, arguing over dairy products.

The man wore a short-sleeved pale blue shirt, open at the neck, with dark expensive-looking pants. On his feet were brown leather loafers with no socks. His dark hair, slicked back from his forehead, had a distinguished trace of gray at the temples, and a pair of expensive sunglasses rested on top of his head. The woman wore Michael Kors high-heeled sandals, a short skirt that displayed her tanned and toned legs with a tight-fitting halter top. Her bleached blond hair spilled just past her shoulders. She was between thirty-five and forty years old, at least ten years younger than her husband.

There was no doubt who they were. The likeness between the man and the boy on the Jet-Ski was uncanny, and it wasn't solely physical. They both projected the same attitude and aura of entitlement.

Charlie's eyes widened when Simm circled around the other end of the aisle and approached the couple.

"You must be Mr. Vaughn." Simm extended his hand to the man. "And Mrs. Vaughn." He beamed at the woman. She preened under the glow of Simm's killer smile.

The man stared at Simm's hand before shaking it with noticeable reluctance. "And you are?"

"Call me Simm. This is my wife, Charlie," he said, holding out his arm toward her. Charlie moved to his side and offered a wide smile to the other couple. She hoped it looked more sincere than she felt.

Marcus Vaughn ran his gaze over Charlie, no doubt noticing her old jean shorts, flip-flops, and messy ponytail.

"We're renting a cottage on the river, near your place." Simm drew the man's attention as Mrs. Vaughn sauntered to the cash register.

"Pete Dunn's place, I guess." His lips curled into a sneer.

Simm pretended not to notice the attitude and offered a sunny grin. "That's right. Met your boy the other day. That's how I knew you had to be his father. Spitting image."

Simm's comments had the desired effect. The man bristled with pride. "Yeah, Tyson takes after his old man."

Charlie was tempted to state Simm didn't mean it as a compliment. Instead, the charade continued.

"That's a nice place you have on the river," Simm said, in the same tone he had given the boys when he talked about their Jet-Skis.

"It's a handy little chalet when we're looking for a change from the city." Vaughn cast a glance toward his wife, as if questioning why it took her so long.

"I hear you're into restaurants and casinos." Simm was determined to keep dredging while he had the chance.

"Among other things." Vaughn shoved his hands into his pockets and rocked back on his heels.

"We have a couple of pubs in downtown Montreal."

The other man's smirk made it clear what he thought of them and their inconsequential business. His wife returned to his side and placed her hand on his arm, a frown creasing her forehead. "We have to get going, Marcus."

"Of course."

The woman sent a weak smile their way, and her husband delivered a brusque nod.

Charlie had a hunch, and she didn't want to waste the opportunity. She took a step forward. "Maybe we'll meet up at one of the charitable events in Montreal sometime." She ignored the grunt of disapproval from Simm.

Marcus Vaughn turned with a mocking smile and a raised brow. "What did you say your name was?"

"Oh, it's not my name that's important. It's Simm. Winston Simmons. Perhaps you knew his father, or maybe you've met his brother, Walter."

Marcus Vaughn froze in place. Only his eyes moved as they shifted to look at Simm. "You're Walt's brother?"

Simm's smile was more of a pained grimace, as if someone pressed a pin into his back. "Yes." He forced the word between gritted teeth.

Vaughn's gaze slid down, taking in Simm's misshapen t-shirt, creased cargo shorts, and beat-up sandals, surely comparing him to his always well-groomed younger sibling. An ingratiating smile replaced his stunned expression. "Why didn't you say so?"

Charlie spotted the tension around Simm's eyes and sensed he neared the limit of his patience. His next words confirmed it.

"Why should it matter?"

Charlie wondered if Vaughn detected the slight trembling of her husband's voice. And did he realize how close Simm was to losing his control? If there was one thing Simm detested, it was classism.

Vaughn's quick, high-pitched laugh betrayed his nervousness, as did his step backward. He waved his hand in a dismissive gesture. "Of course, it doesn't matter. I would've liked to have more time with you. Aren't you a private investigator or something?"

"Yeah. Kinda part-time."

Charlie was surprised Simm admitted it, but it was interesting to see the lines deepen around Vaughn's eyes.

"We should get together some time. We could trade stories about your brother."

"I don't have that many I'd like to share."

"Marcus." The pinched expression on the other woman's face led Charlie to believe she'd like to take a swipe at her husband. He was delaying her preparations for their dinner guests.

"I'm coming." Vaughn answered his wife without moving his gaze from Simm. The showdown lasted a few uncomfortable seconds before the man spun to follow his wife.

As the door swung shut behind the couple, Simm faced Charlie. Before he could speak, she raised her hands in defense.

"I know you don't appreciate that, but you have to admit it gave us something."

Simm placed his hands on his hips. "Really? What exactly did it give me besides a reminder of my parentage?" Tension deepened his voice.

"He knows Walter and not just casually. They run in the same circles. That's certain. They may even be close friends."

"So? My brother is one of the rich and famous of Montreal. Without a doubt, he knows everyone who has money and influence. Why should that make a difference to what we're doing?"

Charlie shrugged. "Maybe it won't change anything, but aren't you the one who always says knowledge is power? The more we know about the people who live here, the easier it'll be to get answers."

CHAPTER 15

"Harley needs a walk. I won't be long."

Simm glanced up from his computer screen. "All right. Take your phone with you."

Charlie tapped her back pocket and smiled. Outside, she hooked Harley's leash onto his collar and took a left turn out of the driveway. This was uncharted territory for her. Apart from driving to Pete's house, they never came this way, but she had noticed walking paths she longed to explore before they headed back to the city.

Charlie had gotten over her fear of the great outdoors. She even wondered if she hadn't developed a liking for it. She would see how much she missed it once she was amid the hustle and bustle of Butler's Pub and downtown Montreal.

Harley remained by her side until she curved onto a trail a little over three feet wide. A mix of gravel and moss made up the path. On either side of them, leafy trees, evergreens, and shrubs tussled for attention. The pug's curly tail wagged as he bound ahead of her, pulling on his leash. Her pet would also miss the excursions in the country.

Charlie inhaled the fresh air and the scent of pine trees and vegetation. She deviated onto another path, mulling over the possibility of it leading her to the water. She wished Simm had come with her. He should have a last chance to enjoy their surroundings without the constant sounds of traffic and people. They never experienced this at home.

The low rumble of a growl drew her out of her peaceful musings. Harley stopped, and the hair rose on the back of his neck. His stiff body pointed toward the trees to the right of them.

"What is it? An animal?" Charlie peered into the greenery, looking for movement and bracing herself for an attack from a bear or a moose. She cursed herself for not bringing the bear spray with her. Tugging on Harley's leash, she took a step backward, but the stubborn dog dug his paws into the ground. His growls turned to furious barks.

"Stop it, Harley. Come on." Annoying the unknown creature wasn't a good idea. She pulled harder. The dog's paws dragged a few inches in the dirt. "Let's go," Charlie said, her gaze pinned on the bushes as her heart pounded.

When the sound of splintering branches grew louder and the trees trembled, Charlie took matters into her own hands. Literally. She snapped up Harley and fled. Beast or human, she wouldn't hang around to find out.

Charlie ran like the devil chased her. And it may have been the case. A quick glance over her shoulder offered her a glimpse of a broad form clothed in black. Definitely human and unfriendly. The heavy club-like object in his hand confirmed the latter. Charlie increased her pace with Harley bouncing in her arms.

Her pulse throbbed in her ears as she veered from one path to another. She hoped to lose him amongst the labyrinth of trails. But she had also lost her way back to the cottage, Simm, and safety. Charlie didn't know where to turn. She was terrified to swerve the wrong way and come face-to-face with the person she most wanted to avoid.

Charlie made a hasty decision. She dived behind an immense rock that towered four feet above her. Pressing her back against the cool, hard surface, she pulled up her knees and cradled Harley to her chest. The dog quivered against her but understood the need for silence. He pressed his little nose to the base of her neck and accepted her soothing touch.

Charlie strained to hear intrusive sounds above the pounding of her heart. There was nothing; no footsteps, no branches snapping. She dared to hope but not to move. She was aware of the phone in her back pocket, but she couldn't call Simm. The man, whoever he was, might hear her. And how could she explain her predicament in a text? She didn't even know where she was.

A cool breeze swept over her as clouds darkened the sky.

After what seemed like an interminable time, she struggled to her feet. Between the weight of the dog and the cramps in her legs, she had to steady herself against the rock before she stepped away and peered around it. There was no sight nor sound of anyone. She slid behind the rock again and wrapped her fingers around her phone. Simm's voice helped to settle her nerves, but she yearned to have him by her side.

"Where are you?" he asked.

"I don't know."

"You're lost?"

Charlie drew in a deep breath to calm the trembling of her voice. "There was a man chasing me..."

"What? Where are you? Are you all right?"

"I'm holed up behind a huge rock, but I don't know where I am." She described the general direction she had taken from the cottage but explained her haphazard escape route.

"Call 9-1-1. I'm on my way."

Charlie repeated the same story to the emergency operator. Knowing both the police and Simm looked for her, she ventured from behind the rock with Harley on his leash. Depending on her instincts, reliable or not, she headed to her right. Her gaze swung from side to side. Tension flowed through her veins. The slightest sound would send her into another full-out sprint.

As she thrust through the clinging branches of a line of shrubs, her chest swelled with hope at the sight of a well-worn path. It signalled civilisation and a connection to the main road.

Charlie stumbled onto the path and recoiled when she spotted a man jogging in her direction. A few seconds passed before her mind registered it was Marcus Vaughn. A smile lit his face, and he raised his hand in greeting. He slowed in front of her but continued to jog in place. His gaze moved over her disheveled hair and clothing before he glanced toward the bushes.

"Doing some off-trail this morning?"

Charlie took in his all-black attire and tried to slow her pounding heartbeat. A quick glance over her shoulder assured her she wasn't alone. A few people strolled the paths within eyesight of them.

"I tried something different." Her words came out in a rush. She wanted Simm by her side. She pointed to her right. "I'm heading to the cottage."

His laugh sent shivers up Charlie's spine. "It'll take you a while. The cottage is that way," he said with a nod in the opposite direction. His narrowed gaze drilled into her. "You should be in Montreal, taking care of your business. Things can go wrong if you're away too long."

Before Charlie could respond, he swept past her, a smirk on his lips. She swiveled to stare at him and spotted a police car slowing to a stop beside her. He lowered his window.

"Did you call 9-1-1?"

Charlie felt foolish. She was rattled, but unharmed. Had she overreacted? Had someone really wished to harm her? "I did. A man was chasing me. In there," she said, pointing into the wooded area beside her. Her path through the shrubs was apparent with broken and twisted branches. The cop cast a sceptical gaze between her and the bushes. Charlie was certain she detected a deep sigh before he disembarked from the car and advanced toward her.

"Who were you talking to? Was he the guy who followed you?"

Charlie gazed at the retreating form of Marcus Vaughn, almost invisible in the gloom of the advancing storm, and puzzled over how to answer. Could it have been him? By speaking up, she would open a can of worms and perhaps falsely accuse someone. Why would he come after her? Were his parting words a threat?

"I don't know who it was. I didn't have a clear look at his face. He was dressed in black. That's all I know."

Charlie jumped when a heavy hand came around her shoulders. Her breath left her lungs in relief when Simm hauled her into his embrace.

"You okay?"

"I'm glad you're here." Reaction set in and her limbs trembled. Charlie hooked her arms around Simm's waist.

The police officer followed them as she tried to retrace her path through the woods, but nothing identified the mysterious man or showed he had even been there. A long series of questions followed, but Charlie had nothing more to add. Her sense of folly increased as the minutes passed, and she regretted calling in the emergency.

Fat drops of rain pounded the trio. The policeman offered them a ride to the cottage, an invitation they readily accepted.

CHAPTER 16

"Sounds like you had a wonderful weekend." Frank leaned back in his chair and stretched his long legs in front of him. "Apart from a strange man chasing you and not solving the mystery you set out to solve." The sun shone through the office window as he and Charlie caught up on the weekend news, both in Montreal and the Gatineau Valley.

"Yes, of course, apart from all that." Charlie sipped her coffee as she gazed at the computer screen and studied the sales numbers for the weekend. "It's a beautiful place, and it was nice to have a change of scenery, but I'm happy to be home, safe and sound, and among my own things."

Charlie had come to terms with her experience in Wakefield. The more she considered it, the more she thought the man hadn't been as menacing as she had imagined. He may simply have been a man hiking with a walking stick. The cop's offhand attitude to the incident had solidified that theory in her mind.

Simm's reaction was altogether different. He alternated between chastising her for going off on her own—although she had informed him of her intentions beforehand—to watching her like a hawk watches his prey.

The one thing that carried over was the confrontation with Marcus Vaughn and his implied threat. She had warned Frank to be extra vigilant around the bars, but she had no idea what they needed to be vigilant about.

"Yet you're going back." Frank's casual tone jolted her back to the present, and Charlie detected a smile in his voice.

"We may. It's not decided yet. We have nosing around to do first."

"Who's the detective? You or Simm?" Frank chuckled.

"I'm his assistant."

"That works out well. He's your assistant here."

"You're right. We're the perfect team."

Charlie had contacted Craig first thing in the morning, and he accepted to drop by for lunch. The plan was for Simm to fill him in on most of what they had learned over the weekend. Certain parts her husband would keep to himself until he talked to more people.

Just before noon, while Charlie filled a bar order, she spotted Craig as he came through the doorway. He separated himself from a crowd of people and headed toward her. Charlie thought he looked nervous, or perhaps anxious. Or maybe she overanalyzed his behavior and should wait to talk to him first.

"Simm has a table for us in the corner," she said after she greeted him. "It'll be private."

Charlie led him to the booth where Simm had settled with a tall glass of water. Craig declined their offer of a drink with a wave of his hand.

"Is it good news or bad?"

Charlie had been right. His breathless question revealed his anxiety level.

"Neither. But I'll let Simm explain."

"To tell you the truth, I have no actual news for you," Simm said. "We discovered nothing the cops didn't already know. We met the owner; we talked to the hermit who lives in the woods; and we mingled with the pub crowds. Not much came out of it. The consensus seems to be that Damon drowned and was washed downstream."

"I'm sorry, Craig." Charlie laid a hand on his arm. "I realize you hoped for more."

"Part of me did, yeah. Another part knew there wasn't much to find." He stared at his clenched fingers. "We gave it a shot, right?"

"I wouldn't mind talking to your friends who were with you that weekend," Simm said.

Craig's head shot up. "What do you expect to gain from that?"

"Probably nothing. But I don't like to leave loose ends, and that's what they are. Would you mind giving me their contact info?"

"I guess not." Craig hesitated. "You want Holly's too?"

"Yeah, she was there. I'd like to talk to her."

"I need to warn you." His eyes flitted from Charlie to Simm. "She had this crazy idea I was involved somehow."

Charlie pretended surprise. "Why would she think that?"

"I don't know. It came out of the blue."

"It's none of my business, but did that have something to do with your breakup?"

"Maybe. I have a hard time figuring out what goes through her head. She and Alanna are thick as thieves. Holly was really upset over everything, and she suddenly turned on me, like it was my fault." His wide-eyed gaze focused on Simm, as if another man would sympathize with him.

Simm gave him a supportive shrug. "It helps to know all this. We'll keep everything in perspective."

Craig texted contacts from his phone to Simm's, and they wound up their meeting. Charlie offered to order lunch for Craig, but he declined.

Charlie frowned as she watched her friend exit the bar, his shoulders hunched more than they had been when he arrived. "I think we're in for a couple of delicate conversations," she said.

"Could be. I know they'll be interesting, at the very least." Simm gazed at his phone. "I'll set them up and we'll take it from there."

CHAPTER 17

Simm and Charlie had a late breakfast. Some might call it an early lunch. They liked the routine they'd established at the cottage, despite only spending a few days there. Although Simm liked to take his time in the morning, Charlie preferred to get up early and tackle the administration side of the business. This was not one of those days.

Charlie swallowed her last sip of coffee as the intercom squawked.

"Simm, you have someone who wants to talk to you."

The couple's gazes met. Frank's voice didn't hold its usual cheer. Something was up. As Simm pushed back his chair and stood, so did she. Whatever it was, she wouldn't let him face it alone.

Charlie followed Simm down the staircase and stifled a groan when she spotted the man standing beside the bar. An elbow rested on the counter, and a grin lit his face. For all the times she wanted Simm to reconnect with his brother, this wasn't one of them. The first sign was the stiffening of her husband's shoulders, and the second was the plastic smile on her brother-in-law's face.

Charlie's past interactions with Walt had been brief and not unpleasant. The last time had been at Winston Simmons Sr.'s funeral the previous year. Her husband had detested his father, but Walter and Susan, Simm's two siblings, tolerated the patriarch of the family. Simm claimed their 'love' for their father stemmed from the purse strings he wielded and that Simm had decided to live without.

Winston Simmons, the father, had been a powerful, intelligent, and successful businessman. He had also been a controlling, ruthless, and immoral human being. He stopped at nothing to get what he desired, when he desired it. If it meant using his money and influence to destroy the lives of others for his benefit, he did it without hesitation.

Fortunately, his wife, although having poor taste in men, loved her children and tried to give them a moral compass to balance out the sins of her husband. She fell victim to breast cancer when Simm was thirteen years old, but with her eldest child, her efforts paid off. The jury was still out on Susan, and it didn't look good for Walter.

Charlie knew Simm's father deserved his hatred. After all, he had written off his son when he took on the lowly profession of law enforcement. But she didn't think her husband should write off his siblings so quickly. As an only child, she would have loved a brother or sister. And from what she understood, the siblings had gotten along well as children, but Simm claimed Walter followed too closely in his father's footsteps to be endured.

Charlie was lenient before judging people, but she was protective of her husband, and he had enough to deal with right now. Walter's timing wasn't ideal.

"Ah, dear brother, you're looking well."

It wouldn't have surprised Charlie if the man had adopted an upper-crust British accent. With his charcoal gray suit, white shirt, and navy tie, along with his raised nose, he had a lord-of-the-manor look. Although two years younger than Simm, his light brown hair had thinned, and he had a mini comb-over going on. The brothers stood at the same height, but the weight Walter had gained since she'd last seen him contributed to the illusion of being older.

"What are you doing here?" Simm remained unmoving, three feet away from the brother he hadn't seen for over a year.

"It's time for a visit, don't you think? We need to catch up." Walt's ingratiating smile widened, but when Simm's eyes narrowed, he rushed on. "I heard you expanded and bought another place. That's great."

A steady stare from Simm and an uncomfortable silence followed. Walt's gaze swung to Charlie. "And there's my beautiful sister-in-law. Sorry I couldn't make it to the wedding. I'm sure it was lovely."

Charlie directed a smile at Walt, certain it appeared as insincere as his. Everyone in the room knew Charlie and Simm were married in a quiet civil ceremony, with only Frank and Melissa beside them. She didn't know where Walt got his information, but it didn't come from her husband, of that she was sure.

Walt glanced at his Rolex. "I realize it's early, but I think I might have a drink, anyway. I think the occasion calls for it." He asked Frank for a glass of whiskey on the rocks and strolled to a booth with the glass in hand. "Please, join me," he said with a sweep of his arm toward the bench opposite him.

Simm sent Charlie a look she interpreted to mean, "Let's hear what he has to say and get this over with."

Once sitting, Simm wasted no time. "Get to the point, Walt. We're busy."

An artificial laugh burst from Walter's mouth. "The point, as you call it, is to see my brother and catch up. A friend of mine said he met you, and it made me think it's been too long since we've seen each other."

Charlie stiffened. She knew what was coming, yet she couldn't predict the outcome.

"Friend?" Simm asked. The casualness of his tone may have fooled Walt, but it didn't take Charlie in.

"Yes. Well, actually, he's an acquaintance. Marcus Vaughn. I think you met him near his place in Gatineau somewhere. He mentioned it in passing."

"He sent you to figure out why I was in his area?"

"Not at all. You're allowed to go wherever you want. I was simply surprised. I thought with two booming businesses, you wouldn't take vacation time."

Simm didn't rise to the derision in Walt's tone. "We weren't on vacation. We were there to help a friend, an acquaintance actually." Simm sent his brother a mechanical smile as he echoed his words, but his stare never wavered from his sibling. "A man disappeared last summer, and we're trying to find out what happened."

Walt examined his whiskey as he swirled it, the ice clinking on the side of the glass. "Disappeared? How?"

"That's what we're trying to figure out, isn't it? Do you know anything about it?"

Walt's head jerked upward, his eyes wide. "Me? How would I know anything? I don't even know who you're talking about. Are you accusing me of something?"

Simm held up his hands in mock surrender. "You don't have to get defensive. I'm still trying to figure out why you're really here."

Walt slammed his glass on the table and propelled himself from the booth. Redness blotched his face. "It's pretty sad when a man can't drop by to visit his brother once a year without being accused of murder. And I thought you gave up your PI gig. What's that about?"

He tunneled into his pocket and removed twenty dollars from a black leather billfold. He dropped the money onto the table, cast a venomous glare at Simm, and strode from the bar.

Simm leaned toward his wife with an innocent look. "Did I mention murder?"

CHAPTER 18

Charlie recognized Holly from when she had shown up with Craig, but she'd changed. Charlie recalled her as a girl-next-door type, with a down-to-earth, relaxed attitude.

Holly's natural brown hair was now a brassy blond, and her features seemed harsher. Whether it was from weight loss or life experiences, Charlie found hard to tell.

As decided beforehand, Simm led the questioning. They met at Holly's house on the West Island, and Simm filled Holly in on the purpose of the visit. He explained that Craig had asked them to look for recent developments in the case.

"You found nothing at the cottage?" Holly set glasses of water on the small table beside them before she settled into a rattan chair. They were on the back patio of her bungalow, where she lived with Craig before their breakup. Evidently, she took possession of the house in the ensuing divorce.

"Nothing new to add to the case," Simm said. "Of course, we only spent a weekend there. Nothing turned up."

"I don't want to sound rude, but why talk to me?"

"We'd like to get everyone's take on what happened." Simm smiled.

Holly's face remained somber. "I told the cops everything."

"Would you mind going over it one more time?" Again, Simm flashed his megawatt smile.

With a pinched expression, Holly complied. Nothing she said about the sequence of events differed from Craig's version.

"Apparently, your first reaction was to ask if Craig was responsible for Damon's disappearance."

Color rose in Holly's cheeks. "It was a gut reaction. I shouldn't have said it. It just brought on a lot of questions and heartache."

Charlie spoke for the first time. "You think Craig had something to do with it? Why would he want to harm Damon?"

"He always resented him, that's all. Not enough to murder him."

"He seems pretty broken up over it, not like someone who didn't like the guy," Charlie said with a perplexed frown.

"He liked Damon enough, but the resentment was still there."

"What was behind it?" Simm asked.

"He didn't tell you?" A smirk appeared on her lips. "Of course, he'd never admit it. He and Alanna were an item before Damon arrived on the scene and swept her off her feet. Craig never got over it."

Charlie didn't mask her surprise. "He must have. He married you, didn't he?"

"He still had a thing for Alanna. Now he's free to go after her."

"Does she return his feelings?" Charlie asked, intrigued by the twist.

"No. That'll be hard for him to accept. Even though she and Damon had their problems, I don't think she thought twice about Craig. She'll move on to someone else soon."

"You still in touch with her?" Simm asked.

"Not much." Her gaze strayed toward the neighbor's house. "We were close before, all six of us. But we've each gone our own way now."

"Craig is determined to unearth what happened to Damon." Simm's narrowed eyes sought a reaction.

"It's a charade or he wants to make sure no one will ever find him." A sour tone coated Holly's words.

Charlie leaned forward. "So, you think he's responsible."

Holly waved her hand in dismissal. "Of course not. Craig is a wuss. He's incapable of fighting for anything. But that doesn't mean he's not happy Damon is out of the picture."

******

"That is a very bitter woman."

Simm drove through the late afternoon Montreal traffic. It would be a long journey to their downtown pub.

"Don't you think it's strange Craig never mentioned the little bombshell about him and Alanna?" Charlie asked.

"It doesn't show him in a good light." Simm's brows lowered into a frown.

"Do you think there might be something there? He resented Damon enough to get rid of him?"

"He doesn't come off as a guy who's happy to lose a friend and a wife. Nor does he look like he's capable of violence, like she said."

Charlie gazed at the scenery that progressed from suburbia to big-city, her mind racing with thoughts. "If he is, he's a great actor. I never would've guessed. And why would he ask us to look into it if he's involved?"

"To throw us off? It's possible." Simm stopped at a traffic light and sent a smile to his wife. "At least it gives us a little more ammunition when we talk to Alanna. Knowledge is power."

Alanna preferred to meet them at the pub. Unlike Holly, her appearance had changed little over the past year. She was still slim and willowy. Her blond hair was stylish and her complexion flawless. But Charlie detected a tightness around her eyes that was caused by the stress of meeting them and unearthing painful memories, or the anguish of the past year.

Alanna settled at the table, deposited her handbag in her lap, and folded her arms. She pressed her lips into a tight line. It was clear she didn't intend to socialize or spend more time than necessary with them. Simm noticed her desire for expediency and got straight to the point. "What do you think happened to Damon?"

"I wish I knew. I'd like closure." Despite the cool attitude she tried to project, Charlie heard the grief in her voice. She longed to reach for the other woman's hand, but she suspected her overture wouldn't be appreciated.

"Do you believe he's dead?" Simm asked.

"Yes." Her tone didn't leave any room for doubt. "He didn't run off like the cops said he did. He wouldn't do that."

"Do you think Craig was involved in his disappearance?"

Charlie knew Simm intended to sideline her with that question. She studied Alanna's expression, and genuine surprise transformed the woman's face.

"What? Of course not. Why would you say that?" Her gaze shifted from Simm to Charlie and back again.

"Apparently you were a couple." Simm kept his tone casual.

"Yeah. So. That was a long time ago." Alanna's body stiffened, and she placed her hands on the table as if ready to spring up and take off.

"No feelings still hanging on?"

"Are you crazy? I married Damon, and Craig married my best friend. That's old news, and it won't change."

"Holly seems to think Craig still has feelings for you."

Alanna rolled her eyes. "Holly never got over that. That's the kind of guy Craig is. He was more serious about me than I was about him. He put too much importance on everything. And Damon wasn't serious enough. There was no happy medium with those two."

"What do you mean, Damon wasn't serious enough?" Simm spoke smoothly, attempting to keep Alanna calm. She clenched her purse in her hands, her manicured nails burrowing into the soft leather.

"You met him, didn't you? He was a big goofball most of the time. And when he wasn't goofy, he was down in the dumps. Like I said, no happy medium."

Alanna sounded more like a pissed-off wife than a grieving widow, Charlie thought.

Simm persisted. "Did he have enemies?"

"Did everybody love him? Probably not. He wasn't easy to love. Did anyone hate him enough to kill him? Not that I know of." She leaned forward, her eyes wide. "Besides, we went away for the weekend. I don't think someone would've followed us just to stalk Damon."

"Were you happy together?" Charlie didn't know if Simm appreciated her intervention, but she couldn't hold back the question any longer.

Alanna huffed out a breath. "I'm sure Holly told you. We had our troubles. I wanted kids. Damon wasn't so keen on the idea. If I wanted to be rid of him, I would've walked away. I wouldn't have killed him."

"Of course not. No one suggested you did." Charlie certainly sympathized with the woman's desire to have children, but she wouldn't consider murder or walking away from Simm.

"What about Bryan and Megan?" Simm continued his questioning after a brief glance at Charlie. "How do you see them fitting into the picture?"

Alanna calmed as the spotlight left her. She shrugged. "They were there. That's it."

"Did they get along with Damon?"

She waved a dismissive hand. "Sure. They get along with everyone. They never rock the boat; they just float on the surface." She snorted a laugh. "An apt analogy, don't you think?"

Charlie thought about the absurdity of her statements, especially when talking about good friends and a husband who may have drowned. Her flippant tone made it worse.

"This past year must have been horrible for you." Charlie didn't fake her sympathetic tone. Putting herself in the other woman's place made her heart break.

For the first time, they witnessed a crack in Alanna's shell. Tears welled in her eyes and her bottom lip trembled. She straightened her shoulders and gazed at the strangers milling in the street outside the window. When she looked back with dry eyes, her expression held only strength and resolve.

"I cope, but the worst is not knowing if he'll come back."

CHAPTER 19

Charlie peered over Simm's shoulder. "What you working on?"

"Researching the other disappearances. They're bugging me," he said without moving his gaze from his computer screen.

"Notice anything?"

"Not a lot. I'll track down whoever led the cases and see what they can tell me."

Charlie plopped into the chair beside him and tilted her head to the side. "You're getting into this, aren't you?"

"Yeah, I guess. More than I thought I would." Simm squirmed in his chair and avoided Charlie's gaze.

"You know, you're allowed to be interested in something besides the pub. There's nothing to feel guilty about. The case interests me too."

He ran a hand through his hair. "I don't feel guilty. It's just something we're doing for Craig. Nothing more."

Charlie leaned forward and took his hand in hers. "You're a good PI. I never expected you to give it up completely. I always thought you'd dabble in it."

"Yeah, well, I'm certainly dabbling now. And I intend to work at the pub full-time. I'm not giving that up."

Charlie wasn't so convinced about Simm's future, and that bothered her. She could only describe their romance as whirlwind. She had hired him a year ago. They fell in love and got married. Did she have the confidence gained from years of getting to know someone, sharing life events, and working together to get through the ups and downs? No. Did she love him and was she prepared to handle those difficulties? Yes. Was he? She hoped so, but her biggest worry was that he would change his mind and want out.

Simm had done nothing to make her doubt his love for her and his commitment to their relationship, but their lack of a long history together worried her. Yet, Craig and Holly had been together for many years, and they had split up anyway, as did many couples. Nothing in life was guaranteed, but Charlie preferred to stack the cards in her favor.

Simm's phone jangled on the desk beside him. He frowned at the screen before answering and putting it on speakerphone. The voice was deep and resonant, with a slight French accent.

"This is Detective Garnier. I was the lead for the Seth Long case. You left me a message. Are you calling with information?"

"Actually, I hoped to get some from you." Simm took a few minutes to fill the cop in on his background in law enforcement and private investigating. "I'm looking into a similar case. A friend, Damon Verne. He disappeared last summer, in the Wakefield area."

Charlie heard a low grunt before the man answered. "We already looked at that one. We couldn't reveal any ties between the two."

"I wondered if you'd mind if I check out the file. I promised someone…"

The detective cut him off. "I can't let you look at a police file, but I might answer questions."

Simm exchanged a glance with Charlie and raised a brow. She knew he had expected a straight-out refusal, so he'd grab the morsel the detective offered.

"What can you tell me about the victim?" Simm asked.

They heard the clicking of a keyboard, a deep breath, and a throat-clearing. "Here it is. Thirty-two-year-old male, six-foot one, 190 pounds, sandy-blond hair, blue eyes. Athletic build, last seen wearing jean shorts, a blue t-shirt, and black sneakers. He was single, no wife, no girlfriend, no children. Does that help?"

Simm pressed on. "Where did it happen? What were the circumstances?"

"Happened near Wakefield. He lived in Ottawa but used to go mountain biking on the trails in Gatineau."

"Regularly?"

"Every weekend."

"Where did he work?"

"In a restaurant."

"Was he biking when he disappeared?"

"He was," the detective said.

"Alone at the time?"

"Just him and his dog. He was into speed, and he didn't like anyone along to slow him down."

"What was the conclusion about what happened?"

A labored sigh. "Nothing solid. He disappeared into thin air. No trace of him anywhere. Presumed drowning."

Charlie snorted. Drowning seemed to be the fallback death of choice.

"What body of water do you presume he drowned in?" Simm asked.

"The Gatineau River. He was last seen near there."

"Personal thoughts?"

"I got a couple. Like I said, I heard about your friend that disappeared last year. I contacted the cop in charge because of the similarities. We compared notes, but there was nothing tying the two guys together. Chances are they were two unconnected accidental drownings. I'd be happy if you proved me wrong, but I think you're wasting your time."

"What about the dog?" Charlie asked.

"Found dead a few days later."

A sharp intake of breath preceded Charlie's cry. "Who would do that? That's horrible." Her distressed gaze swung to Simm, who gave her a sympathetic look.

"How did he die?" Simm asked the cop.

"Stabbed with a knife or sharp object. A big dog too, a German Shepherd. Wouldn't have been easy."

Charlie slumped in her chair after they assured the detective they would share any findings they had, and they disconnected the call.

"I know you feel bad for the dog. Keep in mind human lives were lost too."

"I get it," Charlie said. "But it takes a heartless person to kill an innocent animal for no reason. Imagine what he'd do to a human."

"Maybe there was a reason. A German Shepherd would've attacked to protect his master. It could've been self-defense."

Charlie groaned. "If it was murder, at least it eliminates Noah as a suspect. He wouldn't kill a dog."

"Honey, even I would kill a dog before it killed me."

******

Charlie reached over and smoothed the frown line on Simm's forehead.

"I'm sorry," he said. "I'm distracted and ignoring you."

"I can live with both as long as you tell me what it's about."

It was a quiet Wednesday morning. They sat at the kitchen table while Charlie went over the bar inventory. Simm was supposed to be dealing with the employee schedule. His hand held a pen, but it never grazed the paper. Instead, he stared at the notes as if they were written in a foreign language.

"Walt," he said.

Charlie groaned. "What did he do?"

"Exactly."

"Honey, are you okay? You're not making sense."

Simm flung himself backward in his chair and sighed. "That's exactly what I'm trying to figure out. What did he do? You and I both know his visit wasn't a social one. There was a reason behind it. There's always a reason behind everything my little brother does."

Charlie clasped her hands on the table. "Okay. So, what's your theory?"

"That's just it. I don't have one. Yet." Simm stood and strode to the rain-drenched window to stare at the busy city street below. "I did a little homework. Walt and Marcus Vaughn are both connected with charity events for the Montreal Children's Hospital, where they pretend to care once a year."

Charlie smiled. Simm usually tucked away his disdain for bogus benevolence. She enjoyed seeing him display his true feelings.

"They're also both members at the Royal Montreal Golf Club."

Charlie gave a low whistle. "That's pretty exclusive."

"Very. My father was a member, and he got Walt in."

"You didn't want to join?"

Simm sent her a look. "Golf isn't my game. And, if I had joined, I would've spent time with dear old dad. So... no." He returned to his seat and leaned forward, his elbows resting on the table. "It's not surprising that Walt and Marcus are both members. But they're also regular partners on the course. Twice a week, they golf together and have dinner and drinks in the clubhouse afterward."

"Walt's story of them being merely acquaintances is a lie."

Simm's lips twisted. "Of course. In true Walt fashion."

"Which leads you to speculate about why he showed up."

"Don't you think I have a right to speculate?"

Charlie's nod was emphatic. "Yes. He's afraid you're sniffing around his friend for a reason."

"And that makes me want to sniff more."

Charlie waved her arms melodramatically. "In that case, I forgive you for being distracted, and I set you free to explore your brother's dastardly deeds. I'll take care of the schedule."

CHAPTER 20

Simm slid onto a seat beside Charlie and stared at Frank, who dried glasses behind the counter with a quick efficiency.

"He's alive," the bartender said with a wide grin.

"Hilarious. I've been busy."

"I know. You rarely come out of that office. Charlie's really got you onto something, hasn't she?" He winked at Charlie and set a bottle of carbonated water in front of Simm along with a newly dried glass.

"As usual," Simm said with a wry smile. "Next time, I'd appreciate a heads-up when you hear her come up with an idea."

Frank laughed. "C'mon. Admit it. You love it."

"That's what I said to him, but he refuses to agree with me," Charlie said.

Frank leaned on the counter. "Fill me in. Where're you landed?"

Simm told his friend about the conversation with Detective Garnier. "It got me wondering if there could be others. I called a buddy of mine. He's a detective with the Ottawa Police. He has access to cases throughout the country."

"Are you talking about Josh Riddell?" Charlie scooted behind the bar to help herself to a soda. They still had an hour before the noon rush would begin. "How is he doing?"

Simm shrugged. "He's good."

"How's Tierney? Isn't she due sometime late summer?" Charlie had met the couple when they'd visited Montreal a few months back and had instantly taken a liking to them. Although she was envious of Tierney's pregnancy, it wasn't a malicious envy. It was simply something she longed to experience. "Josh was on cloud nine when he was here."

Simm averted his gaze. "Yeah, I guess he still is. We talked for a few minutes about the case. He'll look into it and get back to me."

Avoidance. Simm was good at it.

Frank discreetly moved to the other end of the bar and struck up a conversation with Melissa.

"Have they chosen a name for the baby? Is it a girl or a boy?"

Simm grimaced and looked around him. Charlie knew he searched for an excuse to leave the room.

"Does she still have morning…"

"Charlie, I don't know. Okay?"

She drew his hand into the warmth of hers. "I'm just saying…"

"I know what you're saying." His gaze drilled into hers, and she felt the intensity of his grip on her fingers. "You know what I'm afraid of."

"The risk of your father's genes passing down is minimal, and it's something we can work around."

"Look at Walt. A carbon copy."

"Look at you. Anything but."

Simm removed his hand from hers and stared into his glass.

******

"I got a text from Bryan," Charlie said. "They can see us tonight."

"Perfect. Are they coming here?"

"In an hour."

Simm glanced at his watch. "I've got a couple of things to finish up." He bestowed a quick peck on his wife's cheek before he headed toward the upstairs office. Charlie's gaze followed him up the stairs. The previous day's disagreement was behind them. She resurrected the subject of having a child more frequently as time marched on, and it always led to the same ending.

But Charlie's desire to have a baby increased with each day that passed, and she truly believed Simm's fear of his father's ruthless disposition being passed on to a child was misplaced. If anyone should worry about genetic makeup, it should be her. As an adopted child, she didn't know who her biological parents were. At least, Simm was well warned.

At times, Simm seemed to weaken in the face of her reasoning, so she persisted. But his fears were engraved on his soul.

"He's really into it." Frank interrupted her musing. "The case, I mean."

Charlie shook aside her melancholy. "I knew he would be. He seems content, at least."

"What if he goes back to it full-time?"

Charlie considered the question. "Honestly, I don't think he will. But if that's what makes him happy, and he wants to do it, I'll support him."

"You'll have to do bookkeeping." There was a telltale glint of amusement in Frank's eye.

Charlie remembered the torture of paperwork. She had done it for several years because she didn't have a choice, but she wasn't a desk person. Working behind a bar, serving people, and chatting with customers was her style. She knew Frank understood. He was the same.

She grinned at him and sent him a wink. "Nah, I'll give that job to you."

CHAPTER 21

Frank whispered a message in Charlie's ear as she ushered a couple to a booth in the corner. She provided them with menus and a smile before she headed for the stairs and their apartment.

She hesitated on the threshold of the office. Her husband stood looking out the window. Charlie didn't need to see his face to sense he was angry. The tension in his shoulders and the clenched fists on his hips were a sure sign. The mystery lay in what made him so furious.

"Simm?"

He swung to face her, his eyes as cold as a Montreal winter.

"What is it?" Charlie asked. His expression frightened her.

"Walt." The word barely made it past his gritted teeth.

Charlie's first reaction was relief. It had nothing to do with her, the bar, or the employees. Once that emotion faded, irritation flooded her system. Why did Simm's brother have to be so frustrating? What had he done now to deserve such anger?

"The root of Walt's visit was because of Vaughn, right?"

Charlie nodded in response.

"I started my digging with him, knowing there had to be some dirt." Simm took a deep breath. "And there was. A couple of years back, one of Vaughn's employees was involved in a hit-and-run accident."

Charlie stiffened. She didn't like the direction in which this headed, but she didn't interrupt Simm.

"It happened during a party held at Vaughn's house in Montreal. Some employees, those that weren't required as servers, had their own celebration. One of them, a man named Paul Lemieux, hijacked one of Vaughn's cars and was involved in an accident."

Simm hissed the last word.

"What happened?" Charlie's voice was barely audible.

"He rammed another car and killed three people. He took off. Many hours later, they found Lemieux and arrested him. He didn't have a scratch on him." Simm's lips curled in disgust. It was clear he would've liked Lemieux to be maimed.

Charlie groaned. "That's horrible. Was he drunk?"

"By the time they found him, they couldn't prove he was drunk at the time of the accident."

Charlie studied her husband for a moment. "It's too tragic for words. But I don't understand where Walter comes into it."

"Lemieux went to court but scored a light sentence. Claimed mental illness. Couldn't recollect the details. Knew nothing about it until the police showed up at his door. Marcus Vaughn hired a top-of-the-line lawyer to defend his employee."

"And…?"

"And the lawyer is a good friend of Walt's. My brother is involved in this somehow. I don't know what he did or how to prove it. I'll keep looking until I do."

Charlie understood the connection Simm tried to forge, but she worried he focused too much on the end prize, which was exposing Walt as a degenerate like his father, rather than concentrating on the logic of the dots he tried to connect. It was a stretch to link Walt to a drunk driver, a man he had probably never met.

Simm interrupted her thoughts. "Walt was most likely there that night. He and Marcus attend each other's social events all the time. I'm sure he suggested the lawyer."

"So? Why would that matter? It doesn't mean Walt was in the car or that he fed the booze to the guy. I'm sorry, but I don't get it."

Simm threw himself into a chair. "Neither do I, but I will. If Walt hadn't shown up here, I wouldn't have given it a second thought. But he did. It was a red flag. I guess he didn't realize it would have that effect. He hoped to find out what I knew."

"And at that point, you knew nothing. But now you know a lot more."

"I also know the prosecuting attorney on the case. I contacted him, and he's going to email me a copy of the court transcripts. I'm hoping it'll give me another perspective."

"You're a smart man, Simm."

"Isn't that why you married me?"

Charlie grinned. "One of the many reasons."

CHAPTER 22

Their posture was anything but relaxed. Bryan stood ramrod straight beside the table, a forced smile on his round face. He wore a t-shirt that hung over his jeans and concealed a small paunch. When he removed his ball cap, thinning blond hair stood on end.

Megan slid into her chair with a wisp of a smile aimed at Charlie and Simm. It didn't reach her blue eyes, and her thin shoulders remained stiff. In sharp contrast to her husband, she was dressed as if she planned a fancy night on the town. Charlie suspected this was Megan's regular look, whether she was at work, a casual pub, or a chic restaurant.

The interview went much the same as those of the other friends. The version of events coincided with the police's information, but Simm drilled deeper.

"What was your impression of Damon and Alanna as a couple? You were pretty close. You must know if they were happy."

"Yeah, of course they were happy." Bryan spoke without hesitation.

"What makes you so sure?" Megan swung a surprised glance toward her husband.

Bryan shrugged. "They didn't fight or anything. Not much, anyway."

"You're clueless," Megan said with a shake of her head. "Just because they didn't argue in public, doesn't mean everything was rosy."

"How true." Charlie wanted to feed the discussion. She suspected a lot could come of it. "Men don't notice things women see."

"What's your take on it?" Simm focused on Megan.

"I could feel the tension between them. They worked hard to bury it, but it was there."

"Do you know what was behind it?"

"Not really. I know Alanna wanted kids and Damon didn't. And he could be a schmuck sometimes. His fooling around got tiresome."

Megan's frankness surprised Charlie. Most people don't speak ill of the dead, but the other woman didn't hold back.

Simm turned to Bryan and shot out a quick question. "How did you feel about Damon?"

The other man's head jerked, and his hand tightened around his water glass. "We got along great. He was a fun guy. Lots of fun. He kept things lively, you know."

Megan looked at him with lowered brows.

"What? It's true." Bryan's eyes darted between the three of them.

"There were lots of times he annoyed you," Megan said. "You should tell the truth."

"Of course." A forced laugh fled his mouth. "But people annoy me. It's nothing special."

Simm spoke up. "The police were concerned about some time you couldn't account for."

"How the hell am I supposed to justify every second I'm out of someone's sight? I went for a drive. Next time, I'll film myself driving the car. They'll have to believe me then." An angry red flush clouded Bryan's face.

Simm raised his hands in defense. "I'm not accusing you of anything. I just repeated what the police said."

"You were royally pissed at him over that money." Megan's lips twisted, as if she had tasted something rotten.

"Would you stop, please? You're making me look bad." Bryan twisted in his seat to face her, but she kept her gaze averted.

"It's no big secret. I'm sure Alanna already told them." She waved her hand in a dismissive gesture.

"She didn't mention anything about money," Simm said.

"Thanks a lot." Bryan's remark to his wife was biting. He turned toward Simm. "I lent Damon some money a couple of years ago, and it took him a while to pay me back. That's all. No big deal. It's water under the bridge."

"There were no hard feelings?"

"None."

"Nothing to worry about?" Simm asked.

Anger rolled off Bryan in waves. Charlie knew there would be a heated conversation in the car. She ransacked her mind for a funny story to lighten the atmosphere, but nothing appropriate came to mind. Besides, the couple sitting opposite them didn't seem interested in a laugh.

Bryan shot a quick glance at his watch. "We have to go."

Megan tossed them another weak smile as she moved from her seat. She swiveled toward the door, and her husband stalked out behind her.

"That went well." Charlie said with a grimace.

"They seem like a happy couple." Simm shook his head. "I don't get it. Three couples who are supposed to be best friends. They spend weekends together. They rent a cottage together for a few days, yet they don't get along." He threw up his hands.

"They get along," Charlie said.

"Really? Damon seemed to irritate all of them. According to most of the people we talk to, including his friends, he was a rude, annoying prankster. Even his wife seems a little iffy about him. How about her remark about not knowing if he was coming back? Didn't that sound like she wished he didn't?"

Charlie conceded that Alanna didn't seem as brokenhearted as expected.

"And what about the love triangle with Craig, Damon, and Alanna?" Simm said. "I don't think I'd be buddies with one of your exes."

Charlie smiled. "They're completely wiped from my mind."

Simm ignored her shot at humor. "And last but not least, Bryan was annoyed and perhaps angry about Damon borrowing money from him and taking his time to pay it back. So, once again, why would people who don't get along want to hang out at a cottage for the weekend?"

"It's elementary, dear Watson," Charlie said as she brandished a hand in the air. "It's the women."

"The women?"

"They're friends. They held the connection, and the men went along for the ride."

Simm stroked the stubble on his chin. "But Holly and Alanna…"

"Were friends. Holly had enough confidence in Craig that she didn't feel threatened by his past relationship with Alanna. Since then, her confidence eroded, but she placed the blame on his doorstep, not Alanna's. Their friendship withstood the storm. And Megan made up the trio with her ability to get along with everyone."

Simm pressed his lips together and frowned.

"Take my word for it," Charlie said. "The women were the filling that held the sandwich together."

"Until someone pulled off a piece of bread and the sandwich fell apart."

"Are you going to look into Bryan's relationship with Damon?"

"Probably. First, I want to know why Damon needed to hit up a friend for money."

CHAPTER 23

Charlie popped her head around the doorframe. "Honey, are you coming for lunch?"

"Soon." Simm's squinted gaze didn't stray from the computer screen.

"Come up for air."

"Sorry. I have a lot going on."

Charlie advanced into the room and perched on the corner of his desk. "Are you happy doing this? I never wanted it to rule your life."

Simm displaced his focus to his wife and smiled. "I'm fine. Don't worry about me."

"I guess I'll always worry."

"Why?"

"Because something's bothering you, and I can't stand not knowing what it is."

Simm's gaze sharpened. "Why do you think something's bothering me?"

"C'mon. I know you. I've asked you this before, and you always say it's nothing." Charlie bit her lip before taking the leap. "Is it me? Is it because I want to have children and you don't? Do you want out?"

Simm stood, grasped her hands, and pulled her into his arms. "Don't even think it. Never will I want out. Whether we have no children or fifty, I'm not leaving you. Ever."

His adamant tone convinced Charlie, at least for now. She would have other moments of self-doubt, she realized, but she believed Simm meant what he said.

"I don't really want fifty," Simm said with a chuckle. "You may convince me to have one.

Charlie raised her head from his chest and held herself away from him. "Really?"

A glimmer of concern surfaced in his eyes. "I'm not committing to anything at the moment."

She kissed him soundly. "All right. I'll take that as an uncommitted pledge."

"How about we concentrate on this case, and we'll worry about that later? Deal?"

"Deal." A spark of hope burned in her chest. She would take whatever she could get. "Fill me in. What did you uncover?"

"Turns out Damon had a gambling problem."

Charlie groaned. "Oh no. The cops didn't tell us that."

"They didn't know. Megan's mention of the money yesterday was a stroke of luck. And a common reason for borrowing money is some sort of addiction. It wasn't hard to put together."

"Now what?"

"I called Detective Marois and put a bug in his ear. He dug deeper. Seems Damon had another bank account where he filtered money and used it to gamble with. They're tracing it. Alanna probably knew nothing about it."

"I bet she does now. Have the cops reopened the case?"

"They never really closed it. They're asking questions, and because I gave them the tip, I hope they'll transfer a few of the answers my way."

"Should we talk to Alanna again?"

"We'll have to. Let's hold on for a few days for the cops to talk to her. She has to digest this information."

"She'll be crushed." Charlie hurt for the other woman. Even if Alanna's relationship with Damon was rocky, the blow of losing him and learning about his secret addiction could be difficult.

"It'll be interesting to see how it shakes out." Simm leaned back in his chair. "In the meantime, I heard from Josh."

Charlie scooted forward. "What did he say?"

"As everyone repeatedly told us, there are plenty of drownings every year. They usually locate the bodies. Sometimes, they don't. He went through the 'nots' and uncovered another case that resembled Damon's, besides the two we know about."

"You're kidding."

"Nope. This one was further away, on a small lake. He disappeared while out on the water by himself. They dragged it and never found him."

"What's the connection to Damon and Seth?"

"This guy, Kurt Gibson, visited the area of Wakefield a few days before he drowned."

"Okay. So, you've tied the cases together because this guy visited Wakefield at some point?" Charlie worried they used an unsharpened pencil to draw conclusions.

"That's one thing. The fact he disappeared without a trace matches the others." Simm raised a finger. "He was also thirty-two years old, athletic, had sandy blond hair, and was an outgoing guy.

Charlie stood and paced back and forth in front of Simm's desk as he linked his hands over his stomach and observed her.

"Three guys disappear under the same circumstances; all of them athletic, around the same age and description, with the same general type of personality." She counted off the points on her fingers.

"Right."

"But how does that tie in with Damon's money problems? Were the other guys gamblers too?"

Simm grimaced. "We don't know yet. It's not likely. It would be too much of a coincidence. It's just another angle. You can't look at a case through a tunnel. You have to be open to anything that comes along."

Charlie seized his hand and gave it a tug. "You should be open to having lunch. Detective work must make you hungry."

Simm smiled and rose from his chair. Halfway across the room, his phone rang. "It's Josh," he said, checking the display. He headed back to his chair as he answered the call. Charlie settled opposite him and eavesdropped. Several times, her husband said 'yeah' and 'okay' before a final 'send it to me.'

"He can't get me the police file, but he's going to send me newspaper articles and other stuff to set me on the right track. There was nothing to show a gambling problem, but it may be well-hidden, like Damon's."

"Food for thought."

"Yeah, now I need food for my belly."

CHAPTER 24

Charlie came upon Simm scrolling through a document on his computer. She peered over his shoulder to see what it was and realized it was the court transcript from the Lemieux trial.

"Have you found anything yet?"

"I just started, but I'm trying my best to read between the lines."

"That's a lot of reading."

"I don't care. I need to do it." Simm looked up at her, his expression intent. "I talked to the lawyer, Stephane, about it. He said something was off with Lemieux. The defense lawyer pleaded mental illness to get a lighter sentence. They had dueling testimonies by psychologists. The jury sided with the defense. He thinks it was because Lemieux came off like a zombie in court."

"I'd think most people would be shell-shocked in a criminal courtroom."

"Steph thought it was more than that. I'll keep it in mind."

"What can I do to help?"

Simm studied her with an appraising eye. "Can you do internet research?"

"Sure."

He grinned and showed her what to look for.

*****

"You're a genius."

Simm glanced up to see his wife at the office door. She had worked in the kitchen with her laptop to do the assigned research.

"Tell me something I don't already know," he said.

"Plenty. I think what I unearthed will impress you."

Simm smiled. "I'm all ears."

Charlie sat in the chair beside him. "Four years ago, a security guard at the Vaughn home was involved in a fistfight at a downtown bar. Beat the crap out of another guy. They arrested him for assault and sent him to prison."

"Let me guess. Marcus didn't lift a finger to save him."

"Fired him. Said he wanted nothing to do with the scumbag."

Simm nodded, a satisfied gleam in his eye.

"There's more," Charlie said. "About five and a half years ago, one of their personal chefs was accused of sexual assault against a minor."

"I bet Marcus fired him."

"Said he never liked him and always suspected he was a pedophile. Was on the brink of getting rid of him."

Simm shook his head. "Now, another employee steals his car, kills three people with it, and Vaughn is behind him all the way. Supplies a high-priced lawyer and gets him off with a reduced charge and a light sentence."

"It raises a red flag."

Simm snorted and pointed toward his computer. "There's enough for a troop of cheerleaders to march through the room waving red flags."

"Like what?" Charlie said, leaning forward.

"Witnesses testified Lemieux was drinking at the employee party that night. At one point, he disappeared, but no one knows when or where he went. One of them claims they saw the car exit the estate, and they thought it was Lemieux driving it. The defense argued that, without a test, they have no proof he drank anything other than non-alcoholic beer."

Charlie twisted her head. "Okay, it looks suspicious, but it'd be difficult for the prosecution to prove. He confessed, right?"

"They charged him with impaired driving, causing death. He pled not guilty. However, the car was in the driveway of his house; was obviously involved in an accident; and a witness put him behind the wheel. He eventually pled to dangerous driving, causing death. His defense was a history of blackouts. He claimed he had one at the time and recalled nothing that happened."

"Did he really have such a history?"

"He never consulted a specialist, but the psychologist they hired diagnosed him after the fact. Would you like to hear about the giant red flag?"

"What?"

"The man who claims he remembers nothing and was in no condition to know what he was doing had the wherewithal to remove fingerprints from the steering wheel and gearshift. But there were other traces of his prints elsewhere in the car."

Charlie's eyes widened. "He wiped away his fingerprints, but he left the car in his driveway?"

"Again, he recalls nothing and claims mental illness. But he's willing to take the fall for dangerous driving causing death."

Charlie studied Simm's expression and understood there was more to come.

"He got off with a fine of a thousand dollars and thirty days in jail."

Charlie dropped her head into her hands. "He killed three people, and that's all he got," she said, her words muffled.

Simm stood, grabbed his phone, and dropped it in his pocket.

"Where are you going?" Charlie asked.

"I want to sling things against a wall and see what sticks."

Charlie scrambled to her feet. "I'm coming with you."

******

Charlie had called ahead to see if he was in his office. When asked who was calling, she dispensed the name of a rich socialite who regularly made the newspapers. Charlie was told there was no problem.

There was a problem when she showed up in jeans, a t-shirt, and Simm on her arm.

"What's this about, Simm?" An angry Walter yanked off his expensive suit jacket and dropped it on the back of his black leather chair. "For

God's sake, you stoop to having your wife make a fake appointment? You could have showed up on your own. I wouldn't turn my brother away."

"Forgive me if I don't believe you," Simm said.

It took some time for Charlie's eyes to adjust to the brightness in the spacious corner office. She strolled to the floor-to-ceiling windows. Their position on the twenty-third floor of the skyscraper allowed a view of the financial district along with a good chunk of Montreal, and it was awe-inspiring.

She pivoted to see Walt and Simm sitting on opposite sides of the modern stainless-steel desk. Not a morsel of paper rested on it. It held a closed laptop computer, and a framed photo of a smiling woman and two young children, a boy and a girl. Charlie remembered seeing Walt's family at the funeral, but only from a distance. She never had the pleasure of meeting his wife Clarisse and wondered why she would marry such a detestable man.

Charlie took the seat next to Simm.

Her husband broke the silence. "I've been looking into your friend, Marcus Vaughn."

"Acquaintance," Walt said.

Simm snorted. "If he's only an acquaintance, I'd love to see what you do for your friends."

When Walt opened his mouth to protest, Simm raised a steadying hand. "All right, for this conversation, we'll call him an acquaintance. Anyway, you were at a party at the Vaughn mansion when an incident occurred."

Charlie knew Simm guessed about his brother's presence that night, but Walt didn't deny it.

"An employee stole one of Vaughn's cars—I believe it was a Mercedes—and a terrible accident happened in which three people were killed. I don't think you should bother denying it. It'd be hard to believe you didn't hear of it."

"I remember." Walt's gaze was stony. "It was a horrible accident."

"No one at the party was aware of what happened. According to the records from that night, it was the next morning before Marcus realized his car had disappeared. The cops put two and two together, and a search for the missing sports car began. Do you remember that part?" Simm's tone was acerbic, but his brother pretended not to notice.

"Yes, I heard of it."

"Several hours later, the car was found at the employee's residence. He was arrested and charged."

"Thank you for rehashing old news for me. I'm sure you must have a point." Walt accompanied his statement with a smile that didn't reach his eyes.

"I find it curious Vaughn would jump to support this person who had killed three people with a stolen car—*his* stolen car—by hiring the best lawyer and experts to get him off the hook for murder."

"Why don't you ask Marcus? Why are you coming to me with these questions?"

"The lawyer he hired is a good friend of yours."

"What does that have to do with anything? You think I'm the only person who knows him. He's a famous criminal lawyer."

Simm continued as if Walt hadn't spoken. "I'm also curious why Marcus would defend this employee. In the past, there were at least two cases of employees who were justifiably arrested, and he didn't try to help them."

"Again, ask Marcus these questions, not me."

"The third thing I find odd is why I made Vaughn so nervous. As soon as he heard I'm your brother, he summons you and sets you on me."

"I hardly think me paying you a simple visit was an attack. Give me more credit than that."

"I'll give you a lot of credit. How's this for credit?" Simm leaned forward and drilled his gaze into his brother's. "You were at the party that night, and Vaughn needed damage control. You rescued him with a plan and a lawyer."

Simm pushed himself to his feet. "But why did he require damage control? That's what I dwell on. He had two other employees that stepped outside the law, and he chucked them under the bus. Why did he care about this guy?"

Walt made a show of looking at his watch. "I've got a meeting in a few minutes. You'd better get to the point soon."

"I thought you'd cleared your schedule for Ms. Rosenthal?"

"Hilarious. Even she only deserved a small portion of my time."

"Lemieux had something over on Vaughn. He demanded the best treatment, and he got it. Why?"

Walt's smile was more relaxed. "Contrary to what you believe, I don't live in Marcus' head. I have no clue why he likes one employee more than another. If it makes you feel better, he asked me for the name of a criminal lawyer. I gave him one. That's where my implication ended." He stood and faced Simm. "You always created sides, and you always put me on the opposite one from you. I don't know why you did that or what I did to deserve it. Someday, you'll have to realize we've always been on the same side."

"That'll never happen."

CHAPTER 25

"What can I help you with? I feel useless." Charlie massaged Simm's tense shoulders as he hunched over his computer.

"You're helping by taking the brunt of running the pubs while I track ghosts."

"Between Frank and Melissa, I haven't had much pub running to do."

Simm swiveled his chair around to face her. "Then why don't we take another trip to Gatineau? This time, we can track down Seth's mother and see what she knows."

Charlie frowned. She had already gone away for a few days. She didn't like to leave her responsibilities in other people's hands, but she had just admitted Frank and Melissa had everything under control. Her thoughts wandered to the cozy cottage on the river and how much she enjoyed sitting in the little sunroom with her coffee in the morning. "I guess I wouldn't mind going back to the cottage. Maybe we'll uncover something more there."

Simm tilted his head. "You think there's something in the cottage that could offer us some clues?"

"I don't know. I keep thinking we didn't do a thorough exploration of that place. Apart from the impromptu search of the basement," she said with a grimace. "All we did was ask questions."

"It's worth a try."

Frank didn't hesitate when they asked if he'd take care of things while they were gone. "It's about time you took vacation time. You didn't go anywhere for your honeymoon. While you're there, why don't you make a baby?"

Charlie's expression turned pensive. "That sounds like a great idea. What do you think, honey?"

Simm cast a withering look in Frank's direction. Charlie experienced a tiny surge of pain. She didn't know if it was from the reminder about her lack of babies or the fact Frank seemed happy they were going away. She felt inadequate in her own pub.

"I think I'll see if we can book the cottage," Simm said.

******

"I'd rather keep the place empty. There could be some water issues."

"We'll only be there a few days. We'll get bottled water if there's a problem."

Pete hesitated. "There'll be heavy equipment. I wouldn't want any injuries." He paused again before adding a statement that sounded more like a desperate afterthought. "What about your dog? You wouldn't want him to get hurt, would you?"

Simm smiled at Pete's unusual concern for Harley. "We'll keep a close eye on him."

"It'll be noisy."

"Compared to downtown Montreal, it'll be an oasis of peace." Simm lowered his voice to a conspiratorial tone. "Charlie really needs this. I'm worried about her. She was so relaxed and happy when she was at your place, but since then..." He let Pete use his imagination to determine Charlie's current state of health. He winked at his wife as she monitored the phone conversation. She grinned back at him.

"We'll pay your regular summer weekend rate. That's a great deal, isn't it?"

Evidently, the idea of extra money appealed to Pete, and he relented, but not before warning Simm he wasn't responsible for injuries to humans or dogs.

Simm disconnected the call and tossed his phone onto the desk. "We're all set. We'll leave Monday afternoon."

******

A trio of workers bustled around the property. One manned a small excavator that gouged a trench from the back of the cottage to the road. Charlie didn't know the purpose of the work, but she sensed it involved plumbing.

Harley bounded from the car and was torn between wanting to greet the workers and avoid the noisy equipment. He settled on remaining by his owner's side until they were safely inside the house. Charlie knew the pug would take care of the meet and greet when the noise abated.

It was as if she had returned home when she walked in the door. Everything was exactly as it had been during their last visit, and a proprietary feeling swept over her. She banished the noise in the basement, the one small black mark from their last visit, to the back of her mind.

This peacefulness was a curious sensation for her, never picturing herself as the cozy country vacationer. Maybe Simm hadn't been off the mark when he told Pete she needed to get away.

"It looks like they're finishing up for the day." Simm dumped their bags at the bottom of the stairs. "We can settle in and relax."

They unpacked before sauntering, hand in hand, to the water. Standing on the end of the dock, they stared at the rock on the opposite side, the spot where Damon was last seen by his friends.

The gentle lapping of the waves against the dock and the whine and buzz of insects zipping along the surface of the water created a hypnotic aura. The occasional chirp of a bird and the croak of a frog added to nature's performance.

A squeeze of her hand jolted Charlie out of her trance, and she twisted her head to catch her husband's smile.

"Isn't this nice?" he said.

"Beautiful." With the return to reality, her thoughts leapt back to Damon. Her forehead creased. "I feel there's something here that'll give us a clue."

"Like what?"

"I don't know. Maybe something was left behind. Maybe Damon made a cry for help at some point."

"You could be right. Something might pop out at us."

They lapsed into silence again until the sound of slamming truck doors signaled the departure of the workers.

Simm sighed. "I'm hungry. Let's get that BBQ going."

******

Charlie woke before Simm. She made her way downstairs and gathered the makings for breakfast. While the bacon sizzled in the pan, she stared out the window and glimpsed the morning sun sparkling on the water.

The sound of movement overhead told her Simm would soon join her. She cracked eggs into the pan and poured two cups of coffee.

A set of muscular arms circled her from behind. "This looks good. It's a treat to have breakfast ready and waiting for me."

"You don't get spoiled like this at home, do you?"

"We lead busy lives at home, but I could get used to this."

"Don't get too used to it. We're only here for a few days." Charlie took a long sip of coffee. "What's the plan?"

Simm settled at the table in front of a plate heaped with food. A glint of appreciation blossomed in his eyes. "I'm going to snoop around outside. See if anything strikes me as strange."

"I'll do the same inside."

Charlie didn't know what she hunted for, but she hoped it would be obvious when she saw it. Having wandered through all the rooms and looked in closets and under beds, finding nothing, she headed for her favorite spot in the cottage, the sunroom. She sank into a chair facing the river and smiled as she watched her husband meander along the trail to the dock, his fists deep in the pockets of his jeans. Harley found a sunbeam and lay down for a nap. Within seconds, his snores competed with the rumble and clatter of the machinery outside.

Charlie rested her feet on the coffee table. As she leaned back in the chair, something caught her eye. A tiny shelf underneath the table held something that resembled a photo album. She shoved aside thoughts of relaxing and wiggled the book out of its resting place. With an eager eye, she flipped to the first page. There was a date from the summer of 1992 with a handwritten thank you to the owner of the cottage and a brief description of what the guests enjoyed. A photo of a smiling family was taped to the bottom of the page. They posed in front of the main entrance to the cottage. Charlie assumed Pete had taken the picture.

The opposite page and the others that followed were similar, always with a notation gushing over the accommodations. A picture of the guests accompanied it, usually taken in the same location. A few were snapped on the dock or by the firepit. Charlie moved to a point near the end of the almost-complete book and backtracked until she reached the page she wanted. Her breath caught as she gazed at the photo of six smiling friends. Pete had taken it when the group arrived, or shortly thereafter.

Sadness struck her. In the picture, the friends brimmed with excitement. A weekend away from responsibilities. Good food, good friends, and good times. The typical goal of long weekends in the summer. But something had gone bad, and it wasn't the food.

Within twenty-four hours, the lives of these people were torn apart, and one of them was lost. She stared at the image of Damon. His sense of mischief radiated from the photo. Was it in the gleam in his eyes, the devil-may-care grin, the casual arm flung over Alanna's shoulder, or the angling of his hip? Had his adventurous spirit been his downfall? Or was it simply bad luck that he had volunteered to stay behind?

Charlie suspected the former, but she had nothing on which to base her suspicion.

The comment read: So excited about our weekend. The place looks great. Fun times ahead.

Someone had gotten the ball rolling for the inscription but didn't complete their thoughts. The reason was obvious.

There were two entries in the album since that date. No photos were added on either of those arrivals. Charlie guessed the joy had diminished after losing a guest and witnessing the grief of a wife and a group of friends.

She flipped backward through the book, interested more in the pictures than the comments, which always ran along the same lines—everyone was happy, everyone loved the place. Even if they didn't, they weren't likely to immortalize their thoughts in writing. Most people were too polite.

Charlie saw an endless array of smiling faces from every age group. Guests ranged from couples to young families to groups of six, the limit for the three-bedroom cottage. There were two photos of a single guest, perhaps someone who needed a change of scenery. Neither of them had bothered to write a comment.

Charlie closed the book and sighed. The briefness of life and the rapidity with which it could pivot hit her. A cloud pressed on her spirit, and she knew she had to get out of the approaching funk. She deposited the book in its hiding spot. With the trees and shrubbery blocking her view of the dock, she couldn't see Simm. It was time to stroll to the river.

The sun warmed Charlie's skin as she threaded her way over the mounds of dirt created by the work crews. The rugged path through the shrubbery was easy to navigate in comparison. The dock came into view and her gaze scoured the area for her husband. Had he taken another route back to the cottage? She didn't think there was one.

Her heart clenched when she spotted the canoe, bobbing by the big rock on the other side.

"He went there by himself? Why?"

Harley cocked his head and looked at his mistress with concern.

Charlie sprinted to the end of the dock and focused on the opposite bank, hunting for movement or a glimpse of a blue t-shirt. Thoughts of Damon raced through her mind, images of a grieving Alanna, not knowing what happened to her husband, waiting for news of the discovery of a body.

Charlie patted the pockets of her jeans. Nothing. She'd forgotten her cell phone at the cottage. She dashed back, tripping over roots and scrambling over the freshly dug mounds of earth near the house, the dog on her heels. In the sunroom, she plucked the phone off the table, jabbed speed dial, and a few seconds later, heard the answering ring coming from the kitchen. Her heart sank.

"Simm, where are you?" Harley's sharp ears picked up her whispered words. His head tilted toward her. "We'll take the pedal boat to go over."

Harley's snorting breaths grew louder as they descended to the dock again.

Charlie lowered herself into the wobbling watercraft before reaching for the dog and setting him on the seat beside her. Untying the boat from its moorings, she headed for the opposite shore, her gaze still searching for Simm. Harley squatted like a sentinel beside her, his gaze pinned on the same destination.

The closer Charlie advanced, the more anxious she became. Why couldn't she see him? Where had he gone?

The pedal boat thudded against the canoe as she pulled alongside. Without thinking about her sneakers, Charlie surged into the water to haul the boat closer and tie it to a tree. She grabbed Harley in her arms and clambered to the crest of the shoreline.

"Simm!" Blood pounded in her ears. She wasn't sure she would hear him if he answered her, but that wouldn't stop her from trying. "Simm, are you here? Where are you?"

Her words bounced off trees as Harley wriggled in her arms. When his paws touched the ground, he circled around Charlie, sniffing and scratching the forest floor.

"Can you find Simm?" Harley was raised in the city, not foraging in the countryside. If he could track someone, it was purely intuitive.

Charlie's instincts led her toward the stream, where it was believed Damon had fallen in and drowned. She didn't linger to see if Harley picked up Simm's scent. She dashed toward the water, yelling for Simm, and encouraging the pug to follow her.

Charlie's lungs labored as she stopped on the bank of the stream. Her narrowed gaze searched for a sign of her husband in the flowing water. A sharp bark drew her attention to Harley. He stood six feet away, his tail wagging, as he looked at her expectantly. She advanced and kneeled beside him.

"Oh no," she breathed. Her hand reached out and collected Simm's cap, lying mere feet from the bank. "Please, no."

Her fingers clutched the hat as she jogged alongside the bank, heading upstream, her gaze moving from the path to the sparkling water on her right. Harley kept pace beside her as she gathered speed.

This time, the condition of the bridge didn't penetrate her mind. Both she and Harley darted across it, hurdling over the empty spots, with no particular destination in mind. Charlie wanted to cover the most area possible.

She yelled her husband's name as she ran, until a thunderous bark caught her attention. Charlie skidded to a halt and pressed Simm's hat to her chest as she waited for the immense beast to pounce.

His tongue lolled out of his open mouth as he bounded toward her, each step covering several feet. Yet, it wasn't Charlie who attracted the dog; it was Harley's frantic yapping. Leaves and dirt flew in every direction when the mastiff slid to a stop beside the pug, and they engaged in a round of sniffs.

Charlie's gaze met that of the large, bearded man who lumbered through the trees. His lowered brows accentuated the dark gleam in his eyes. Her heart hammered a rapid beat. She didn't need this confrontation. She had to find Simm, and she couldn't waste time.

The man turned and looked behind him. Charlie glimpsed a familiar blue shirt. A high-pitched yelp bolted from deep inside her as she drove past the bigger man and launched herself at a wide-eyed Simm.

Her arms wrapped around him for a brief second before she stepped back half a pace and punched his arm.

"Ow! What was that for?"

"Where did you go? I've been searching everywhere for you." She pitched his hat at him. It bounced off his chest and landed on the ground between them. "Dammit Simm! I looked... I looked..." The words caught in her throat, and her hand waved toward the water that rushed by them.

Charlie's hands clutched her husband's shirt as his arms folded around her and pulled her close. "I was so worried. I thought you'd drowned. Or someone had killed you. What would I do without you?"

"I'm sorry. I didn't think I'd be gone that long."

A voice boomed the mastiff's name. Charlie and Simm broke apart to see the dog send a last wistful look at Harley before he bounded after his master. The dense trees swallowed them within seconds.

"He left without saying anything." Charlie wiped her face with shaky hands.

"He's a man of few words."

"What were you doing with him?"

"I came upon him. Or, rather, Bosco came upon me. I braced myself, or the brute would've knocked me into the river. Your worst fears would've come true."

"You hung out with them?" Charlie had trouble wrapping her head around the thought.

"It was less hanging out and more me asking questions and getting grunts in return."

"Did you get inside the house?"

"No invitation was offered, and I didn't think he'd fall for the old can-I-use-your-bathroom trick. He saw through it last time."

Charlie's hands gripped Simm's forearms. "Swear to me you'll never take off like that again. Not around here."

"Don't worry. I won't."

"You didn't even take your phone." Charlie couldn't keep the accusatory tone from her voice. A tightness still gripped her chest.

"It was a last second decision. I intended to go over and back. I didn't think you'd have time to miss me."

Charlie picked up the cap, shook off the dirt, and poked it into its original shape, or close to it.

"Yeah, I lost that when Bosco tried to tackle me."

Simm took it from her, inspected it, and pulled it on. "I saw something, but it may be meaningless."

Charlie stilled. "What?"

"I saw a section of freshly turned earth."

"How big?"

"Big enough."

CHAPTER 26

"I've got to track down the family of those other guys." Simm focused on his computer screen, his fingers performing a tap dance on the keyboard. His head lifted, and he stared at his wife. "Did you hear me?"

Charlie huddled on the couch with a cup of tea clasped between her hands. "Yeah. I'm still creeped out by that grave."

"I didn't say it was a grave. I said it was overturned earth."

"I won't go there in the middle of the night to dig it up."

Simm laughed. "This isn't a horror movie. If we feel we need to, we'll tell the cops. Let them dig it up."

"Why don't we call them now?"

"The guy could be planting a garden. We can't report everyone who's doing yardwork. Like I said, I'll find someone connected to Seth Long or Kurt Gibson."

"Good plan. What can I do?" Charlie set her mug on the coffee table and stood.

Simm cocked an eyebrow and puffed out his chest. "How about bein' a good woman and rustlin' up some grub for your hungry man?"

Charlie narrowed her eyes. "That's such a sexist remark."

His chest deflated, and he grinned. "What can I say? I'm a sexy guy."

A groan accompanied Charlie's eye roll.

"Actually, I have a better idea," Simm said. "Contact Craig. Quiz him about who had the idea for the weekend getaway and who chose the spot."

"What are you going to do?"

"Locate someone with connections to the rich and famous in Montreal."

Fifteen minutes later, Simm strolled into the kitchen as Charlie poured herself a cup of tea.

"And?" he asked.

"Damon came up with the idea, found the place, and made the reservations."

Simm nodded. "Things are slipping into place."

Charlie thought signs of progress would make Simm happy, but his frown said otherwise. "What did you find?"

"I called an old school friend I keep in touch with. He knows Marcus Vaughn. Said he's a shady character. There're rumors he may be connected to the Mafia, but nothing confirmed. Of course, anyone running casinos is assumed to be connected."

"I thought the Quebec government controlled the casinos."

"They do. That's why he opened them on the American side of the border. He has plenty of other businesses in Montreal."

"Did your friend have anything else to share?"

Simm grimaced. "Nothing good. A sleazeball is the term he used."

Charlie watched Simm remove a water bottle from the fridge. "I'm not surprised," she said. "We had a glimpse of both the apple and the tree it tumbled from."

"Did Craig know if Damon went to the casinos Vaughn owns?"

She shook her head. "He said he'd find out. It didn't surprise him when I questioned him about it. He had suspicions, but never thought it was connected to his disappearance."

Charlie paced, her hands clasped behind her back and her head bowed. "Okay, let's say Damon planned the weekend because of some association he had with Marcus Vaughn. What did he want? Was he going to spy on him? Did they set up a meeting? The trip to the other side was a spur-of-the-moment thing. It doesn't make sense."

"And how did Damon find an excuse to stay over there by himself? He didn't know the boat would take on water."

Charlie faced her husband, her arms folded over her midriff. "If he intended to spy on Vaughn or meet up with him, it wasn't planned."

"Damon may have owed him money, and he wanted to negotiate with him, or force his hand."

A horrible thought invaded Charlie's mind. "Do you think he planned to hurt someone? Kidnap a kid, or something?"

"I think we're letting our imaginations get away on us. We need more information before we can jump to any theories."

"There's something else to consider."

"What?" Simm tilted his head.

"If Damon had a personal vendetta against Vaughn, and it backfired, but it involved his gambling habit, what's his connection to the other men who disappeared?"

"Maybe there's none. The others may be random disappearances. They could've drowned, like everyone suspects."

"What are the chances?"

"Seemingly, the chances are good."

"Do you think Damon had something to do with the car accident?"

"I hope not."

CHAPTER 27

Charlie and Simm didn't call ahead, deciding to stop on their return trip from the grocery store.

The wooden sign at the end of the driveway used an intricate design to advertise a furniture restoration and antique shop. Immense wooden doors stood open and exposed the interior of a well-ordered workshop. Antique and newly built furniture, along with smaller items, including lamps, mirrors, and cookware, were arranged in front of the structure that sat several feet from the main house.

Charlie's steps were eager as she approached the shop. The condition of the furniture and restoration spoke of the talent of the woodworker. She beamed a genuine smile of admiration at Pete when he emerged from the gloom of the interior.

"You have so many beautiful things. You're a natural."

Pete's cheeks turned a shade of pink at Charlie's words, and his smile revealed his pleasure at the compliment. "It's just something I putter at."

"You're too modest." Simm stepped inside the workshop and gave a low whistle. "Quite the set-up you have here. Look at all these tools."

Charlie was also impressed with the quantity of tools and the order in which they were kept. She was convinced Pete had obsessive-compulsive disorder. Either that, or Simm had whatever the opposite of OCD was. His tools were in constant disarray.

"He won't make a mess in here, will he?" Pete pointed at Harley, who strained at the end of his leash.

"Not at all. He's very well-behaved." To put his mind at ease, Charlie bent and picked up the pug.

Simm stood in front of a panel of gadgets and implements, his eyes wide. "You must have every saw known to man."

Pete chuckled. "There might be one or two I'm missing. I guess you'd call it my passion," he said with an expression full of pride.

"And everything's so clean." Simm was clearly awestruck.

"I don't put a tool back unless I've cleaned it to a shine."

Charlie wandered over to the opposite wall. A corkboard covered a wide section. Dozens of photos adorned it. In them, people stood near furniture items, their expressions happy and satisfied. Some were taken in or near this workshop. Others were captured in their homes.

Pete spoke from behind her left shoulder. "Those are my pieces with the lucky clients that bought them."

"It's a good idea to take pictures. They're great reminders."

"I like to keep track of what I've done. People see the quality of the work and how much people love them."

"You have such a beautiful home," Charlie said. It had looked nice from the river, but now she could appreciate the immaculately maintained property.

"Thank you very much. Why don't you come down and I'll show you the boathouse?"

Charlie and Simm followed Pete down the graveled path past huge rhododendron bushes toward the river.

"This is a pleasant surprise. I didn't expect you to drop by for a visit." Charlie wondered if she detected a quiver of wariness in Pete's voice.

"We didn't expect to visit. We drove by and stopped in." Charlie sent him her warmest smile, wanting to put him at ease. "I'm so glad we did. Everything is even lovelier from this angle."

Charlie's gaze took in the manicured lawns, the well-tended gardens, and the boathouse and dock they had seen from the water.

"You must be busy, what with the shop and the rental property," Simm said.

"Busy enough, I guess. As much as I need to be." Pete gave a casual shrug, but his tone sounded wistful. "This place has been in my family for generations. It's just my mother and me who live here now. We don't spend much money."

A buzzing noise interrupted them. Pete grabbed his cell phone from his pocket, and his lips twisted into a slight grimace. "That's my mother. She had a terrible stroke a few years back. I don't leave her alone very often."

Charlie spoke up. "We'd love to meet her, if we may."

A concerned expression crossed Pete's face. "She can't talk."

"That's okay. We'll just say hello." Her natural friendliness drove Charlie, but she also wanted to understand everything she could about the people who had circled Damon's life at the time of his disappearance. That included Pete and his family.

Pete led the way to the house, and the couple fell in behind him. Simm shot Charlie a look that held a mixture of curiosity and pride. On Pete's instructions, they tied Harley's leash to the post of the veranda before going inside.

As expected, the interior of the house was impeccable and neat, but it assaulted Charlie's simplistic tastes. Heavy antiques in dark wood, lovingly restored, filled every corner and hallway. Victorian-style wallpaper and wainscotting embellished the walls. An ornate handrail decorated the curved staircase leading to the second floor.

To the right of the entranceway, in a sitting room, a tiny, frail-looking woman sat in a straight-backed wooden chair. The size and quantity of the furnishings made her appear insignificant. Providing further contrast with the surroundings was the practical wheelchair beside her.

Following Pete's lead, Charlie and Simm stepped into the room. The older woman's eyes shifted toward her son's shoes as she raised a trembling hand to wipe away a line of drool that trickled down her chin.

"Mother, these people want to say hello." His tone still held the wariness, and Charlie wasn't sure if it was because of concern for his mother or if something else was at play.

Charlie stepped in front of the woman and bent forward to place herself in her line of vision. She didn't offer her hand to shake, unsure about physical limitations. "I'm pleased to meet you, Mrs. Dunn."

The woman lifted her head. Her eyes widened as her gaze met Charlie's before moving to Simm. The trembling morphed into a near-violent shaking as she swung her head to look at Pete with a terror-stricken expression. A whimper escaped from deep in her throat.

Charlie took a step back, her hand clutched to her chest. "I'm so sorry. I didn't mean to frighten her."

"It's okay," Pete said, but his swift maneuver to step between Charlie and his mother showed it was anything but okay. "She's not used to seeing people." He put his hands on the arms of her chair and leaned down until they were face-to-face. "Don't worry, Mother. There's no danger. Nothing for you to be afraid of."

The woman's stricken gaze clung to his before it swiveled back to Simm. Charlie saw fear in her eyes, but there was something else she couldn't define. Was it pleading? Did she beg them to leave?

Pete turned to them, his face ashen. "You'd better go."

Charlie followed Simm and Pete outside, throwing a last glance over her shoulder at the woman whose gaze was locked on the trio. Outside, Pete faced them, but his head hung low as he stared at his feet. "I'm sorry. I made a mistake the other day. I spoke to my mother about your friend and how you thought some of the other disappearances were connected. Now she thinks there's a madman running loose."

Charlie's hand covered her mouth, dismayed for the older woman who not only had to deal with a terrible handicap, but lived in fear. "How terrible for her."

Pete met her gaze. "Her mind isn't as sharp as it used to be. I tried to explain she wasn't in any danger, but I guess she didn't understand. I'm sorry for putting you in that situation. I should have explained."

Charlie's first instinct was to reassure him and apologize for the intrusion. Although her heart went out to the older woman, she speculated about what Mrs. Dunn really feared. Was it her and Simm? Was it having strange people in her home? Or was she afraid of her son?

Charlie released Harley from the porch railing. He hadn't been happy about being excluded from the visit, but in hindsight, Charlie was glad they hadn't added the extra complication of a dog to the encounter.

In the car, she raised her hands to her cheeks. "I feel bad for that woman. We shouldn't have gone in there."

"I feel terrible too, but Pete shouldn't have let us in if he thought she'd react that way." Simm pulled out onto the main road that led to the cottage.

"Do you think she was afraid of us?"

Simm sent her a curious look. "Who else would it be? Pete?"

Charlie shrugged a shoulder without removing her gaze from her husband, who shook his head.

"I think you're reading too much into it," Simm said. "The woman is obviously infirm. She's in the house with only Pete for company. Of course, a couple of strangers would creep her out, especially if she's been hearing stories of people disappearing. She might not be the only person who's afraid."

It hadn't occurred to Charlie that the vanishings would create terror among the residents of the small town, and she said so.

"I don't think many people made the connection," Simm said. "The police didn't. And, when it comes down to it, we haven't found it either."

"I think it's there. We have to delve deeper." The encounter with Pete's mother spurred a sense of urgency in Charlie.

Simm detoured to a nearby gas station. As he pumped gas, Charlie's mind wandered. She gazed out the window at the sights of small-town Quebec; the quiet streets, the small shops and businesses, and the comings and goings of residents. A man came out of a diner and strolled down the street. Something about him was familiar.

Charlie straightened and leaned forward in her seat. Yes, his walk and build were similar. The breeze raised his hair and disturbed the careful comb-over. Charlie struggled to open the door as her heart pounded. Simm was in the store paying for the gas. Harley scurried to follow her out of the car, but she slammed the door shut. She couldn't waste time with either a leash or Simm's arrival.

Charlie glanced up and down the street before crossing. Her flip-flops made her movements awkward and far from fast, but she still had the man in her sights. He had reached the next light, and she prayed for it to change so he couldn't cross. Luck wasn't with her.

He traversed the street and merged with a group of eight. Charlie glimpsed the top of his head as she hurried to catch up. Within a few feet of the knot of people, a moment of dread overtook her. She couldn't see him.

She grasped the elbow of the nearest person, a young woman. "Excuse me." Her chest heaved as she forced out the words. "There was a man. Where did he go?"

The woman's startled gaze moved from Charlie's face to her hand. Charlie released her as her friends glared.

"What are you talking about?" the girl said.

"I saw a man. He was walking with you. I need to know where he went."

They traded perplexed looks as Charlie heard a shout from behind her. She whirled to see her husband jogging in her direction with Harley under his arm like a football.

"What happened? What are you doing?" Simm said, as breathless as she had been a moment earlier.

"I saw Bryan."

"Here?" Simm's eyes narrowed as he swung his gaze around the area. With his height, he had a better chance of noticing him. "I don't see him anywhere."

The group of friends moved on once they sensed the lack of urgency.

"There aren't many places to go. I'll look inside each shop," Charlie said.

Within ten minutes, they had investigated all the surrounding businesses with no sign of Bryan. Charlie's shoulders slumped when she met Simm on the sidewalk. "I was sure it was him."

"I believe you, but he isn't around anymore."

"What is he doing here?"

Simm's shoulders hiked in a shrug. "I don't know, but it won't be too hard to find out. We'll call him when we get to the cottage."

******

Harley scurried from the car as soon as Charlie released him from his harness. The workers were there, and the pug was confident he could wheedle snacks. He spun and sprinted back to Charlie when the excavator roared to life.

Simm bundled the dog in his arms and strolled beside his wife on the way to the cottage. "So much for peace. We'll make that call and then we can go for our canoe ride."

Charlie was about to reply when a shout rang out. Their attention swung to the trio of workers. One man bent to reach for something in the hole created by the machinery, but another snagged his arm and reined him in. All of them spoke at once in rapid French, their expressions alarmed.

Harley, sensing adventure, wriggled to get out of Simm's arms and took off as soon as his little paws hit the ground, heading toward the center of the action. He hesitated at the edge of the hole, but as he poised his little body to bound into it, one man caught him and raised him off the ground. Charlie reached the dog a few seconds later, and her gaze followed everyone else's. Her mouth dropped open in shock.

CHAPTER 28

The backyard was crowded.

It was past quitting time, but the workers huddled together beside the heavy equipment. Their boss had joined them, whether from curiosity or for damage control was anyone's guess. A distraught Pete paced beside the house, deep in conversation on his cell phone, his free arm waving in the air. Two police cars and a CSI van blocked the driveway. More cars lined the street. No one could leave.

Charlie and Simm withdrew to the house. They'd wait for the police to interview them, but they had little to tell them except what they'd seen in the trench.

Charlie's shock had kept her pinned to her spot as Simm knelt beside the cavity and used a branch to lift a piece of filthy, stained clothing, just enough to peer underneath. "Call the police."

"Is it…?" Charlie had breathed the words, afraid of his response.

"Yes. I see bones."

"Oh, God." Her worst fears were realized. Murmurs of alarm circled among the men.

Simm stood and looked at Charlie with concern. "Why don't you take Harley to the house and stay there? I'll call the police and Pete. Nobody can touch anything here." His gaze swung over the workers as he spoke.

Charlie clutched the dog in her arms as she stumbled toward the cottage. Even though she realized Damon was likely dead, seeing his bones in a hole was horrible. She had never witnessed anything like it, and it would be an image forever engraved in her mind.

Now Charlie lounged in the sunroom with Harley sprawled on her lap. The dog seemed to sense her desire for his comforting presence.

Charlie had an unrestricted view of her husband as he talked to Pete. The owner of the property flapped his hands toward the excavation, the workers, and the investigators. Although she understood his agitation, the redness of his face and the flare in his eyes suggested he was angry. At whom, she couldn't imagine. Certainly no one here was at fault for burying a body in his backyard. His reaction was probably born of stress and fear. It didn't look good to unearth a murder victim on your property.

She glanced toward the police cars and saw officers questioning the three workers, each of them with a different cop, separated by several yards.

Did the bones belong to someone else, or were they Damon's? It seemed likely to be the man she had known. He disappeared while he was a guest in this very house. She looked around her. The idyllic setting took on a sinister cast. The sky had darkened with low, gray clouds, as if to thrust a cloak of mourning over the scene.

Charlie groaned out loud as she imagined Alanna and the other friends receiving the news that Damon was murdered and buried so close to the cottage in which they had stayed. Whoever killed him bided his time for a few days to dispose of the body, waiting until the coast was clear and the cottage was empty.

Another car parked on the street near the driveway, and Detective Marois made his way to one of the uniformed police officers. They spoke for a few minutes until the cop directed the detective toward Simm and Pete, who observed the newcomer's approach with interest.

The men exchanged handshakes with Marois before the detective strolled to the edge of the hole. Pete and Simm trailed behind. Charlie's curiosity got the better of her, and she was about to head outside when the cop waved the men toward the house.

The detective nodded at Charlie when he crossed the threshold, and his gaze circled the room before he turned to Simm. "I didn't realize you were back. Still carrying on your investigation?"

Charlie didn't miss the forced nonchalance of his tone and knew he battled to conceal his annoyance.

Simm put a casual spin on their presence. "I wouldn't call it an investigation. Just trying to get some answers for our friend." He gave a wry smile. "And enjoying a weekend away."

"A body turned up while you're here."

"You think we made it appear out of nowhere? It was there a while."

Pete, wide-eyed and fidgety, spoke up, his voice bordering on a shout. "I'd like to know how it got there."

The cop's gaze narrowed on the agitated man. "You didn't notice anything? There was growth on top of it, wasn't there?"

"And around it. But I didn't notice anything out of the ordinary."

"Who maintains the grounds?"

"I do, but I never bother with that corner. There's no grass to mow, just shrubs. I concentrate on the front lawn and the gardens."

The cop gave him a long speculative stare, and Pete squirmed under his attention.

Marois finally shifted his gaze to Simm. "We'll know more with the forensics."

"You'll keep me posted?"

"As much as I can." With that enigmatic response and a nod, the detective took his leave.

"I don't believe this is happening." Pete ran a shaky hand through his hair. "Of all things... your friend buried in the backyard of my property."

"How do you know it's Damon? Did you recognize the clothing?" Simm asked.

Pete's eyes bulged. "Who else would it be? He was staying here. Whoever killed him must've thought it was a sick joke to bury him in the backyard." He shook his head in confusion. "I can't believe you'd think it could be someone else." The color drained from his face. "God, do you think there are others buried here?"

Charlie was worried about Pete. A sheen of sweat covered his reddened face, and he trembled with nerves. She rushed to reassure him. "I'm sure there's only one. There's no point in agonizing over something we can't control."

Pete didn't react to Charlie's comments. Instead, his anxiety seemed to increase, his face reddening further.

"They would never have discovered it if it wasn't for the workers. What were they doing? There's nothing there to work on."

Charlie's brows lowered in puzzlement. Pete made it sound as if he wished they hadn't uncovered the body. Didn't he realize how important it was to solve the crime and grant the family closure?

"From what I understand, they were looking for the water main," Simm said. "The layout they had on the plan wasn't clear."

"God, this is crazy." Pete flung out his arms. "It was probably the hermit who lives downstream. It's exactly something he'd do."

Charlie glanced at Simm. She knew he pictured the overturned earth on the man's land and wondered if there was another body buried there. Now wasn't the time to bring it up.

"It could be that damn Marcus Vaughn. He's the type."

Charlie questioned how Pete had determined Vaughn was the type to murder someone and bury him in someone else's yard. Because he was rich and arrogant?

"At any rate," Simm said, placing a steady hand on Pete's shoulder. "There'll be questions, and hopefully they'll lead us to an answer. That's the silver lining, as difficult as it is to see."

A sour expression contorted Pete's face. It was obvious he disagreed with Simm's philosophy, but he withheld his comments.

Simm turned to Charlie. "I think we should stay a few more days. Do you think we can swing it?"

Charlie consented to talk to Frank and see if it would work.

"Pete, would that be okay with you?" Simm asked. "Is the place rented?"

The other man said it was fine. Other things occupied his mind. He mumbled something unintelligible and left the house. Charlie's gaze followed him as he crossed the lawn to speak to the workers' boss.

Leaving an unhappy Harley inside the cottage, Simm and Charlie tracked down the detective and pulled him aside. "I don't really feel right doing this," Simm said. "I may be off track, but I paid a visit to Noah Wolfe the other day, and I noticed a pile of freshly worked earth.

The cop frowned. "On his property?"

"Yeah. It could be something innocent. Maybe he's putting in a garden, but after this…," he gestured toward the depression in the ground surrounded by yellow crime scene tape.

"I get it. We'll check it out."

Charlie watched the detective move toward his car before her gaze strayed to the hole in the far corner of the yard. "Poor Damon," she said.

"I don't think it's Damon."

She swung to face her husband. "You don't? Why not?"

"The decomposition of the body was too advanced. Damon's only gone ten months. In this climate, it would take over a year to reach that state. I'm not an expert, though. Maybe the tests will identify Damon. If not, it could be one of the others."

Charlie's stomach sank. She didn't know which was worse; knowing Damon was buried nearby, or not having the closure of finding a body.

CHAPTER 29

Charlie sat on the edge of her seat, waiting for Simm to hang up the phone. The person on the other end was chatty. All she heard were Simm's muttered acknowledgments and the occasional question, but prompting was rarely required.

Charlie remained glued to the chair. Pieces of the puzzle were still missing, and she was convinced a clearer picture would materialize.

She sat straighter when her husband punched the disconnect button and set down the phone. He pushed himself from his chair and stretched long and hard.

"What did she say?"

He glanced over his shoulder on the way to the fridge. "Who?"

"Winston Simmons, the Third. Don't you tease me."

Simm took his time unscrewing the top of the water bottle and taking a long drink.

"Did I ever tell you how lucky you are to have a patient wife like me?"

A grin spread over his face. "Many times. I also appreciate that you don't talk my ear off."

"What did Kurt Gibson's wife have to say?"

"A lot, as you saw. They'd been in the area a few times. Interestingly enough, Maya Gibson has an interest in antiques." Simm paused and seemed pleased with the widening of Charlie's eyes. "Yes. As you guessed, they visited Pete's shop. Spent quite a lot of time there. I imagine Mrs. Gibson had a lot to tell Pete about their life, habits, interests, and everything else. She purchased two items. Would you like to know exactly what they were and where they are in her house?"

Charlie waved her hand. "No. Skip to the important part."

"Well, they were large items and required a truck, so Pete was nice enough to deliver them to their home in Aylmer. For a fee, of course."

"Naturally."

"However." Simm held up a finger. "While they were there, Kurt showed an interest in acquiring a boat and asked Pete for recommendations, both for what type of boat and where to buy one. Two weeks later, he went to look at boats and never returned."

Charlie groaned. The sadness of it struck her.

Simm's tone deepened with the weight of Maya Gibson's sorrow. "She was frantic, of course. Called the police. She got the same song and dance about waiting twenty-four hours before being declared a missing person. They traced his steps to a place downriver where Pete had suggested he look for a boat. Apparently, Kurt had shown up, tested one, returned it, and said he was going to look somewhere else. The salesperson said he acted strange but couldn't pinpoint what it was. They found his wallet on the riverbank." Simm held his hands out to his sides. "Presumed drowned."

"Of course." Charlie shook her head. "Where did they find his wallet?"

"Close to the big rock. On the other side."

A sigh slipped from her chest. She needed no more explanation. Charlie's gaze snapped back to her husband's. "Why did the sales guy think he acted strange? What could that mean?"

"It could mean a lot of things. One person's strange is another person's normal. He could have been seasick. He could've been uncomfortable telling the guy his boat was crap. It's hard to know."

"Did you get the salesperson's name?"

Simm held up his notepad and smiled. Charlie recognized his illegible scribble.

"Shall we go?" she asked.

Simm stood and dropped his phone into his pocket. "You don't have to ask me twice."

In the car, Simm programmed his GPS before they set off. The store was on the river a little past Wakefield. It wasn't a big operation. The shop itself was in a house divided in two sections. Half served as a residence, and the other half was a store that sold second-hand boats and boating paraphernalia. In the yard were vessels of various sizes, ages, and degrees of seaworthiness.

As they pulled into the driveway, Charlie spotted more examples of watercraft on the incline leading to the river. There was a dock with a couple of motorboats and rowboats bobbing alongside it. A few customers milled about.

A man in jeans, a greased-stained t-shirt, and work boots met them as they strolled toward the door of the shop. He shook their hands and introduced himself as the owner, Bill O'Neill. With skin like cured leather and not an ounce of extra weight on his scrawny frame, Charlie estimated his age at mid to late sixties.

"Can I help you? You interested in a boat? We got all kinds."

Simm smiled. "We have questions about someone else who showed up here to buy one."

Bill gave them a confused frown.

"A couple of years ago, a man took one of your boats for a test run. He brought it back, and later that day, he disappeared."

The frown cleared. "Oh yeah, I remember that. The police had a lot of questions. Are you another cop?" His gaze shifted between Simm and Charlie.

"No, I'm a private investigator," Simm said, embellishing the truth a little. "Hired by a friend. Would you mind if I asked you some questions of my own?"

"I got a few minutes," he said with a shrug. By the gleam in his eye, Charlie suspected he enjoyed the attention.

"The detective said when Kurt Gibson returned with the boat, you thought he acted strange. What did you mean? Strange how?"

"Like I told the cop, he was excited about the boat when he left with it. I was sure I had a sale. When he came back, he was in a hurry to take off. Said it wasn't what he wanted. But he wouldn't look me in the eye. Kinda like he was lying. And then he left."

"Do you recall seeing which direction he went in?"

"Sure did. He turned right and headed south." The man gestured with his arm.

Simm nodded toward the line-up of boats. "Did you ever sell the one he was looking at?"

"Yeah. We roll those over pretty fast."

"What was it like?"

Bill squinted his eyes and surveyed his inventory. A gnarly finger pointed toward a red boat near the river. "Exactly like that one, only it was blue, not red."

Simm headed to the vessel in question. As he got closer, he sent a glance toward Charlie. She caught his meaning. The boat was exactly like Pete's.

CHAPTER 30

Simm disconnected the call. "No answer."

"He was the one who took off when they were looking for Damon. He couldn't account for where he was." Charlie ran her fingers through her hair. "Should we contact Megan?"

With the discovery of the body in the backyard and their investigation into Kurt Gibson, the mysterious spotting of Bryan in town had been jammed to the back of their minds. Now it moved to the forefront as another loose end to be tied.

"Why not?" Simm found the woman's number in his contacts and shot a smile at Charlie when Megan answered. He put the device on speakerphone and set it on the table beside him.

After the preliminary greetings, he got to the point. "I tried to get ahold of Bryan, but he didn't answer his phone. Is he around?"

"He's away right now. He's gone on a business trip."

"I don't remember what he does for a living."

"He's a buyer for an auto parts distributor. Sometimes, he goes to the head office in New Brunswick."

"That's where he is?"

"Yeah. He should be back tomorrow. Do you want me to have him call you?"

"No, that's all right. I'll get back to him. Thanks."

"If that was him I saw, he's a long way from New Brunswick," Charlie said.

"Other than staking out the streets in town, I don't know how else to locate him. Unless we contact all the hotels and rentals in the area."

Charlie was about to suggest it was a good option when knuckles rapped on the door.

Detective Marois stood on the other side, his lips set in a tight line. Charlie couldn't recall ever seeing him anything other than grim. She offered him a seat and a coffee. The seat, he accepted, but he declined the beverage.

"I won't stay long. I just wanted to tell you we paid a visit to Noah Wolfe yesterday."

"I guess it didn't go well," Simm said.

"You guess right. But there was something buried in his yard. A goat."

Charlie's voice squeaked with surprise. "A goat?"

"Yep. One of his goats died, and he buried it. He told us that right away, but I insisted we check, so we dug it up."

"Did he ask who led you to him?" Simm said.

"No. I don't think he needed to ask." The look the detective gave Simm was the only answer they needed.

"I guess Noah and I won't be exchanging postcards, will we?"

"Don't count on it. But, to be honest, I don't think Wolfe ever yearned to be your friend."

"Did you get inside his house?" Charlie couldn't help it. The inside of the hermit's house obsessed her. There was a reason he didn't want anyone to go in.

The cop shrugged. "Had no reason to. There's nothing to lead us to him, and it's not against the law to bury your goats when they die."

"He wouldn't let us into his house," Simm said. "Even when Charlie asked to use the washroom."

"No law against that either."

"Pete suspects him." Charlie hated to point the finger at Noah, but the detective needed as much information as possible, even if it was based on Pete's rant.

The detective snorted. "He also suspects Marcus Vaughn. He can't decide who's more evil. He spends his time looking over his shoulder, expecting an ax murderer to be behind him."

"How long before we'll know who was in that hole?" Simm's words echoed Charlie's thoughts. It was horrible for anyone's bones to be in there, but she dreaded to hear they belonged to Damon.

"It should only be a few days." Marois stood. "Thanks for your time."

Simm watched as the detective pulled out of the driveway. His expression was thoughtful as he turned to refill his coffee cup.

"Now what?" Charlie said.

"First, I have to contact Seth Long's mother again. She never got back to me," Simm said as he took a chair opposite her. "I also have to find a connection between Damon and the other victims. And I need more information about Wolfe."

"That's a long list. I'll call Frank and find out how things are at home."

CHAPTER 31

"I don't like that look."

"I don't like wearing it."

"What did you find out?" Charlie was torn between fear and curiosity. She didn't know what to expect from her husband's research.

Simm leaned back in his chair and placed his palms on the armrests. "Unfortunately, not much yet. I spend my time waiting for people to get back to me. But I've got a video call with Seth's mother, Evelyn Long, in a few minutes. Like to join in?"

"I won't say no."

Simm set up the call and, seconds later, the image of a woman in her late fifties appeared on the screen. Her short, dark, curly hair framed a round face with laugh lines around her eyes. Her lips curved in a nervous smile. Simm thanked her for taking the time to talk to him and Charlie.

"If I can do anything that'll help bring justice for my boy, I'll do it."

Charlie's heart went out to the woman, whose unsteady voice betrayed her grief. "We appreciate it, Mrs. Long,"

"The detective told us Seth liked to bike in that area," Simm said. "How often did he go?"

"Whenever he had a day off. Even if it wasn't nice, he'd go. That boy loved to bike and spend his time outdoors. I always worried about him. One time, he told me a dog the size of a small horse chased him. And a man that looked like Big Foot."

Simm flicked a glance at Charlie, but neither of them commented. Instead, Simm asked, "Did he do any boating?"

Evelyn frowned. "Not that I know of. He never mentioned it."

"How often did you talk to him?"

"Every Sunday evening." Her eyes welled with tears. "I miss those calls." The last word was barely audible.

"We understand, Mrs. Long," Charlie said. She relayed a warning glance to Simm. They shouldn't drag the conversation on too long. Simm nodded.

"He lived and worked in Ottawa, didn't he?" Simm asked.

"Yes, he did."

"Did he ever rent a cottage in Gatineau?"

"No. Never. He lived nearby. There was no need, and he wasn't one to waste money. He didn't earn that much. Any extra cash went into his bike."

"Where did he work?"

"He was a bartender at The Wayfair Club."

Simm's frown was barely perceptible, but Charlie noticed it. "Isn't that owned by Marcus Vaughn?" he said.

Charlie fought to keep her expression impassive. Not another tie to Vaughn?

"I don't know," Mrs. Long said. "He never told me who owned it. Does it matter?"

Simm smiled. "Not at all. It's because my wife and I are pub owners, and I've heard the name."

"How long had he worked there?" Charlie asked.

The older woman's face creased as she tried to call the memory to mind. "I'd say it was about three or four years. He liked it there."

"Do you know if he had a friend named Damon Verne or Kurt Gibson?"

She moved her head side-to-side slowly. "The police asked me the same question. Those names mean nothing to me, but that doesn't mean he didn't know them. Seth had lots of friends."

The interview was taking its toll. As Evelyn Long wiped her eyes, she reached for something beside her. "Do you want to see my boy?"

In her hand, she held an eight by ten photograph in a wooden frame. The young man in the picture stood on a hilltop with his treasured bike leaning on his right hip. A bright smile lit his face. He was tall and lean, with light brown hair. Charlie's stomach twisted.

The bereaved mother seemed to forget she was on video as she stared bleakly at the photo of her son. Her gaze refocused when Simm thanked her and ended the call. He circled around to face his wife. "What are the chances?"

"I don't like it." Charlie ran a hand through her hair.

"Vaughn probably didn't know he existed. Seth was a bartender in one of his many businesses. A small cog in a big wheel."

Charlie frowned. "I'd know if something happened to one of my employees."

"Of course, you would, but thankfully you're not like Marcus Vaughn."

Charlie held up her index finger. "Seth Long was an employee." Another digit popped up. "And Damon was a regular client. What are the chances the third guy has a connection?"

"We have to keep in mind Marcus has his fingers in many pies. It could be a coincidence."

"And is it a coincidence that they all have a strong physical resemblance, or at least the key features of being in shape and having light brown hair?"

Simm shook his head. "I have a hard time with that, too."

Unease roiled in Charlie's gut. She could blame a lot of things: horror, grief, confusion. But the sense she had forgotten something niggled the back of her mind. She hated it.

"In the meantime, I learned more about our friend, Noah."

"Do tell." Charlie settled back and prepared to hear a report about the odd man's criminal past.

"Apparently, Noah Wolfe wasn't always a hermit. He had a job, a wife, and a family."

Charlie's eyes widened more with each word Simm spoke. "You're kidding me. What did he do for a living?"

"He was a photographer. Did weddings, grads, babies, all that stuff."

Charlie had difficulty imagining the big, scruffy man coaxing a smile out of a baby. She jerked her head to clear it and focused on Simm. "What happened?"

"Lost his wife and kids in a car accident. A drunk driver. Noah tossed everything away to live in the bush by himself."

A maelstrom of emotions flowed through Charlie: pity, sadness, confusion, and fear. "You think he cracked?"

"Maybe. It affected him deeply enough to sacrifice life as he knew it and live in total isolation."

"How horrible." Charlie whispered the words. Her heart felt heavy with pain for the man's suffering.

"It's even more horrible if he killed people to get revenge against the world."

Charlie realized Simm was right. It seemed as if one tragedy may have fed another, making it even worse. "Of course. Do you think the police know this?"

"If they did their homework, they do, and they decided not to share it with us."

"What can we do?"

"We can try talking to him again."

Charlie drew a deep breath. "Do you think we need a weapon?"

Simm seemed to consider the question. "No. We're two, and we'll be careful. We'll just pay him a friendly visit and pose a few questions. There's no reason for him to feel threatened by us."

As they crossed the river in the pedal boat, Charlie thought of the fateful day when the group of friends had done the same. They had no inkling anything tragic would happen that glorious sunny afternoon, probably a day much like today. Had she and Simm put themselves in the same situation?

Thirty minutes later, they approached Wolfe's cabin. The huge dog didn't sprint to greet them. And there was no sign of the hulking man.

"He isn't here?" Charlie realized she shouldn't feel surprised. The man wasn't obliged to stay at his house. He had to get supplies at some point, didn't he?

Simm peered around the corner of the house. "Doesn't seem to be. I'm sure Bosco would've heard us and reacted by now."

They exchanged a look. Simm rapped his knuckles on the solid wood door. Silence reigned.

Charlie sent a nervous glance over her shoulder.

"I think we should make sure he's okay." Simm reached for the knob, and it twisted in his grasp. "I guess he doesn't worry about locking his doors."

"Maybe we should…"

"Noah? Are you there?" Simm shouted through the narrow opening. He paused a few seconds before he gave the door a gentle shove. Harley rushed through the gap before it fully opened. When it did, it revealed a small rudimentary kitchen and an old white refrigerator with rounded corners. A teal green laminate counter with chrome edges ran along one wall, interrupted by a deep sink that had a rust stain running down the middle. A wooden table crisscrossed with scratches and two mismatched wooden chairs completed the kitchen decor.

Charlie massaged the back of her neck. It felt as if someone had her in their sights. "I don't know about this."

"I'll be fast. I'll just check on him. Stay here." Simm took a step over the threshold.

"No. I'm coming with you." She wouldn't stay behind, a target on the doorstep.

To the left, Charlie spotted a tattered plaid couch and a low coffee table. A small tube TV rested on another table on the opposite side. The room, though dated from the sixties and seventies, was tidy and clean. It was impossible to know how long the man and his dog had been gone.

Simm headed straight for a hallway that had three closed doors along it.

"Noah?" Simm shoved open the first door. "Holy shit."

"What?" Charlie's fist covered her mouth, preparing herself for whatever horror lay inside the room.

"It's crazy. You gotta see this." Simm stepped forward with Harley close on his heels, and he disappeared from Charlie's view.

Comforted by the fact Simm hadn't screamed in terror, Charlie peered around her husband. The room wasn't spacious, but hundreds of photographs were taped to the wall in precise rows. Her gaze swept over them. Most of them seemed to be of the same woman and two children. A noise alerted her as she was about to set foot inside the room. Before Charlie could turn, she was flung against the doorjamb, and two enormous paws held her there, pressing on her shoulder blades.

Charlie had a glimpse of Simm's alarmed expression before he shouted. "No. Leave her alone."

A similar shout came from behind her, while Harley barked with a fury far beyond his size. The weight lifted from her shoulders seconds before Simm's arm slipped around her waist and yanked her to his side.

Noah Wolfe, framed by the gaping front door, stood in stark contrast to the peaceful vista of greenery and smoothly flowing water behind him. He seemed larger than life, his hands curled into fists at his side and his hair ragged and windblown. Fury blazed in the man's eyes as his chest heaved with suppressed rage. Charlie's fingers grasped Simm's shirt, bracing for an explosion.

"What are you doing in my home?" He forced each word from his throat as if it took every ounce of control to keep from ripping his unwanted visitors limb from limb.

Simm's voice held a confidence Charlie was far from feeling. "You didn't answer. We thought something was wrong."

The man took a menacing step toward them. "You take me for a fool? It never occurred to you I might not be home?"

"With what's been going on, we didn't want to take a chance." Simm stuck to their fabricated story while Charlie remained flustered and dumbstruck, terrified of where this confrontation was headed.

"What did you expect to find? A dead body in my home? Or did you want the cops to dig up my whole yard?" His fury hadn't abated. Even the dogs sensed it, both silent. Bosco stood still and tense beside his owner, while Harley cowered behind Charlie's legs.

"Noah, I realize you're upset…"

"Upset is not even a fraction of what I am. Get out. Now. Don't come back. Or you'll regret it."

A solid five seconds passed while Noah pierced Simm with his glare. He leaned sideways, allowing them just enough room to sidle past him to reach the front door. Bosco quivered at attention, too well-trained to budge, as Simm kept a hand on Charlie's back and guided her outside.

Neither of them looked back as they headed toward the boat.

CHAPTER 32

They maneuvered the pedal boat across the river in silence. Charlie's stomach was tied in knots, and her mind raced over the details of the encounter. She glanced at her husband and recognized the look on his face. Something bothered him, something more than what they had gone through, and he wasn't ready to talk about it.

Charlie had been petrified in that cabin. Between the man and the beast, she hadn't expected to come out in one piece. Now, all she craved was to get to the other cottage. At that point, she'd try to convince Simm to go back to Montreal right away.

The boat scraped against the dock. Harley scrambled onto the wooden structure and scurried to shore. He hurled his squat little body on the grass and rolled and twisted, as if demonstrating his joy to be in friendly territory. Charlie wasn't alone in her desire to put the event behind her.

"I can't say that was the best part of this week." Simm grasped Charlie's elbow and assisted her onto the dock as he delivered his understatement of the day.

"I'd like it to be the last part before we go home."

"You want to go home?" Simm raised his brows in surprise.

Charlie held her arms out to her sides. "What more can we do here? The police have reopened the investigation. They'll tell us if the bones belonged to Damon. And even if they aren't his, they have to believe something may have happened to him other than drowning."

"You're right." Simm gave a last tug on the rope that secured the boat. "But I can't go back yet."

"You didn't even want this case." The irony wasn't lost on Charlie. She had been the one to encourage him to take it.

"I can't." He shook his head as he reached into the boat for his cap.

"I'll ask you again. What more can we do?"

Simm sighed and faced her. "I have to find out about Noah's photos."

"Wasn't it obvious? Those were his wife and kids."

"I had a few more seconds in there. I saw pictures of a certain man. Plenty of them."

"What about him? What are you not telling me?"

"I think I recognize him, but I'm not sure. I have to check it out."

Charlie stared at the dog stretched out on the grass as she digested this information. She raised her gaze to her husband. "Okay. I get it, but can't you do that research from Montreal?"

"The short answer is yes, but I'd rather wait another night. Let's get out of here. We'll head into town and grab something to eat. As a special treat, we'll have ice cream after."

"You're the ice cream-aholic, not me."

"Then you can watch me enjoy it." He held his elbow out and Charlie slid her arm through it. They ambled up the path, each of them deep in thought.

******

A Wednesday night in downtown Wakefield was not usually a big deal in the off-season, but in the summer, it was hopping. Charlie guessed the owners were into the hunting and fishing scene. Framed photos of sportsmen with their catches or kills adorned the restaurant, and a stuffed moose head graced a back wall. Charlie was a meat eater, but she still considered it over the top. They probably didn't attract many vegetarian clients.

There was a delay for a free table at Archer's Pub & Restaurant, so Simm and Charlie had a drink at the bar. As was normal for her, Charlie befriended the bartender, and they shared stories about their respective establishments.

"Where're you two staying?" Joan, the bartender/owner, was a heavyset woman in her early fifties. Her dark brown hair, though cut short, had a natural curl to it.

"A place downriver," Simm said. "A guy named Pete Dunn owns it. Do you know him?"

"Oh, yeah." Joan accompanied her statement with an eye roll. "I know him real well."

Charlie's pulse quickened at the prospect of speaking to someone close to Pete, but her expression must have betrayed her speculation. The other woman set out to correct her in short order.

"Don't even think it. We were not romantically involved and never will be." She shook her head as she wiped the counter in front of her, scouring a little harder than Charlie thought the surface warranted. "His mom was a good friend of my dear old mother. Like an aunt to me. After my mom passed away five years ago, I kept in contact with Pamela. Until I couldn't."

Charlie leaned forward, intrigued. "Why couldn't you?"

"Pete. He was always protective, but after the accident, his mother had her stroke, and he went a little nuts. Wouldn't let anyone near her. I offered to help with her care, but he wanted nothing to do with me."

"Did he say why?"

"He said she didn't want anyone but him." Joan snorted a humorless laugh. "Which is a pack of bull, if you ask me. More like, now that she couldn't talk, he decided for her."

"Are you worried about her safety?" Charlie found it difficult to imagine the soft-spoken man being violent, but she didn't like the picture Joan painted.

"No. If I was, I'd call the cops right away. He's definitely devoted to her. But I can't believe she wouldn't want to see anyone."

Simm spoke up. "You mentioned an accident. Do you mean what happened to Pete's brother?"

Charlie realized she had missed that part and was grateful Simm had picked up on it.

Joan ceased her perpetual motion long enough to shoot Simm a look. "You heard about that? Did Pete tell you? No, I don't think so." She held up a finger and swung around to pour a beer for a customer. She prepared a gin and tonic for someone else before she returned to stand in front of Simm and Charlie. "How much do you know about Eddie?"

"Not much," Simm said. "Only that he drowned."

Joan nodded. "Yeah, that's about it. The accident happened about four years ago. Pete and his older brother, Eddie, went camping down past here a ways, on the river. Something happened. I don't know the details, but Ed plummeted into the water and was washed downstream. They hunted for days but never found him."

"That's terrible." Charlie was horrified by the picture that had formed in her mind—a frantic Pete, searching for his brother. "It must have been a shock."

"It was. Eddie was everything that Pete isn't. He was handsome and charming, a real outgoing guy. A football star at university. He lived in Montreal, worked as a financial advisor. When he visited, he had everyone eating out of his hand," Joan said with a wistful smile. "Of course, he knew it. He loved the attention. But you couldn't avoid seeing the difference between him and Pete." Joan gave a deep sigh. "He was the apple of his mother's eye."

"Was there friction between the brothers?" Simm asked.

The bartender tilted her head and narrowed her eyes. "Maybe a little. Pete's not the type to display his emotions, but I can't imagine he wasn't resentful. The irony is that he's the one taking care of his mother. And to be honest, he always was. I'll grant him that. I just don't like him not allowing me to see her."

"There must've been an investigation into the brother's death. No one suspected Pete?"

Joan drew her head back and blinked several times. "No. Never. Pete may be a lot of things, but he's not violent. If anything, he's too soft. It devastated him." She paused and tears pooled in her eyes. "Not long after, Pamela had the stroke. I'm sure losing Eddie brought it on."

"That poor woman." Charlie sympathized with Pamela Dunn, but her mind spun with all the implications of what they'd just learned. Simm would pitch himself into a swirl of research after this conversation. In the meantime, Charlie couldn't let this opportunity pass. Joan was a fountain of information. She pretended ignorance. "So, Pete always lived with his mother?"

"Oh no, he was married at one point. They lived in the house you're renting. It lasted about five years. She packed up and relocated to Montreal. We never saw hide nor hair of her ever since. Myriam and Pamela got along real well. I'm surprised she never contacted her after she left."

Charlie controlled her reaction to Joan's revelation as a smiling hostess approached them and told them their table was ready. The young woman waited as Simm asked Joan one last question. "Could you describe Eddie for me?"

"Sure. Like I said, he was handsome. Tall and lean. Gangly maybe, but in top shape. He had light brown hair, almost blond, and lovely blue eyes."

Simm thanked Joan and left her a generous tip before following his wife to their table by the window.

"My mind is reeling," Charlie said. She leaned forward as if Joan might hear her. "He lied to us about his wife. She didn't die. She left him."

Simm snapped up the menus and offered one to Charlie. "I have a lot of mining to do into Pete's background."

"We should try to talk to his wife."

"Good idea."

Charlie tapped the menu on the table. "I have a problem picturing Pete murdering three men because they resembled his brother."

"So do I, but we can't ignore what Joan said. His brother's death affected him. It may have tipped him over the edge." Simm's frown deepened. "What really pisses me off is that Detective Marois didn't share the details."

CHAPTER 33

Charlie rolled over and extended her arm. Her fingertips came up against… nothing. She pushed herself onto her elbows and peered around the room. Simm was many things, but an early riser he wasn't.

Padding down the stairs, she found him parked at the kitchen table, his laptop in front of him and a large mug of coffee in his left hand.

"Something wrong?"

His gaze met hers. "Why do you think something's wrong?"

"You're up before me."

"It happens," he said. "And this early bird caught a worm. Actually, I found two."

"Good or bad?"

"One is mysterious, bordering on creepy, and the other is terrible."

Charlie studied Simm's face to see if he was joking, but the look in his eye told her his words were dead serious.

She rested a hand on his shoulder as she peered at the screen. "Who is that?" The photo showed a woman in her late thirties. The backdrop of a beach scene emphasized her dark, shoulder-length hair. Unexceptional was a word Charlie would use to describe her. Neither ugly nor pretty, but the glimmer in her eye hinted at a mischievous character and a certain charm.

"Myriam, Pete's ex-wife. Her Facebook profile."

"You found her. Good job." Charlie patted her husband's back.

"I found her profile, but not her. She has no posts, no sign of activity in the last four years."

"Okay. She gave up social media," Charlie said with a shrug. "It happens."

"Why didn't she shut down her page?"

Charlie wasn't an active user and couldn't express an opinion. "Can't help you with that one."

"That's the tip of the iceberg. I checked with my contact, and it seems the ex-Mrs. Dunn was reported as a missing person around the same time. They never solved it."

Charlie lowered herself onto the nearest chair. "You've got to be kidding me. But... how... where?"

"She was last seen in Montreal. After leaving Pete, she moved into an apartment in the Westmount area. Secured a job as an administrative assistant. One day, she phoned in to say she was taking the day off. The next day, she didn't show up for work. After a couple of days of being MIA, someone checked on her. It was as if she walked out of her apartment and never returned."

Charlie flung up her hands. "Is this the Canadian version of the Bermuda Triangle? So many people disappeared without a clue. Didn't the police look for her?"

"Of course, but the case went cold and was put aside. It remains open, but unsolved."

"Pete?" It was inconceivable, but Charlie needed to ask.

"He never left this area. Maybe he was involved somehow. Maybe she left Montreal to come here, but there's nothing to point in that direction. He was questioned, seemed to be upset, but couldn't enlighten the police. He also had an alibi. He was with his mother."

Charlie leaned back in her chair and ran her hands through her hair. "Talk about a coincidence. His ex-wife vanishes, his brother dies, one of his renters disappears, along with a couple of other men in the area. And a pile of human remains turns up on his property."

"It smells like week-old fish."

"He told us she passed away. I thought it was while they were still together. I felt so terrible for him. But now..."

"He made up that story. Unless he knows for sure that she's dead, in which case, he would've been the one to kill her."

"You'll call Detective Marois?"

"I did. I'm waiting to hear. Although, I doubt anything I have to tell him will come as a surprise. He had this information and chose not to tell me."

Charlie wiped a hand over her face. "I want a coffee." On her way to the kitchen, she spoke over her shoulder to Simm. "That was the terrible worm, I take it."

"No."

Charlie spun around. "It wasn't? What could be worse than a missing ex-wife?"

"You won't believe this one. I checked out my bad feeling from yesterday."

Charlie returned to the chair facing Simm, the need for caffeine wiped from her memory.

"Remember, I saw pictures of a man in Noah's house yesterday?"

Charlie nodded; dread clenched her stomach.

"It's Paul Lemieux," Simm said.

"Paul? The same guy who stole Vaughn's car and killed those three people?" Charlie stifled a squeal when her hands clapped over her mouth and her eyes widened. "No. Please don't tell me those people belonged to Noah."

Simm remained silent, but his miserable expression said it all.

Charlie wanted to scream. She buried her face in her hands, but all she saw were images of a beautiful woman and two lovely children. An employee of the man who lived opposite Noah had killed those people.

Charlie lowered her hands and stared at her husband. "I don't understand. What does it mean? Is Noah stalking Marcus Vaughn? Does he blame him for his family's death?"

Simm lifted his hands and let them drop back onto the table. "It's too much of a coincidence for him to ditch everything, to end up staring at a man who is at least indirectly related to the deaths of his wife and kids."

"Is it related to Damon?"

"We don't know, and I'm afraid the only person who can hand us the answers won't talk to us."

"Not only won't he talk to us, but he's likely to feed us to his dog for dinner."

Simm's phone jangled next to his elbow. He glanced at the display, and his frown deepened. Charlie listened to the one-sided conversation, but all she heard were Simm's grunts. He grabbed a pen, wrote one word on a notepad, and circled it. Seth. When he looked at her, Charlie understood.

"It was Seth Long in that hole," she said when he disconnected the call.

Simm's nod confirmed it for her. Her thoughts fled to the mother, who would have received the news and lost all hope. Charlie's thoughts circled to the friends who might feel relief and hope for Damon. Or perhaps a lack of closure.

CHAPTER 34

Charlie sat in the sunroom where she usually found calm and relaxation. But not this day. Her thoughts churned, skipping from one idea to the next, without stopping long enough to make any sense. The beauty of the landscape outside the windows remained a blur to her. Something teetered at the edge of her consciousness, and she willed it to tilt closer, into the view of her mind's eye.

She blinked as Simm slipped into her peripheral vision, and she turned toward him. His brows formed a question.

"I don't know," she said. "Something's bugging me, and I can't zero in on the root."

"Let's take the canoe out."

"You have something planned. What is it?"

Simm smiled. "I thought we'd drop in on Noah."

Charlie's stomach clenched. "It's not safe to go see him. We should let sleeping dogs lie. And large dangerous dogs, too."

"I can't let it go. We have to talk to him about the accident and why he's living across from Marcus Vaughn."

"I don't see why. He's allowed to live wherever he desires." Charlie hated the idea of going there.

Simm pushed himself away from the doorjamb. "All right. I understand if you don't want to go. I'll fill you in when I get back."

Charlie vaulted to her feet. "No. You're not going alone."

"You don't have to. I'll be fine."

"You'll go no matter what I say, but I can't let you go alone. It's way too dangerous."

"If it's dangerous for me, then it's too dangerous for you."

"At least if we're two, one of us can distract Bosco while the other runs for help."

Simm laughed and grabbed her hand. "We have Harley to protect us."

The little dog wagged his tail, eager to be included in their adventure.

******

The weather had cleared, and the sun reflected off the dark water as they made their way downstream. Charlie locked her gaze on Wolfe's side of the river, searching for a sign of him or the dog. She chewed on her lip, weighing if she should try once more to change her husband's mind.

"What the hell?"

Simm's exclamation put Charlie on high alert. Her heart pounded as she peered into the gloomy forest. "Where? What is it?"

"Not there. On the other side."

Charlie wheeled to face the opposite way. Her mouth opened, but no sound came out.

White and blue lights flashed from the tops of cars and vans. Cops and civilians roamed the lawns on both sides of the line between Marcus and Pete's properties. Officers attempted to set up a restricted area with yellow tape while another moved people out of the way.

Simm didn't hesitate. He swung the canoe in the dock's direction. Charlie had doubts about whether they'd be allowed anywhere near the action, but she didn't voice them. The need to know flowed in her veins.

No one noticed their approach until they set foot on the lawn. Detective Marois' head swiveled in their direction and his frown deepened. Charlie braced herself when he strode in their direction. He clearly intended to head them off.

"I forgot to tell them to blockade the dock. I didn't think anyone had the nerve to infiltrate through there." An insincere attempt to smile accompanied the detective's words.

Simm ignored the dig and got to the point. "What happened?"

The other man sighed. "Another body."

Charlie gasped, drawing the cop's attention to her. He held up his hands. "We don't know who it is."

"Workers again. This time they belonged to Vaughn," Simm stated.

"Yeah, they were putting up that wall of his. They freaked out."

Charlie sympathized with them.

"How did Pete and Marcus react?"

Detective Marois gave Simm a level stare before he answered. "Come up and see for yourself. You'll only ask me a hundred questions afterward, anyway." He held up a warning finger. "But don't forget two things: I'm being generous, letting you anywhere near this scene, and if anyone says anything worthwhile, I need to know about it."

"Deal," Simm said. He sent a sideways glance at Charlie, and she nodded.

They followed the cop to the heart of the action. Charlie darted anxious glances toward the trench, so similar to the one at the cottage. She knew what lay in there. Part of her sought confirmation; the idea horrified the other part. The latter won out. While Simm accompanied the detective to the site, Charlie remained on the opposite side of the yellow tape.

A raised voice snagged her attention. She altered her position and caught sight of Pete on the far side of a crowd of law enforcement people. His hair was in disarray, and his head jerked from side to side.

His voice had drawn her attention, but she couldn't understand his words. However, his arm-waving, his reddened face, and his wild eyes convinced her he was furious. From the direction of his pointing, she knew who the target of his verbal assault was.

Her gaze drifted to the property on the other side of the hole. In the dispute over the trees, Pete had won his case. But evidently, some trees grew on Vaughn's side of the line, and he had removed them to make way for his wall. Charlie had a clear view of the businessman as he exchanged glares with Pete. Vaughn's wide, rigid stance and his tightly clenched fists completed the aggressive look. Beside him stood his wife, dressed like she was prepared for dinner at the club. But her expression betrayed the same unease as Charlie felt about the discovery.

Charlie inched her way closer to Pete. She overheard a cop demanding Pete remain calm.

"Arrest him." Pete lowered his voice to a growl, but the words were clear.

"We'll do our job."

"What if he escapes?" More hand-waving in Marcus' direction. "He has the money to make himself disappear."

Charlie sympathized with the police officer. She had the arduous task of soothing Pete. Unsure if she would step into a quagmire, Charlie moved to Pete's side and laid a hand on his forearm.

"This is horrible. A second body. But you're obviously taking it on the chin."

Pete blinked at her as if he couldn't place who she was. Charlie glanced at the cop in time to witness her relief. At least Charlie had forestalled his rant. Or redirected it toward herself.

Pete bent until his face was mere inches from hers. His eyes glimmered with something resembling madness. "He did it."

Charlie didn't pretend to misunderstand him. "Marcus."

Pete shot a triumphant smile at the cop who stood by their sides. "It's buried on his land." He glanced toward the hole. "Mostly."

Charlie adopted what she hoped was a conspiratorial look. "But why? Why would he kill these guys and bury them on or near your property?"

"He wants me to leave. He wants to buy my property… and put a casino here."

It was obvious Pete made this up as he went. Charlie didn't challenge him. When a hand stroked her shoulder, she gazed up at her husband with gratitude. She was even more grateful for Detective Marois, but his glare told her he didn't want her anywhere near his witness or suspect, whichever the case might be.

"Mr. Dunn, I'd like you to come with me. I have questions for you."

"Are you arresting me?" A voice like a squeaky door.

Marois was brusque. "It's too early to arrest anyone. But, since the body was exposed partially on your land, we need to ask questions. Let's go."

The detective nodded toward the uniformed officer, and she got the message. Her hand grasped Pete's elbow and guided him toward the police van that doubled as a command post.

Marois wheeled toward Simm and Charlie with a hard look. "Don't leave the area. We may have questions for you."

The detective traipsed after Pete and the other officer.

Charlie and Simm shifted their attention to Marcus. He stood in the shadows of the remaining trees on his property, his gaze glued to Pete's retreating back. He looked as if he was ready for the golf course, with a white polo shirt and a pair of gray Bermuda shorts.

Two cops stood on either side of him and his wife. A slender form materialized at Vaughn's side; their son, Tyson. His gaze bounced from his parents to the hole and back again before he spoke to his father, his expression concerned.

The older Vaughn's gaze found Simm and Charlie, and something flashed in his eyes that Charlie couldn't interpret. He rounded on his son and barked an order at him, the muscles in the side of his neck rigid. The boy's expression morphed to perplexity and hurt, and Charlie easily read his lips. "Why?"

Again, Marcus said something through gritted teeth, his eyes wide and angry. Tyson shoved his hands into the pockets of his jeans and swung toward their house, dragging his feet as he went.

A firm grip on her elbow drew Charlie's attention to her husband. Her heart pounded as she saw the look on his face. His gaze was glued to the antics of the Vaughn family thirty feet away, his eyes wide with shock.

"What's wrong?"

"Let's get out of here," he said, as he tugged her toward the dock.

CHAPTER 35

Charlie watched her husband pace. She yearned to relieve his anguish, but she couldn't think of any way to put a positive spin on things. She suggested his imagination was working overtime, but her heart wasn't in it. The more Charlie thought about it, the more sense it made.

"It doesn't mean Walter was involved in everything. It's unlikely Marcus would have shared the details."

Simm barked out a humorless laugh. "I assure you Walter does nothing without knowing the details behind it."

"How can we prove it?"

"That's my problem. I don't know how, but I'll get something." Simm ran frustrated hands through his hair.

"Let's go over it again. I'll write down your theory, and we'll organize our thoughts." Charlie poised a pen over a large notepad.

Simm took a deep breath. "There's a party at Vaughn's place in Montreal. Walter is there. On the sidelines, somewhere on the property, a few employees have their own shindig. Lemieux is one of them. So far, that follows the official storyline." Simm held up a finger. "Here's where it veers off. The Mercedes is taken. I won't use the word stolen here, more like borrowed. Not by Lemieux. By Tyson."

Charlie nodded as she scribbled notes in point form. She glanced up at her husband as he planned his words.

"Tyson is the one who caused the accident and killed Wolfe's family. He calls Dad in a panic and tells him what happened. A terrified Marcus contacts his good friend Walter to help him out of a tough situation. Walt, always ready to be of service to the rich and pampered, comes up with a scheme."

Charlie interrupted him. "You know, it could have been Marcus' scheme."

"You're right. I think Marcus was too upset to be level headed and depended on Walt to help him out. But I'll concede the possibility."

"Okay. Continue."

"They quickly consider their options. They can ditch the car and thus remove the evidence, but someone's going to notice the car is missing from his fleet, and it could circle back to him, anyway. They check with Tyson and think no one witnessed him leaving with the car, so they decide to find a fall guy. To be on the safe side, they make sure it's someone with the same hair color and general shape as Tyson."

"Lemieux."

"Right. He drew the short straw. Maybe his level of inebriation was higher than the others. I think he was unfortunate enough to leave the party as Walter prowled around, hunting for a victim. My brother coerced or bribed him into accompanying him somewhere. He plied him with booze and/or drugs until the man didn't know which way was up."

Charlie hesitated in her note-taking, thinking about the poor man who innocently staggered into a trap that would transform his life forever. She hurried to catch up as Simm continued.

"They took him home and hid the car on his property, in a spot where he wouldn't immediately see it when he got up the next day. Otherwise, he may have reported it, or at the very least, returned it to Marcus with his deepest apologies for driving it and causing damage to his car."

"But they found his fingerprints in the car."

"I suspect he was an employee who took care of the cars. Cleaning them, taking them for maintenance work. It would be normal to have his fingerprints in the car. But there were none on the steering wheel or gearshift. That means someone wiped it clean. Someone who doesn't drive the car. It doesn't make sense for Lemieux, supposedly blind drunk, to wipe down the steering wheel if he regularly drove the car as part of his job."

"Then they found the car on his property," Charlie said.

"Marois told us the cops received an anonymous call reporting a damaged Mercedes."

Charlie groaned. Simm didn't need to explain that point any further.

"Marcus steps up to the plate for his employee, offers to hire the best lawyer and make sure he has the greatest deal," Simm said.

"He could've slung him to the dogs and let him go to prison for life."

"Yeah. Maybe the creep felt a sliver of guilt for framing someone for a crime his son committed. Or he made Lemieux feel so grateful for helping him get off lightly he would never question whether he was actually guilty."

"Maybe Walter convinced Marcus it was the right thing."

Simm's upper lip curled. "I doubt it, but miracles happen."

"Let me play devil's advocate for a minute."

Simm reclined, clasped his hands behind his head, and stretched his legs out in front of him, giving her the floor.

"First," Charlie said. "If Tyson was going to take his father's car during a party, he must've been trying to impress someone. What are the chances he would've been alone?"

Simm pursed his lips and nodded. "Maybe that friend he was on the Jet-Skis with. Marcus might have bought his silence."

"True. But why would Lemieux roll so easily? We're talking about his life here."

Simm rubbed the tips of his fingers together.

"Money?" Charlie said. "Yes, Marcus probably assumed his legal fees, but do you think he bribed him too? Offered to pay him off as a trade-off for prison?"

"I wouldn't put it past him."

"But that would clue Lemieux in to the fact he wasn't guilty. He would've realized someone else was behind the wheel of that car, and the person was closely connected to Marcus." Charlie gathered her thoughts. "My last point is Vaughn could have organized it on his own. Walt didn't have to be involved."

"Why did he visit me? Why the interest in my random meeting with Vaughn in a store? He wanted to know if I suspected something."

Charlie held two fingers in the air. "My last questions: How do we prove this? And how does it tie into the disappearances of three men?"

Simm groaned and pitched his head back. "The first answer is: I don't know. The second one is: I'm not sure if it ties in at all."

Charlie's gut twisted. That's what she was afraid of.

CHAPTER 36

The canoe jostled against the wooden posts. Charlie dropped her paddle inside the vessel and grabbed onto the dock while Simm leapt out and wound the cord around the cleat. He steadied the canoe as she heaved herself out.

It was hard to believe that only yesterday they had pulled up to the same dock and witnessed a full crew of law enforcement officers and technicians scattered throughout the property. The yellow crime scene tape drew Charlie's attention. She knew the authorities had moved the body, but a chill still crept up her spine.

The door to the boathouse opened, and Pete emerged with a frown. Simm strode toward him and laid a hand on his shoulder.

"How you holding up?" Simm said.

Pete shook his head and shifted his gaze to his feet. "I wish this nightmare would go away. The police act like I was behind it."

"That means nothing. They think everyone is a suspect at the beginning."

Pete looked at Simm with narrowed eyes. "You think?"

"I do. I used to be a cop."

Pete seemed reassured by Simm's words, until his eyes hardened, and he nodded his head toward Marcus Vaughn's property. "I hope they're giving him the same treatment. Or worse."

"I'm sure they are."

Her husband's reassuring tone had the desired effect on Pete. It was time to move to the second step.

Charlie gazed up at the house. "If you don't mind, Pete, I'd like to inspect your beautiful flower gardens. They're giving me ideas for our place." He didn't need to know they lived in a second-floor apartment above a pub with only enough space for a potted plant.

Pete seemed taken aback but swept his arm for her to lead the way. When he moved to follow her, Simm forestalled him with a bogus interest in buying a boat. Simm led him into the boathouse as Pete cast a concerned glance in Charlie's direction.

Charlie held a genuine attraction to Pete's meticulously maintained flowers, but today horticulture took second place to another goal. The men safely out of sight, she sprinted up the steps and slipped over the threshold. If caught, her backup plan was the overused I-needed-to-use-the-washroom excuse. With luck, it wouldn't come to that.

Her memory of the interior of the house remained true. Within seconds, she was in view of Mrs. Dunn. The woman wore her black dress and, again, had a tissue grasped in her right hand.

The old woman's eyes widened upon seeing her, but this time, Charlie was certain fear wasn't the cause; it was surprise. Charlie didn't think she frightened Pete's mother, and that fact handed her the courage to step closer.

"Do you remember me? My husband and I were here a few days ago. We're renting the cottage from Pete."

The woman nodded as her nervous gaze bounced from Charlie to the front window to the doorway.

"Pete's in the boathouse with my husband," Charlie said, answering the unspoken question. Intelligence and perception shone in Pamela Dunn's eyes, but her brows lowered in concern.

"It's okay. There won't be a problem, and I'll only stay a minute." Charlie glanced at the walkie-talkie resting beside the woman's right thigh. Mrs. Dunn did not reach for it, further confirming her confidence in Charlie.

Charlie knelt in front of her. She wanted a clear view of the woman's face and reactions.

"Why were you afraid the other day? Were you afraid of us?"

The woman gave a quick jerk of her head. Her right hand flapped, helplessly trying to convey a message Charlie didn't understand.

"Were you afraid *for* us?"

Mrs. Dunn waved toward the boathouse.

"Pete? Has he ever harmed you? Are you in physical danger?" The thought of this lovely frail woman being abused alarmed Charlie.

An adamant shake of Mrs. Dunn's head reassured her, but the older woman again waved her hand toward the boathouse. Charlie foraged her mind for a reason.

"You were afraid for Pete? You thought we would hurt him?"

A quick, frustrated quiver of her head.

"You were afraid for Simm?"

Yes, she nodded.

"You thought Pete would hurt my husband?"

The last words cleared Charlie's lips as the front door banged on its hinges. Charlie straightened and spun toward the entrance of the sitting room.

A breathless Pete rushed in. "What are you doing here?"

"I came in to say hello to your mother," Charlie responded, forgetting her initial plan and falling back on a lie that wasn't altogether a lie. "I didn't think it would be a problem."

Pete moved to stand beside his mother, planting a hand on her frail shoulder. "She's not comfortable with strangers. You know that. You're frightening her."

Charlie's gaze shifted from the son to the mother, whose eyes held fear, a fear that hadn't been there a few moments earlier.

"I'm sorry. I wasn't thinking." Charlie didn't want to make things worse for Pamela. She connected with Simm's gaze from where he stood behind Pete, and he caught her message.

"Maybe we should go," Simm said.

"Yes, of course." Charlie turned toward Pete and his mother. "I'm sorry if I upset you. I thought it would be nice to say hello."

Pete's expression softened slightly, perhaps in relief, and he left his mother's side to see them to the door. Charlie felt his stare on her back until they climbed into the canoe.

Simm and Charlie didn't speak until they were moving upstream.

"She's afraid of him, not us," Charlie said. "But not for herself. She was afraid he'd hurt you."

She didn't need to elaborate further. Simm may not be an extroverted prankster, but his physical description resembled that of Damon. Perhaps Mrs. Dunn knew more that she couldn't verbalize. Maybe she had discerned a pattern.

"Pete isn't a big guy. I could've taken him on."

"What if he struck when you turned your back?"

"I didn't turn my back on him." His grin was crooked. "Besides, I knew you would've saved me."

"This isn't funny. I'm worried. It's not safe here."

"We'll be fine. Tomorrow, we'll see Detective Marois and tell him what we're thinking."

Charlie nodded. That sounded like a good plan. Once the police knew their suspicions, they'd take charge, especially after uncovering two bodies on Pete's properties.

CHAPTER 37

Simm's exclamation drew Charlie out of her troubled thoughts as they emerged from the path into the view of the rented cottage. The sight of the black Tesla didn't register in her mind, but when Simm swore under his breath, she guessed it belonged to Walter. This was not a good time for him to show up. On the other hand, she didn't think any time would be good.

"What are you doing here?" Simm said, echoing his words from the last time Walter had shown up unexpectedly.

"I visited Marcus, and he told me you were here. I thought I'd drop by."

"Are you his go-to man for damage control? Did he demand help after yesterday's fiasco?"

Walter laughed, but to Charlie's ears, it sounded forced. "You and your conspiracy theories. Don't you ever tire of imagining me as a villain?"

"I'd love to imagine you as something else, but nothing plausible comes to mind."

Walter held out his hands. "Simm…"

"No. No more bullshit. Tell me why you're here and then leave."

Charlie was paralyzed. She rarely witnessed anger in her normally calm husband, but this had gone past the threshold of anger. Rage burned in his eyes.

Walter swallowed and studied the ground before he raised his wide-eyed gaze to Simm. "Marcus wanted me to talk to you. He thinks you have it in for him. I don't know why, and I explained you were unlikely to listen to me. But I said I'd try it."

"You're right. I'm not interested in what you have to say." Simm advanced toward his brother. "Because I know how you guys pulled it off."

Charlie didn't think it was a good idea to launch accusations. She stepped forward and laid her hand on Simm's arm. "Maybe we shouldn't…"

Simm's gaze didn't waver from that of his brother's. "It's okay, honey. It's just me tossing around some ideas with Walt. I'm sure he'll let me know if I'm right."

"Why don't we get something cold to drink?" Charlie tried again to diffuse the situation, but her husband was having none of it.

"We're okay here. Walt won't be staying long."

Charlie looked at the other man. His lips were pressed tightly together, and his shoulders were stiff. He braced himself for the onslaught, and Charlie considered why he would go to such lengths for Marcus Vaughn.

"To make this as quick as possible, I'll go with the abridged version," Simm said. "Tyson Vaughn took his dad's car for a spin one night. He may or may not have been drunk. That's beside the point. The result is the same. He killed a woman and her two children. Marcus had to get the kid out of this mess, so he turned to his old friend Walter. You found a fall guy, made sure he had no recollection of events, set the car up on his property, and made an anonymous call to the police. They hired a lawyer, paid off an expert witness, and *voilà*, an innocent man goes to jail so that Tyson Vaughn can feel entitled to do whatever he desires."

Walter breathed heavily through his nostrils, and his face reddened. With fists clenched by his sides, Charlie worried he'd take a swipe at Simm. She knew her husband could fend for himself, but her gaze swept her immediate surroundings for a shovel or something to use if it came down to protecting him.

"I don't believe you," Walter said in a snarl. "Ever since Dad wrote you out of his will, you've been out for revenge. You always thought the worst of me and Dad. Probably Susan too." He thrust his arms in the air, and his voice rose in pitch. "You've invented these rigid standards for everyone to adhere to, and if we set a toe over the line, we're lying, thieving, murdering despots."

"You set more than a toe over the line. You did a full body dive."

Charlie stepped between the two like a referee during a fight at a hockey game. "Okay. I've heard enough. You both spoke your mind, and you got nowhere."

Walter pointed a furious finger at Simm. "You're rambling. You have no proof about anything you've said, and if you mention it to anyone, you'll be sued for slander."

"I realize I've got no proof. I admit it. But I won't forget, and if I ever get that proof, I'll use it."

"Good luck with that," Walter shot back before he exited the premises, gravel spraying behind him.

CHAPTER 38

Charlie removed cold drinks from the refrigerator, hoping to cool her husband's temper. He seemed more depleted than angry at this point. She knew these confrontations affected him more than he let show.

Her cell phone rang as she made her way to the sunroom. Frank's name appeared on the display. Charlie hoped he would deliver a ray of sunshine to their day. The tone of his greeting dispelled that notion.

"What's wrong?" she asked.

"It's nothing for you to worry about. I just wanted to let you know."

"Get to the point, Frank."

"There was a fire…"

"A fire!"

Simm got to his feet and advanced toward her.

"What happened?" she asked. "Is anyone hurt? Are you okay?"

Frank's voice was soft and reassuring, but Charlie knew him. He'd do anything to protect her.

"No one's hurt. It was a small fire in the kitchen after we closed. We have a bit of smoke and water damage. The kitchen will be off limits until we get the work done, but the bar will only be shut down a couple of days."

Charlie lowered herself into a chair before her knees gave out. Her worst fears were eased. However, she detected the 'but' in Frank's voice. "Tell me the rest."

"The fire inspector thinks it may be criminal."

Charlie was stunned. It would never have occurred to her. "You're kidding. Who would do such a thing?"

"I have no idea. Apparently, they used a device with a timer. It could have been anyone. It's easy to reach the kitchen from the bar. They planted it inside a cupboard."

Charlie's gaze met that of her husband. She realized he shared the same thoughts. Marcus Vaughn's retaliation had materialized. He had gone after their business, but even worse, he had endangered lives. Frank could have been in the bar after closing. It could have destroyed the homes and businesses of the neighbors. Charlie couldn't fathom what she would have done if anyone had been hurt or killed.

Fury tore through Charlie. This had gone too far. She knew the police would do their job and search for the perpetrator, but if it was Vaughn, she would see he paid for it.

******

The atmosphere in the sunroom was glum. Charlie and Simm had hashed over the details with Frank for close to an hour, and they were ready to pack up and leave. But Frank has assured his friends they didn't need to rush home. There was nothing they could do. The case was in the hands of the police and the insurance company. A quick-witted neighbor, who had spotted something unusual from his apartment window, had saved their business and home. If not for him, the damage would have been substantial, possibly involving loss of life.

Simm sprawled in a chair and stared out the window. Charlie knew he not only worried about the pub but rehashed his argument with Walter. She also knew he didn't regret a word he'd said. He was angry and frustrated because he had no means to prove anything against Vaughn or his brother.

Charlie leaned forward and placed a hand on Simm's knee, concerned by the intensity of his expression. "What are you thinking?"

He leaned his head back on the chair and stared at the skylight above them. "I can't let it go. It's possible a man is in jail for a crime he didn't commit." He returned his gaze to Charlie, and she saw the bleakness in his eyes. "But to set Lemieux free, it could incriminate my brother. He may even be implicated in the fire."

Despite the animosity Simm felt toward his brother, Charlie understood it pained him to think of Walt being accused of a crime. As youngsters, the siblings had been close, and Simm was the protective older brother. However, upon their father's death, things turned sour. The glimmers of unpleasantness that Simm had witnessed in his brother broke to the surface. Walter took on the mantle of ruthlessness that Winston Simmons, the elder, had weaved. The disagreements and arguments between the brothers grew rancorous, and their respect for each other disintegrated.

"I can't sit back and let it happen. I'll have to report my suspicions to the Montreal police and let them take it from there," Simm said.

Charlie squeezed his hand and nodded. She hated to think of what would follow, but she acknowledged justice had to be served. She would support Simm's decision, no matter what.

Her husband stood and withdrew from the room with slumped shoulders as he extracted his phone from his pocket. His call would set the wheels in motion. If their suspicions held true, or even if they didn't, it would be the final nail in the coffin between him and his brother.

She listened to the murmur of his voice and shot him a sympathetic smile when he lowered himself into the chair beside her. He laid his head back and shut his eyes.

Charlie granted him his space as her mind ran through everything that had happened. Despite the urge to go home to her precious pub, she had to place her faith in Frank to handle the fallout from the fire. They would be there soon enough.

For now, they needed to find out who was responsible for the deaths of the men, but she had no idea where else to look or what more they could do. Her gaze settled on the shelf under the table, and she stared at the photo album that rested there. Her mind wandered for several moments until the bothersome questions at the back of her mind slid to the forefront and clicked into place.

"Oh my God."

Harley bounded to his feet, his little body quivering with excitement, when Charlie dived for the album, pulled it out, and slammed it on the tabletop. Simm's attention veered to his wife.

"What?"

"The photos," she said. "I remember now. I knew something was off." Her hand flipped back and forth through the pages, rummaging frantically for the pictures.

"Slow down. Take your time, and you'll find whatever it is."

Charlie inhaled a deep breath and willed herself to follow Simm's instructions. Panicking would do no good. She turned the pages until she found the first one and thrust a finger at the photograph.

"There. See it?" She rotated the album to offer Simm a clear view. It was of a young man on a grassy hilltop. His long legs were sprawled in front of him, and a bike lay on the ground at his side. He wore a crooked grin on his handsome face. The photo itself was small and obviously snipped from a larger one. The sides were worn, as if it had been carried in a wallet.

"It's Seth Long," Simm said as he raised his gaze to hers, his eyes wide and stunned.

"Yes. His mother showed us his picture. That's him. But he never stayed in this cottage. Why is his picture here?" Charlie flipped more pages. "Here. Look at this one."

Simm stared at the picture of a couple standing in a living room on opposite sides of a bulky rocking chair and shook his head. "Who is it? Kurt Gibson?"

"I think it is. That's probably the chair he and his wife bought from Pete. That picture wasn't taken here. It's in their home. It may have been on the wall in Pete's workshop. Those are the only pictures that weren't taken on this property, and they're of the two men who disappeared. The third one is Damon." She turned to the second last page and showed him the picture of the friends from the previous year.

"Pete put them in there," Simm said.

"Yes, because he likes to keep track of things." Charlie's words ended on a note of misery. The horror of the man's crimes lay in front of them. They were on his property, had been in his home. He had taken them downriver in his boat. A frail old woman was in his care, controlled by him. "We have to call the police."

"I'm on it." Simm punched a few buttons on his cell phone and left a message for Detective Marois.

"How did he do it?" Charlie said. "How could he overpower three grown men, kill them, and bury their bodies? Apart from the fact that it's a heinous, cold-blooded crime, how did he physically do it?"

"Pete's in better shape than we give him credit for. He may look meek and mild, but he does physical labor. He has an impressive quantity of tools. All of which are meticulously cleaned. You won't find any DNA on them. And he's got boats, equipment, and property."

Charlie couldn't remain still. She paced the room. "But I don't get it. Damon was on one side of the river, and Pete's place is on the other side. We don't know yet if that was Damon's body on his property, but if it was, how did he get him there?"

"By boat."

Charlie wrung her hands as her mind raced. She needed to get it clear in her head. "Let's go look again while we're waiting for Marois to call."

Simm didn't hesitate. Within minutes, they were in the pedal boat with Harley settled between them. Dark clouds veiled the late afternoon sun, and a cool breeze blew over the water. Charlie held Harley closer, both for warmth and comfort.

Ashore, they tried to retrace Damon's last steps but spotted nothing that told them how Pete could have captured or killed him. They followed the line of the river until they neared Noah's property.

"I don't feel up to confronting him today," Charlie said. The day was stressful enough.

"Neither do I. We've got other things to worry about. Hopefully, he's not around, and if he is, he won't sic Bosco on us."

Charlie's stomach lurched. "Ugh. I didn't think of that."

Simm glanced over his shoulder at her. "Just keep going. Hopefully, he won't notice us."

Charlie thought it unlikely Noah wouldn't notice two people and a pug, but she pinned her gaze on her husband's back and kept pace. Harley must've realized he crossed familiar territory and caught the scent of either Bosco, Noah, food, or all three. The pug trotted in the direction of the man's cabin, his flat nose high in the air and his curly tail wagging.

"Harley. Come back here." Charlie used her firmest tone. The little dog paid no attention to her. The draw of the cabin held more promise for him.

Simm's harsh repeat of Charlie's order made Harley glance over his shoulder, but he didn't switch direction or slow. Charlie had no choice but to follow. When she jogged to catch up, Harley took off at a furious pace, loving the game.

As they burst through the trees and faced the cabin, the door flew open, and Bosco charged out. Noah Wolfe loomed in the doorway, a dark scowl on his face.

Grass and dirt sprayed into the air as the colossal beast skidded to a halt beside the smaller dog. They playfully chased each other, while the adults traded looks, one menacing and two apprehensive.

"We're heading back." Calm and controlled, Simm pointed behind him.

"Take that thing with ya." A long, hairy finger pointed at Harley.

Charlie would never leave him behind. "C'mon Harley. Let's get a treat."

The pug gave Charlie a long look, as if weighing the likeliness of a treat versus the excitement of staying with Bosco. Seeming to reach a decision, he took up the rear of the small convoy along the riverbank.

The thick forest swallowed up the trio, and the cabin dropped from view. Charlie's shoulders slumped as the tension fled her body. "I don't know what makes me more nervous, the man or the dog."

A muffled ringing came from Simm's pocket. Neither of them slowed their pace as he answered the call and put it on speakerphone. Marois' voice echoed in the open air.

Simm delivered a quick overview of their suspicions about Pete, mentioning the photos and what they had gleaned from Mrs. Dunn's interactions. The cop asked them to come to the station with the photo album. Charlie detected a sense of urgency in the usually composed man.

"Will do. We're on our way to the cottage now," Simm said. "At the same time, we want to discuss Pete's ex-wife with you. She seemed to vanish a few years back."

A heavy silence filled the rapidly cooling air. A perplexed glance passed between Charlie and Simm.

"Are you still there?" Simm asked.

"Once again, you have perfect timing. I just got a call. They found a car on the bottom of Cascade Lake. It's been there a while. Had human remains in it."

Charlie's heart pounded as a grim-faced Simm dropped a puzzle piece into the conversation. "The car belongs to Myriam."

"We have to talk. Get down here."

Simm slid the phone into his pocket and looked at Charlie with a deep frown. His voice was solemn. "I guess I shouldn't be surprised. There are too many people around Pete who have dropped out of sight."

Charlie was too stunned to speak. They were in direct contact with a serial killer and never suspected. But the evidence was clear.

"We'll go pack and get out..."

A thud interrupted Simm's sentence. A hand over Charlie's mouth and the overpowering stench of chemicals squelched her scream. In her peripheral vision, she saw her husband's body sprawled on the dead leaves and moss of the forest floor. The last sound she remembered hearing was Harley's yapping, followed by a yelp of pain.

CHAPTER 39

She woke up to the warmth of a hand smoothing her forehead. Groggy, Charlie forced her eyes open. A second later, her body stiffened, and those eyes bulged. Solid darkness surrounded her. She jerked with fear, afraid of the dark and the unknown hand, until Simm's soothing voice sounded in her ear, so close the heat of his breath fanned her cheek.

"It's okay. It's me."

"Where are we?" The slurring of her words surprised her, but the trace of a smell brought back the memory of what had knocked her out. Another memory, even more frightening, followed. "Are you okay?" Charlie's hands struggled to locate her husband in the darkness and reassure herself.

"I'm fine, apart from a splitting headache and a desire to rip someone apart." Simm's voice was rough and gravelly.

Charlie's eyes adjusted to the blackness of her surroundings. The hard-packed earth beneath her emitted a damp, musty odor. She shivered and pressed herself against her husband's solid chest. "Where do you think we are? A cave?"

"My guess is it's a root cellar."

"A what?"

"A root cellar, a place to store garden vegetables."

Charlie's thoughts swirled in confusion. "How would you recognize such a thing? You've been in one before?"

"No." His tone was grim. "Pete described his to me."

Neither of them spoke as Charlie digested that information. A heaviness settled in her chest. "It's him then. I guess I had hoped to be wrong."

Simm's shoulders rubbed against her as they lifted and dropped.

"I don't think he's the only local to have a root cellar. It wouldn't surprise me if Noah has one."

"Marcus Vaughn wouldn't."

Simm snorted. "He might know where to find one."

"Everything points to Pete. I can't believe he'd do something like this. The photos, the missing wife, everything." Charlie's voice rose. She battled to hold back tears. "Why us? Because we're looking into the case? He figured he has to get rid of us?"

"This'll only channel more attention his way."

A tear rolled down Charlie's cheek. "He's left us to die in here."

"He won't succeed."

Charlie pushed herself up and faced Simm, even though she couldn't see his features. "How will you get us out? Did you find a door?"

Simm wriggled to a sitting position. "I did. It's locked tight and barred with something on the outside. That doesn't mean I won't find a way to get through it."

The enormity of their situation descended on Charlie. She hung her head, her chin on her chest. "I'm so sorry."

Charlie knew Simm didn't require light to realize tears flowed down her cheeks. His arms folded around her and tugged her close. "This isn't your fault."

"I convinced you to take this on, this whole stupid case."

"I could've said no."

"You did say no."

"I could've said it with more emphasis."

Charlie leaned her head against his chest. She wondered how much time she had left to spend with him. Another thought occurred to her. "I think he may have hurt Harley. Or worse."

Simm's hand massaged her shoulder. "Don't think about that now. We'll find Harley when we get out of here."

Her husband's optimism made Charlie love him all the more, but she had no clue how they'd find a way out of this dungeon.

"He'll be back, and we'll be ready for him," he said, as if reading her thoughts.

"I wish I could be so sure he'll come back, but at least planning for it will give us something to occupy our minds."

"That's the spirit."

"Pete isn't that big. He'll know the two of us can overpower him. What if he's armed?"

"We have to count on it."

"Or he might have an accomplice."

"Equally possible. We'll plan for both."

They devised a simple plan. It involved separating to opposite sides of the limited space at the first sound of someone unbarring the door. Simm circled the cellar to learn the size and shape they dealt with and to search for a weapon. His second goal came up with a result of zero.

Simm decided where to stand to overpower Pete if and when he arrived. Simm would pounce on him and try to get whatever weapon he had. Meanwhile, Charlie could flee, and her husband would follow close on her heels. If there were two captors, the plan ran along the same lines, but the chances of Simm following Charlie greatly diminished.

Charlie didn't care for either strategy, but she couldn't come up with anything better.

A few hours later—they weren't sure how long—the sound of wood grating against wood, followed by a key scraping in a lock, brought them both to attention. Simm found Charlie's face and gave her a quick kiss before scuttling to the other side of the cellar.

A cold sweat broke out on Charlie's body. Her heart skipped a beat when a bright light illuminated the stairs and heavy boots clumped down the few steps onto the dirt floor. She lifted an arm to protect her eyes from the pain of light after hours of complete darkness. She longed to look her captor in the eye.

"Don't try anything stupid. I know you plan to jump me, but I've got a gun aimed at your wife."

The voice was muffled and unrecognizable, as if the person wore a face covering. Charlie peered from between her fingers, trying to gauge the danger she faced. The man's headlamp was fixed on her, rendering her blind.

Charlie realized Simm wouldn't risk her getting shot.

The light flicked from her face for an instant, but her eyes didn't have time to adjust.

"Get up off the floor, girl. Head up the stairs. Go outside. Stand with your back to the door. I'll watch you. If you don't do exactly what I say, he gets shot."

Charlie's knees trembled as she forced herself to her feet.

"No. Take me instead." Fear choked Simm's voice. The man swung his head in her husband's direction, and she had a fleeting view of Simm's face. His expression matched his tone. Charlie wondered if it was the last glimpse she'd ever have of him.

"Don't worry. Your time'll come."

The distorted voice and the movie script words made the scene surreal. But Charlie knew there was nothing fake about it. This man was responsible for the deaths of several people, possibly including his ex-wife and brother. Evil was too kind a word for him.

The light swiveled to Charlie, and she twisted her head from the piercing shaft of brightness. "Move it. Now."

"Simm." The word was a murmur; her steps faltered as Charlie shuffled to the stairs. Tears flowed down her cheeks. She would never again see this man who had given her so much happiness.

"I'll be fine, honey. I'll find you." Confidence found its way into his voice.

Charlie set her foot on the bottom step. The glare of the light pinned her husband, but she was convinced the gun remained trained on her. Shaky legs carried her up the stairs as she pressed her hands on the cool damp walls for support.

The evening air enveloped her, warm compared to the underground vault. Her eyes adjusted to the deepening dusk. Drifting clouds would make the moonlight scarce, another point against her.

As instructed, she faced the river, her back to the cellar door. Charlie didn't dare turn her head. She recognized her surroundings from where she stood—on Pete's lawn, facing his dock and boathouse.

Feet pounded up the steps, and the door slammed into place; Charlie stiffened. The twisting of the key in the lock brought a pain that penetrated deep into her heart.

Boots crunched on the gravel while Charlie's entire body trembled with fear. She didn't think Pete would shoot her in the back on his lawn, but he had definite plans for her; she was certain of that.

The coarse rope that tied her arms behind her back revealed the first part of the scheme. The second part involved a smelly rag shoved into her mouth. Bile rose in her throat.

"Go," he said, jostling her forward with the barrel of the gun. Charlie didn't need to be told the destination. Moonlight revealed a motorboat tied to the dock, ready for them. Dwelling on where he intended to take her made her tremors ratchet upward.

Rough hands steadied her as Charlie stumbled into the boat, unable to balance herself. Seconds later, with her back to him, he shoved the boat from the dock and slipped into the middle of the river. They floated for several feet before he started the engine. Keeping it in a low, quiet idle, they headed downstream.

Houses and cottages that had grown familiar to Charlie wafted past her vision, their windows dark, but their shapes visible in the eerie light. She considered heaving herself overboard and attempting to swim to one of them. The thought was brief and tossed aside. Charlie wasn't a strong swimmer. With her hands tied and the pull of the current, she would drown, if Pete did not recapture her.

She had to wait. She might find a safer means of escape. A makeshift weapon, a moment of inattention on the part of her captor. Someone might come to her rescue. Would Frank notify the police if he didn't hear from them? Would it be too late?

The boat slowed, and Charlie gaze flitted from side to side, seeking a sign of a house or a dock. Instead, the vessel curved toward the shoreline and a thick line of trees.

"Duck your head," the voice mumbled from behind her.

At the last second, that's what she did, avoiding a heavy branch. The leaves skimmed over her scalp. He motored to a dock obscured by dense trees and vegetation that sabotaged its discovery.

Rough hands yanked her from the boat onto the modest and shaky wooden berth before shoving her toward land. Charlie headed forward, urged by the gun that prodded her back. She pushed through shrubs and crawled over rocks, worried she couldn't break a fall without her hands.

A rundown shack entered into view. A rusty tin roof sported a few spots of gleaming metal patches. Knotted boards enclosed the windows, and paint peeled off the once-white door. Charlie shivered as a horror movie came to mind. How long would this be her home? Or would it be her ultimate resting place?

A long arm reached over Charlie and unlatched the door. The tip of the gun shoved her in. Diminishing natural light displayed torn linoleum floors. Bare basics equipped the room: a sink, table, and two chairs. Dirty dishes were scattered on chipped laminate counters. To her right, a threadbare couch and coffee table made up the living area.

A short corridor led to two doors, presumably a bedroom and a bathroom. Neither of them appealed to her. The gun offered her no choice.

Charlie lurched forward, knowing she had no say in her destiny, at least not now. Her captor nudged her toward the door on the left. Her gaze fixed on the dull grey paint as he grasped her hands and untied them before tugging the rag from her mouth. He opened the door and thrust her in. The slam of the door and the clinking of the key suggested a permanency.

The total darkness created a terror fed by a vivid imagination.

CHAPTER 40

The most troublesome part was over. He'd separated them. The woman wasn't a risk. Easy pickings. She wanted to be with her husband, and she'd get her wish. Once they were dead, they'd share a grave. Another detail to work out.

He shook his head. Why can't anything be easy?

His vision clouded, and a twitchy feeling darted along his extremities. His goal had been within reach, the knife ready to twist. He didn't need the complication of these people. Their nosing around, their speculation, their questions.

The desire to inflict pain surged through his veins. He snatched the headlamp and jammed it on his head.

The trip upstream was uneventful, usual for this time of night. This was when he truly lived as himself. His mind reeled with everything he ached to do. But he had to deviate from his usual routine. He'd award himself the gift of one night, but longer than that was too dangerous.

He took his time opening the door. The magic was in the anticipation, the build-up of fear. He slipped the mask over his face. His prisoner wouldn't see him once he turned on the headlamp and put its blinding force to good use, but the mask distorted his voice.

He descended the steps and smiled when Simm shielded his eyes with his arm as he stood in the corner. He didn't cower. Not this man. He admired that. In another life, at another time, they could have been friends.

"We finally have time alone." He advanced until he was within a few feet of his captive. The rifle was ready, his finger on the trigger. Simm was smart and experienced. He didn't trust him not to try something.

The ex-PI squinted and tried to focus on him, but it was impossible. "Where's my wife?"

He ignored Simm's desperate question. "You've caused me a lot of trouble. You should never have stuck your nose in my business."

Simm dropped his arm, but kept his gaze averted from the light. "And let you get away with murder?"

"That doesn't concern you."

"As a human being, it concerns me. Why did you kill them?"

"Why should they live if I can't?" He enjoyed the confusion that dashed across Simm's face. It was a riddle for him to puzzle over in the coming hours. But he wanted to put the icing on the cake.

"Don't worry about your wife. She's at peace now. Not to say it was peaceful for her, but at least one of us enjoyed it."

The pain and anguish he witnessed was worth the sacrifices he needed to make.

CHAPTER 41

During the long hours that followed, Charlie contemplated her situation. She had too much time to do so. It led her down a path of fear and grief.

Pete had killed at least three men. Of that, she was certain. Was he also responsible for the death of his brother and ex-wife, or were their deaths the catalysts that drove him to kill others?

She knew the chances of her and Simm surviving were slim. If the others hadn't overpowered or outsmarted the killer, how could they? No one else had lived to tell the tale.

Charlie had shuffled around the space until her knees jammed up against a bed. Turning around, she sat gingerly on the surface, hoping she didn't share it with another body.

If there was a window, it was sealed. No moonlight made its way through. A musty smell, like damp newspaper, permeated the room. Charlie shivered from fear and cold.

Her thoughts looped to Simm. What did the killer have planned for him? Pete couldn't afford to let him live, not now. He might take the simple route and let him die of starvation, coming to collect the body in a few weeks. He might do the same with her. Or would he have mercy on them and kill them quickly, like old, crippled horses? Surely, he understood someone would look for them. If Frank didn't have a call from Charlie by tomorrow, he'd worry. He wouldn't delay before he contacted the authorities.

Could she trick Pete when he came back? How? She didn't know if she could physically take him on, and she didn't have a weapon.

Charlie tried not to let herself plunge into despair. She needed to stay positive and believe she'd find a way out of here to rescue Simm.

She lay down on the bed with trepidation. How many people had he captured and held in this room? What atrocities had been committed against them?

Stop it, she told herself. This is not a horror movie, no matter how much it may resemble one.

******

Charlie woke, startled, and astonished that she'd fallen asleep. Without moving, she shifted her gaze around the room. Her breath whooshed from her lungs. She was alone. It was daylight, and she acknowledged her misconception from the night before. A tiny sliver of light seeped between the boards into the room, but only enough to give her a dim view of her surroundings. There wasn't much to see; simply the bed she lay on. Thankfully, it was void of bodies and bloodstains. She couldn't attest to the cleanliness of the blanket, but she was alive.

Noises came from the front of the cabin. Someone was there. Had Pete slept here last night? No, he wouldn't do that. He always stayed with his mother. He must have gone home and returned this morning.

Charlie tensed at the sound of the key in the lock. She waited for the doorknob to turn and tried to decide on her best move. A muffled voice took the decision from her hands.

"Turn around and face the wall. I have a gun."

Not having any choice, Charlie stood and faced the boarded-up window. The door creaked and heavy boots crossed the room. She braced herself for whatever was to come. Would it be a violent beating or a gunshot?

Something landed on the floor with a soft thud.

"There's your breakfast. Turn around after I leave."

Charlie grasped at the tiny display of kindness and hoped she could reason with him. "Pete, let's talk about this. We can work it out."

An open palm slammed the back of her head, flinging her face-forward onto the bed. Before she could rise, the door slammed shut and was locked.

A dazed Charlie puzzled over what she had done to deserve the slap. Did speaking his name anger him? Had he thought they hadn't figured it out?

Groaning and kneading the back of her head, Charlie turned to look at her meal. It was a sandwich of sorts, accompanied by a bag of potato chips and a bottle of water. She considered whether he might poison her. If he wanted to kill her, he had the means to do it with his bare hands.

Besides, she was hungry.

Charlie devoured the sandwich and chips and lay on the bed to analyze her predicament or to wait for death by poison, whichever arrived first.

Hours passed with no alteration of either her situation or her health, but the light gradually dimmed until she lay in complete darkness again. Throughout the endless day, she heard sporadic movements in the cabin. At times, it fell quiet. She assumed he was gone. He couldn't abandon his mother for long, after all.

Perhaps her prison was positioned within walking distance of the Dunn house. Or maybe Pete had an accomplice. The more Charlie considered that possibility, the more sense it made. Pete could have teamed up with someone else to carry out his killings. Maybe this man wasn't Pete, but his partner. That could explain the mask and his desire to keep his identity a secret.

It also gave her hope. If he fed her and cared about her seeing him, maybe he didn't plan to kill her.

Once full darkness fell, Charlie heard him leave, and he didn't return. There were no more visits, no more meals. She strained to hear a motorboat, but there was only silence.

Instead of being comforted by the fact she was alone, her heart raced with fear. Charlie knew in her bones he had returned to the root cellar. He went to visit her husband, and thoughts of what he might do terrified her. She was certain it wasn't for something so innocent as the delivery of a sandwich.

Charlie paced the floor of the room. Despite the darkness, she knew how many steps took her from the mattress to the wall and back. Her nervous energy bubbled over, and she longed to break out of the room and make her way to Pete's house.

She had inspected the room in daylight. There was no way to escape. The boards on the window were solidly hammered in place. And she had nothing to loosen them with. The mattress was made of foam. There were no springs to use as a weapon or a tool. She was out of ideas.

Charlie skidded to a stop and cocked her head, her eyes wide. He was back. She'd heard a noise. She spun to face the door. Something was different. These footsteps were heavier. And there was something else. Strange clicking noises.

Under the door, a sliver of light shone through, but it wavered like a probing flashlight. Another door banged. A grunt followed. How many people were there? Pete and his partner? The light shone on the door, and the knob was tested. Whoever it was didn't expect a lock. Something massive crashed against the door, once, twice, until it flew open and banged against the wall. Once again, a light blinded her.

CHAPTER 42

A familiar yipping, a resounding deep-throated bark, and the clawing of tiny paws on her legs preceded Charlie's tears. She avoided the slobber of the mastiff as she grabbed Harley into her arms with a squeal and hugged him to her chest. She rushed toward the man holding the glaring flashlight.

As she reached out for the familiar shape of her husband, her hand encountered a taller, broader shape. She drew back and her brain connected her rescuer and Bosco.

"Noah. I... I..."

"Never mind your ramblin'. We gotta get out of here."

Wolfe's suggestion seemed sound. Charlie set aside her questions and followed the beam of his flashlight to the door. Harley sprung from her arms and pranced ahead of them with his long-legged friend, as if they were invited on a grand adventure. In essence, they were.

The group trudged to the riverbank. Charlie spotted the canoe at the dock, and after a glance at the big dog, she cast a dubious look at her rescuer.

"It went okay on the way over. Get in front and take a paddle." He kept his voice low, and Charlie smothered the desire to ask if he'd rescued Simm. She'd wait until they were a safe distance from the cabin. Her worry lay more in the thought they might meet Pete or his accomplice on the water.

Charlie settled in the canoe's front, and Harley wiggled his way onto her lap. Bosco, with surprising grace, parked himself in the middle while

Noah took up the rear. Charlie helped glide the canoe into open water and work their way upstream. Her arms ached, but she overrode the pain, fixated on reaching Simm as soon as possible.

The branches of the trees appeared menacing in the overcast night sky. A cool breeze raised the hair off the back of her neck, sending a shiver down her spine. Yet, the fresh air mixed with the scent of algae delivered a rush of appreciation for her freedom. It also fueled the desire to free her husband.

Unable to delay any longer, Charlie glanced over her shoulder at the large man propelling them through the water. "Is Simm safe?"

"I have no idea. I thought he was with you."

"No." Charlie's arms slumped to her sides. She almost lost her grip on the paddle. "He's in Pete's root cellar. Pete left hours ago. Simm may be dead by now." She forced the words past her tears.

"Pete's the one behind this?" His voice showed no hint of surprise.

"He's got a gun."

"So do I."

Charlie absorbed that information as she gripped the paddle, drove it into the water, and increased her pace. She had to find Simm before any shots were fired. "Where's your phone? Did you call the police?"

"Don't have a phone."

Charlie rolled her eyes and gave an extra boost to her paddling. "How did you know where we were?"

"I heard the boat last night. I had an idea where it stopped. I kept watch tonight to see where it came from."

"And Harley? Where was he?" The dog's ears flipped up at the sound of his name.

"He found us. I knew something was wrong. I kept him. And I watched."

"Thank you so much." Charlie's gratitude was heartfelt. If they survived, it would be because of Noah. Her cheeks burned as she recalled how she and Simm had suspected him of being the killer.

"Don't thank me yet. We still have to fetch your husband."

"We have to go somewhere and phone the police."

"We don't have time. Quit talking and let me handle this. We're almost there."

Under normal circumstances, Charlie would resent the gruff orders, but her gratitude outweighed the sting of his stern words.

"What about the dogs?" Charlie hoped he heard her whispered question.

"Mine will do as he's told. Can't speak for yours."

Charlie wasn't sure Harley would obey anyone's orders. They had no choice but to go ahead with whatever plan Noah had.

They eased the canoe to the dock. The man didn't budge. Charlie followed his lead. She listened for movement, a gunshot, a shout, anything, but it was eerily peaceful.

For a man of his size, Noah moved with stealth and agility. Barely rocking the canoe, he climbed onto the dock and secured the rope around the metal cleat.

"Stay here," he said.

"What?" It was less of a question and more of a low, drawn-out squeal. Charlie desperately needed to locate her husband, alive and well. She had no intention of sitting alone in the dark with a killer wandering the grounds. She clambered out of the canoe without requesting permission of her rescuer. The dogs followed suit.

"I don't need somebody gettin' in my way." He bent down to deliver his message inches from her face, as if his tone didn't already convey his annoyance.

"I won't get in your way. I'll help you. Besides, that's my husband up there." She pointed a shaky finger toward the root cellar.

A growl rumbled from deep inside his throat. He drew Harley's leash from his pocket and attached the little dog to the same cleat as the canoe. "I don't trust this one." He pointed a finger at Bosco and barked an order. The imposing animal sat on the dock beside the affronted pug.

Noah tilted and snatched his rifle from the canoe. "Stay behind me."

The improbable twosome followed the tree line until they reached the root cellar. In the dim moonlight, Charlie spotted a wooden shaft on the ground.

She clutched Noah's arm, gestured to the object, and whispered toward his ear. "He's in there with Simm. It's not locked."

Noah nodded and shrugged off her hand. He looked like he wanted to speak but changed his mind. If it was to tell her to stay behind, he was wise to not waste his breath.

They crept forward.

Noah took up position beside the door and signaled for Charlie to stand behind. She didn't argue. She peered around the big man for a view of the opening.

Noah wrapped a large hand over the latch and heaved up the door. His movements were slow and silent, but he attracted the attention of the man inside. A gunshot rang out. Noah dived toward Charlie, his weight knocking her to the ground. The air whooshed from her lungs as he landed on top of her.

Charlie tried to shove Noah off her. "Simm. I have to get to him." Her voice was a desperate squeal. "He shot him."

"No. He shot at me."

A voice resounded from the darkness of the root cellar. A shiver streaked through Charlie at the familiar muffled sound.

"Get down here. Both of you. You got ten seconds before I kill him."

Charlie's eyes widened, and she strained harder against Noah's chest, but he was already hauling himself to his feet.

"Run and get help." The scruff of his beard scraped her face as he mumbled in her ear.

"I will not risk Simm's life, or yours. We'll both go."

His frown deepened, and anger shot from those dark eyes. "Stay close behind me." Noah grabbed her by the elbow and dragged her to her feet. He shoved the rifle into her hands. "Hide this."

The cold metal of the rifle barrel was a shock. Charlie had never held a gun in her life. She couldn't fathom what he expected her to do, but there was no time for discussion.

"Now, I said. Go." The voice seemed closer. Had he climbed the stairs?

"We're comin'."

Noah moved toward the opening. Charlie followed behind, her heart hammering in her chest. She knew Noah meant for her to smuggle the gun between them, and he didn't want her to fire it, but she slid her right hand down the barrel until her finger settled on the trigger. She might not have experience, but this was a need-to-know situation.

As they started down the steps, the flashlight on Pete's head illuminated their path and highlighted the weapon in his hands. But it rendered his features invisible and blinded the focus of its light. On the plus side, it exposed Simm to Charlie's eager gaze. Her husband stood in the corner of the space, his hands clenched in fists by his side, his eyes hunting for a glimpse of his wife.

Their gazes met and clung until an order burst from the gunman. "All of you in the corner. Now."

The newcomers shuffled toward Simm. Charlie remained behind Noah, her prize carefully concealed. She wrapped her arms around her husband, clenching the gun behind him. His powerful arms crushed her to him, and his apparent health brought tears to her eyes.

Simm's right arm left her side and reached behind him to secure the rifle. Noah's height and breadth covered their movements.

"You, move over. I want to see all of you." The masked man motioned with his gun. Noah obediently shifted to Charlie's side.

Agitation marked Pete's movements. He transferred his weight from one foot to the other, and his breathing was ragged.

"Damn you. All of you. You can't keep your noses out of anything, can you?"

No one answered his rhetorical question. Charlie tried to imagine a way out of their situation. She hoped the man's distress helped them.

"Do you realize how hard it is to stash a body? Now, I'll have three. That wasn't in my plans."

The situation was surreal. He must realize this wasn't in their plans, either. A real-life Jekyll and Hyde stood before them. The soft-spoken landlord who fussed over his mother had morphed into a homicidal maniac who was inconvenienced because he had three bodies to bury. Charlie wanted to scream at him. She wanted to see him suffer.

Simm fumbled for her hand and squeezed it, apparently guessing her thoughts. As his hand withdrew from hers, she tensed, anticipating his next move. She sensed Noah's tension on her other side, and she wondered what they expected of her.

She didn't have long to wonder. They took care of the decisions.

Everything happened at once.

Simm raised his arm and drew the rifle to his shoulder. The flashlight swung toward him as he caught Pete's attention. Noah shouted a command. A huge shape soared through the air to land on the man at the bottom. A gunshot rang out, the sound echoing through the small space, deafening the occupants.

An immense, growling beast pinned the man to the ground. Bosco's bared teeth dripped drool on the mask, and he was poised to strike once he received the command from his master.

"Get him off me." Their captor's voice trembled.

Simm moved the rifle to his left hand and approached the prone man. Bending down, he wrenched the flashlight from his forehead and used it to illuminate the man's face. Wide, frantic eyes stared back at him.

"Take off his mask."

"No! Get away from me. Let me go."

Charlie tugged the mask off his face and stumbled back two steps.

CHAPTER 43

Charlie cradled Harley in her arms, more for her own comfort than his.

After the initial shock, Simm had told her to dart up to Pete's house and get help. She hadn't wasted a second arguing. Her desire to vacate the cellar outweighed everything else. At the top of the stairs, Charlie scooped up her agitated pup, not questioning how he'd released himself. She raced to the house and banged on the front door.

His face was ashen when he swung it wide. He looked thin in a baggy t-shirt and sweatpants.

"What are you doing here? What was that noise? It sounded like gunshots."

"Call the police. There's a man in your root cellar. He's the killer."

If possible, Pete's face grew paler. "What?"

"Simm and Noah have him. And Bosco." Charlie grasped his forearm. "The police. Call them. Please."

The urgency in her voice seemed to reach him. He seized his cell phone off a nearby table.

"Who is he?" Shaky fingers punched in the emergency number. "How do you know he's the killer?"

"I don't know who he is, but he pretty much admitted to killing the others, and he intended to kill us."

Pete barked information into the phone, an inner strength taking over. The operator told him to stay on the line. His response to her made it clear he had other things to do. Charlie reached out to take the phone from him, but it was too late.

"I'll come down," he said as dropped the phone into his pocket. "Is it safe? Do I need a weapon?"

Charlie worked to reconcile this new Pete with the old one. Where did this ferocity appear from?

"He's under control for now."

Charlie was in for another surprise when Pete removed an ax from the closet.

"Let's go," he said, the ax dangling by his leg. A moment of doubt prompted her to hold the door and let him pass. She felt safer behind him.

As they neared the underground room, angry swearing, still in that muffled tone, reached their ears. Charlie snagged Pete by the elbow of his free arm.

"I need to warn you," she said. "This guy is severely disfigured. Something terrible destroyed his face."

Pete blinked in surprise, but straightened his shoulders, gripped his ax in both hands, and followed her down the stairs. The trio of humans were in the same position, their guns pointed at the prone man. Bosco stood to the side. His behind wiggled when he saw Charlie and Pete descend the steps, but he didn't budge from his spot.

Noah's intense gaze remained pinned on the man in front of him, but Simm swung to face his wife. He gave her a quick once-over before he focused on Pete's ax with a frown.

"Are the cops coming?" he asked.

Charlie moved to stand beside her husband. "Yes. I don't know how long it'll take." She stared at the man lying flat on his back. His face looked as if Picasso had remodeled it. Scarred and twisted skin surrounded non-existent lips. Only his eyes and forehead had been spared whatever tragedy had befallen him.

Hatred filled his eyes. Charlie followed the trajectory of his gaze to the man who stood beside her.

Pete stood stock still, his facial muscles slack and his gaze dull. The ax slid out of his hand to land with a thud beside his foot. When he swayed to his left, Charlie leaped forward to take his arm and lower him to the damp earthen floor.

She knelt in front of him, trying to connect with his gaze. "Pete, are you okay?"

Pete's focus hadn't wavered from the man on the floor, but the stunned denial in his eyes transformed into terror. Tremors raged through his body.

"Simm, something's wrong with him." Her voice quaked with fear.

Noah spoke up. "Bosco and I have this guy. Take care of the other one."

Simm went to Pete's side, knocked the ax out of harm's way, and put his hand on his shoulder. "What is it? Do you recognize him?"

"He's dead."

Simm and Charlie both swiveled their gazes to the man trapped between the dog and the hermit. The loathing in his eyes confirmed his existence in the living world but raised the subject of the reason behind his animosity for Pete.

Despite the chill, damp air in the chamber, drops of sweat rolled down Pete's face. His motor skills returned, and he used his heels to drive himself further away. His back bumped up against the wall, yet his boots continued to gouge in, as if he could bulldoze his way through the wall and elude whatever horror he experienced.

"It… it can't be."

"It is." The other man spat out the words like rancid meat. "You failed to get rid of me, just like you fail at everything."

"No. I didn't mean to. It was an accident. I tried to save you. Believe me."

Simm and Charlie's gazes met. Pete's babbling revealed the mystery of the stranger's identity. It was the brother everyone had believed dead.

"You'll pay for this. I'll find another way to make you pay."

Screeching sirens and pounding feet encroached on the tense atmosphere in the cellar. A voice shouted from beside the entrance.

"Police! Who's there?"

******

Charlie's eyes threatened to slam shut. She had gone too many hours without sleep. Stress brought on a fresh wave of fatigue she could barely battle. The only thing that kept her going was the comfort of Simm's arm around her shoulders and the steady beat of his heart under her cheek as she leaned against him.

The questioning was interminable. Charlie and Simm huddled in a waiting area while investigators grilled Noah. Their day wasn't over. Detective Marois wanted to see them. Charlie prayed for the chance to steal some sleep for a few hours. But she worried about what she would see when she shut her eyes. She'd never forget the terror and stunned surprise on Pete's face, nor the hatred and vengeance on that of his brother.

It was obvious Pete had believed his brother dead. It was also obvious the man had survived and vowed to wreak vengeance on his sibling, probably because of the disfigurement caused by the accident. The details were yet to be revealed.

Charlie felt concern for Pete's mother. It was full daylight, and she'd worry about where her son was. Detective Marois reassured her that Pete had called Joan, who had consented to take care of the older woman. There was much to explain, and it would be a horrific shock for Pamela Dunn to learn her oldest son lived and was the perpetrator of multiple murders.

"Simm. Charlie."

They raised their heads to see the detective. He looked as tired as they felt, Charlie thought.

"Why don't you two come into my office?"

The chairs were more comfortable in the cop's office, but Charlie missed the warmth of Simm's side.

The man leaned his elbows on the desk and studied a paperweight. "What a mess." He shook his head in despair.

"Did you get a confession?" Simm asked.

"We did. There's still a lot to piece together, but we'll get there." Another shake of his head. "I've seen some twisted things, but this has to take the cake."

"What happened?" Charlie couldn't suppress her impatience.

"I'm pretty sure what happened to Eddie Dunn was an accident, and Pete truly believed he was dead. Hell, I was the investigating officer, and we were all convinced the man was dead. But he survived and was so enraged about the damage to his face that he set out to make Pete pay."

"What was the point of murdering the others? Why let Pete live, if he felt that way?" Simm said.

An exhausted sigh escaped the detective's chest. "His mind is too damaged for me to figure out. Apparently, he planned to frame Pete and have him suffer in jail for the rest of his life. He lived in his own type of prison."

"That's what he meant." Simm spoke slowly. "Why should they live if I can't?"

Charlie's expression was confused. "What do you mean?"

"That's what he told me. I think he selected men who were like him, both in looks and character. He decided that if he couldn't live a normal life, they shouldn't either."

"He could have returned, had surgery, and lived a normal life." Charlie didn't understand Eddie Dunn's reasoning.

Marois nodded. "I agree, but according to him, without his looks and the adoration of his friends, he had nothing." He gave them a go-figure look. "Not long after the accident, he paid a visit to his mother. He's the reason she had a stroke. Her reaction may have contributed to his quest for revenge."

"How horrible." Charlie imagined the fright the older woman experienced; seeing her son, who she believed to be dead, in such a condition.

"He had always been the golden boy. Handsome and athletic. He couldn't live with what was done to him. So, he hid in that abandoned cabin, moving around mostly at night, stealing food and whatever else he required. He learned everyone's habits, what was unlocked, what he could get away with."

Charlie looked at her husband as a thought occurred to her. "The basement. He was in there." Simm pressed his lips into a thin line as he nodded. Charlie addressed Marois. "There was a noise in the basement one night. Harley sensed it too."

"It would've been him," the detective said. "He had keys to all the properties. He even had a hiding place in Pete's workshop. That's how he discovered Kurt Gibson and knew where he lived. Seth Long was a guy he'd seen many times in the area. As for your friend Damon, he stowed away on the grounds of the cottage and spied on the group."

"How did he do it? No one fought back?"

"He pretended to be handicapped, kind of like the Hunchback of Notre Dame. He'd cover his face as much as possible and solicit help with his boat. Once they were close enough, he'd hammer them over the head and dump them in. He enticed Kurt Gibson with a sign for a boat for sale. A real deal. When Gibson showed up, Eddie rushed him from behind."

Simm massaged the back of his head, and Charlie knew he recalled the thump he'd received. Her stomach clenched at the thought of how close they'd come to losing their lives.

The cop continued his explanation. "I don't know if you noticed it, but there's a little inlet among the trees. He'd hide the boat in there until dark and transport his prisoners to the root cellar. He'd torment and torture them for a few days until the searches were called off. Then he'd kill and bury them."

"How did he kill them?" Simm asked.

Marois sent an apologetic look at Charlie before he spoke. "He slit their throats with a specialty knife, used for carving wood. He stole it from Pete's shop. Intended to put it back with a little DNA on it."

"Oh, no." Charlie covered her face with her hands. She had hoped their deaths were quick and painless. Knowing the men had suffered, hoping for freedom and life, only to be brutally murdered, made it ten times worse.

"The plan was to point everything in Pete's direction. The placement of the bodies and the photos you noticed were meant to lead us to his brother and make him suffer."

"It's crazy. Why kill those innocent men?" Charlie said. A thought occurred to her. "What about Pete's wife? Did he have anything to do with that?"

If possible, the cop's expression grew grimmer.

"He bragged that, prior to the accident, he was having an affair with Myriam Dunn. Afterward, he pretended to be someone else and enticed her to Wakefield. He didn't appreciate her reaction to his looks. As payback, he gifted her with a new home at the bottom of a lake."

The information didn't surprise Charlie. It was as if she was beyond shock, her spirit battered.

Simm leaned forward. "Tell me something. Is Eddie connected to Marcus Vaughn or Noah Wolfe?"

The detective rubbed his chin. "We didn't find any connection. I know the second body was partially on Vaughn's land, but from what we can see, Eddie didn't care about him. And I don't know why you'd think Wolfe was involved. He was only guilty of burying a goat, and that's not a crime." His gaze held a question.

Charlie held her breath. Was Simm going to bring up the accident that killed Wolfe's family and his belief that Vaughn and his own brother were involved? There was something going on with that trio, but Charlie didn't believe it was connected to Eddie and Pete Dunn.

Besides, she and Simm owed their lives to Noah.

Simm smiled. "It's nothing. I just wondered. We mulled over the idea of them being suspects."

"We looked at everyone, but we had nothing to tie them to the disappearances." The cop spread his hands on his desktop. "That's all I have for you. I appreciate the input you gave us. Eddie confessed, but we may still call you to testify at his sentence hearing. You're free to go back to Montreal, if you like."

"I very much like," Charlie said, eliciting a laugh from the usually stern-faced detective.

******

Pete answered their knock within seconds. A feeble smile graced his lips.

Charlie didn't hesitate. She stepped forward and gave him a quick hug before she stood back and looked him in the eye. "How are you doing?" she said. "How's your mom?"

"I'm okay. Still getting over the shock. Mother seems better than me. Of course, she realized Eddie was alive, and she suspected he was behind the killings." Pete guided them to the porch, where they reclined in white rattan chairs. They had a beautiful view of the grounds and the river, but the still-present yellow tape marred the scenery. "She tried to write Eddie's name, but I assumed Eddie's death still distressed her, and I ignored it."

He stared at his shoes for a moment before he continued. "I could've prevented the deaths of those men if I'd listened."

Charlie reached over and squeezed his hand. "You can't blame yourself. It was Eddie's twisted mind that caused it." She glanced at her husband. "Pete, I have to get something off my chest." She waited for Pete's expectant look. "We had reached a point where we thought you were the killer. I'm sorry."

Pete held up a hand. "Don't feel bad about that. Eddie planned to set me up as the suspect. He did a good job. If I'd been in your shoes, I would've thought the same."

Pete's words lifted a weight off Charlie's shoulders, and Simm's eyes reflected the same relief.

Before they left, Charlie asked to say goodbye to Mrs. Dunn. Pete led them into the sitting room, where the woman sat in her usual spot, but her bearing differed this time. Although weak, her smile was genuine. The terror that had hung over her head for the past few years was eradicated. Even though Eddie was her son, Pamela Dunn would no longer have to worry about his murderous rampage. Charlie was thankful for the old woman's relief. She had lived through too much already.

They departed with a promise to return. In Charlie's mind, it wouldn't be for a long time.

******

They had one last stop before they left the Gatineau Valley. The pedal boat bumped against the rock and Charlie was happy this was her final crossing of that river. She and Simm held hands as they watched Harley scamper through the forest. He sensed exactly where they headed.

Noah sprawled on an old wooden chair outside his cabin, looking as if he'd expected them. And maybe he had. Surely, he understood they wouldn't leave without saying a proper goodbye.

He stood as they approached, and Charlie thought she detected a glimmer of a smile through the density of his beard. It may have been wishful thinking on her part.

Bosco took a moment from frolicking with Harley to greet them, transferring a dose of slobber to their clothing, before rushing off to join his little friend.

"I want to thank you, Noah," Charlie said.

The man held up a large hand. "Don't say it. There's nothing to thank me for."

Charlie wouldn't be put off. "Yes, there is. You saved our lives. Especially after..." Charlie glanced at Simm. She didn't know how to phrase her next statement.

Noah took the task off her hands. "Especially after you suspected me of being a serial killer."

Redness seeped into Charlie's cheeks, but Simm chuckled beside her. "If it's any consolation, we suspected a lot of people," he said.

Noah's lips twisted in a wry grimace. "Yeah, that makes me feel a lot better."

Charlie took a bracing breath. "Noah, I may be sticking my nose where it doesn't belong, but I have to ask. Why are you here? Why do you look at this guy every day?" She swept her arm toward the enormous house that towered above the trees in front of Noah's cabin.

A pained expression crossed his face. "You're right. You are sticking your nose in my business, but I guess it's something you can't control." His gaze fixed on the ground. When he spoke, his voice was soft. "You don't know how painful it is to lose your entire family. Everyone that I loved most in this world was instantly gone."

Tears rushed to Charlie's eyes, and she did nothing to stop them from flowing. Her heart broke for this man.

"My life no longer had meaning," he said. "I wished I had died with them. Nothing mattered anymore." He straightened and shifted his wounded gaze to Charlie. "Except for one thing. I wanted to be near the people responsible for their deaths. I understand Lemieux is in prison, but Vaughn helped him get a light sentence." Noah gestured with his chin toward the water. "I know it sounds crazy, but it became an obsession for me. Ironically, it was the only thing that kept me sane."

Charlie swiped the wetness from her cheek. "Sane maybe, but constantly angry and in pain."

Noah nodded glumly.

Charlie looked at Simm to gauge his reaction. She didn't think it was the time to offer unproven theories. Her husband shook his head slightly in agreement.

Charlie laid her hand on the much larger, rougher one of the tormented man. "I can't even imagine what you're going through, but I truly hope you come to terms with it. I'll be thinking of you."

Simm stood. "If there's ever anything we can do for you, call us." He handed Noah a business card as his wife attached Harley's leash to his harness.

"Charlie," Noah said, straight-faced. "You don't want to use the washroom today? I don't mind."

Charlie's surprised expression turned into a wide smile. Noah had made a joke. She didn't know he had it in him.

CHAPTER 44

Charlie dipped a spoon into the steaming pot of spaghetti sauce. She tasted it with trepidation. Cooking wasn't one of her strong points, but she was determined to master the basics. As she added salt to the pot, she caught Simm's skeptical look.

"Trust me," she said. "It'll be good."

"Should I order a pizza, just in case?"

"No. You're going to like this."

"Is that a promise or an order?"

"Smarty-pants. It'll be as good as anything you make."

They had made their return to Montreal with mixed feelings. Charlie looked forward to leaving the cottage behind, with its stark memories of death and grief. She wanted to be in her home, in safety and comfort. But they knew they returned to a pub that an unknown hand had assaulted. The police hadn't caught the perpetrator, and the closer they got to Montreal, the harder Simm frowned. She realized, like her, he suspected Marcus was connected to the fire. And Vaughn was a direct link to Walter.

The bang and clatter of construction work rose through the floor to invade their apartment. Frank and the insurance company did everything possible to get the kitchen back in order, and the progress had pleasantly surprised Charlie. No traces of fire or water damage remained to ruin their homecoming.

Now, Charlie welcomed Simm's teasing. It was good to see a smile on his face and a glint in his eye.

An abrupt knock interrupted their banter. Their heads pivoted toward the apartment door as it swung open, and Walter Simmons stormed into the room.

"There you are." His voice trembled with rage. "What do you think you're doing?"

Charlie looked at her husband and saw his expression morph from surprise to anger to controlled calm.

"I was about to have a delicious meal with my wife. We didn't expect company." Simm spoke in a slow drawl.

"Don't be funny. You know what I'm talking about." Walt advanced toward them, his face twisted in anger. "You've invented some crazy theory about Tyson Vaughn, and now they've reopened the investigation. They caught the guy. Lemieux is in jail. Can't you keep your nose out of other people's business and leave things alone?"

"And what if Paul Lemieux is innocent?"

"How can he be? All the evidence pointed in his direction."

"Yeah, that was very convenient."

Walter's scowl deepened. "You better be careful with your accusations."

"And what will you do, Walt? Frame me for a crime I didn't commit?"

"I didn't frame anyone." His finger poked his own chest as he spoke.

"Marcus Vaughn did. Both of us know it." Simm leaned forward and placed his palms on the table that separated him from his brother. "What hand did you have in it?"

"I found him a lawyer. That's all."

Simm straightened. "I hope that's all. And, for your sake, I hope you had nothing to do with the case of arson here."

******

An uncharacteristic nervousness disturbed Charlie. It had nothing to do with the argument between Simm and his brother. Walt had taken off with a snarl, a frown, and a promise to return if things didn't go his way.

Simm, to Charlie's surprise, took the confrontation in stride and was at ease with his initial decision to talk to the police.

No, her jumpy nerves had to do with the imminent arrival of guests and the subject they would discuss. Charlie wanted to put the events in the Gatineau Valley behind her. Although the setting was lovely and she hoped to return one day, it would be a while before she'd purge the memories of the gruesome events that took place there.

Before she could do that, they had one last hurdle to leap.

Craig was the first to arrive. He strode a little straighter. His smile came a little easier.

Charlie wondered if she had over thought this day. Maybe it wouldn't be as difficult as expected.

Bryan and Megan advanced through the doorway as Charlie gave Craig a hug. They exchanged greetings and slid into the booth in the farthest corner of the bar. Holly and Alanna were the last to arrive, and awkward glances and smiles filled the silence.

Frank provided the much-needed distraction of taking drink orders while Charlie and Simm pulled up chairs beside the booth.

The police had informed the group of the findings in the case. The body found on the construction site of the wall had been identified as Damon's. The police unearthed Kurt Gibson's remains buried among the trees behind the root cellar.

Detective Marois had updated the family about the killer and his motives, however crazed they were, but Craig had called on Charlie and Simm to answer their remaining questions. The couple had agreed to do the best they could.

It was a disheartening hour as Charlie and Simm took turns revealing the details of the investigation and the discoveries. At Charlie's behest, they'd skirted the issue of possible torture and torment. Instead, they claimed the killer had kept the men captive before killing them quickly. The result was distressing but knowing your loved one had suffered for days before dying was too painful to bear or share.

A lightness filled Charlie when she saw the benefits of the get-together. Tears were shed, but long-suppressed questions were answered. The awkwardness of the situation lifted. She even witnessed a few hopeful glances between Craig and Holly.

Bryan cleared his throat and raised his hand to gain everyone's attention. All eyes swerved toward him, but none were more eager than Charlie's. Would they finally learn the mystery of his strange behavior?

"I have a small announcement," he said. "Megan and I are leaving Montreal."

Gasps of surprise and murmurs of disbelief followed his statement. The redness of Bryan's cheeks was visible despite the low lighting of the pub. "I bought a business in Wakefield."

It was Charlie's turn to gasp. Of all the explanations for his presence in Gatineau, that was the last one she suspected.

"That's what I was doing when Damon disappeared. And I've been back a couple of times since." Bryan's expression turned sheepish. "I didn't mention anything to Megan in case it didn't pan out, but we've wanted to move to a small town for a while." He shot a smile at his wife and took her hand. "Now, we're finally going to do it. But we'll be back to visit often. Our families are still here. And you guys, of course."

A weight lifted from Charlie's shoulders. Bryan wasn't involved in Damon's death or anything else illegal or immoral, and that made her feel better.

When the evening ended, they promised to keep in touch. Craig suggested a regular meeting at Butler's to catch up on each other's news, and everyone agreed.

Charlie and Simm held hands as they ascended the stairs to their apartment. The pub was locked down, and the employees were gone.

"I think we've ended that chapter of our life, don't you?" Charlie asked.

"Yeah, most of it wasn't pleasant." Simm stood with his back to her as he poured himself a glass of water.

"Most of it? What parts did you like?" Charlie leaned against the kitchen counter and crossed her arms.

Simm swiveled in her direction and smiled. "I enjoyed getting away alone with you. The pub is fun, and I enjoy being around people, but I like having you to myself."

"Likewise." Charlie circled her arms around his waist and leaned her cheek on his chest. "What else?" She needed to hear him speak the words, although she wasn't certain what they would be.

"I've learned I have two important things to consider."

Charlie grew impatient. "What are they?" she said.

"I may have missed private investigating more than I thought. I enjoyed getting back into it, especially with you by my side."

Charlie leaned back to look him in the eye. "Are you going to hang out your shingle again?"

Simm pursed his lips. "I don't wish to do it in a big way, but if someone asked me for help again, I'd probably go for it. Would that bother you?"

"Not at all. I see how much happier you are. It did you good to wet your feet again." She narrowed her eyes. "What's the other thing?"

Simm drew a deep breath. "I may consider having children. You're probably right about the nature versus nurture business. Look at Pete and Eddie. If it hadn't been for that accident, they may have lived their lives as brothers without a problem. Fate wasn't on their side." He kissed her. "Although, after what happened with Walt today, I don't understand why you'd want to have anything to do with our family genes."

Charlie smiled. "Your brother I can live without. I don't enjoy seeing the stress he causes you. But seeing how you handle him reassures me you'll be a great father. You'll make our kids toe the line."

An exaggerated pensive expression covered Simm's face. "If only I can figure out how to get you to do it."

THE END

ACKNOWLEDGEMENTS

There are many people who affect a writer's life, and some may not realize they've contributed. I'd like to acknowledge a few here.

First, thank you to my daughter, Rachel, who acted as a beta reader for this novel. Her insights and advice were encouraging, valuable, and greatly appreciated. To Timothy Sojka, a very talented thriller writer: your honest and sometimes brutal opinions helped shape this story into what it is, good or bad. I hope I've done your advice justice.

Howard Bruce answered questions about legal technicalities, and I thank him for taking the time to do so.

My brother-in-law, Tom McCarthy, and his partner, Donna Babin (a close friend of mine from high school) served as hosts and tour guides in the lovely region of Gatineau. Thank you for your hospitality and the sauna.

Thank you to Bosco for being who you are. Hopefully, Brianna and Jesse will let me borrow you again for another story. As Bri's mother, I claim certain privileges.

I'm often asked where my ideas come from. Some come out of nowhere, but most are planted with a tiny seed that someone slips into my ear. That is the case with *The Other Side*.

A few years ago, a weekend trip to a cottage with two other couples led to that seed. The cottage in this novel is the same as in real life, as is the pedal boat with the weight limit. The location was moved to Gatineau. The characters and the plot grew from my imagination. During that weekend, Margaret Baker McBain said, "Wouldn't it make a great book idea if someone went to the other side of the lake and vanished?" The seed. Thank you, Margaret.

I hope you enjoyed reading this story as much as I enjoyed writing it and watching it bloom.

ABOUT THE AUTHOR

The author of six mystery suspense novels, A.J. McCarthy is always on the lookout for new ideas. Her friends and family are cautious, concerned they may become a victim in her next novel. Those who are more adventurous offer up ideas and are willing to sacrifice certain family members for the cause. A.J. bides her time, waiting for the right moment and the perfect victim. She hides behind a quiet façade, and few know what she's really thinking. A.J. grew up reading Agatha Christie, Sidney Sheldon, and many other masters of mystery and suspense. A lifelong love of the genre evolved. She's a member of Crime Writers of Canada, Sisters in Crime, and International Thriller Writers. When she isn't writing, chances are she is reading.

NOTE FROM THE AUTHOR

Word-of-mouth is crucial for any author to succeed. If you enjoyed *The Other Side*, please leave a review online—anywhere you are able. Even if it's just a sentence or two. It would make all the difference and would be very much appreciated.

Thanks!
A.J. McCarthy

We hope you enjoyed reading this title from:

BLACK ☙ ROSE
writing™

www.blackrosewriting.com

Subscribe to our mailing list – *The Rosevine* – and receive **FREE** books, daily deals, and stay current with news about upcoming releases and our hottest authors.
Scan the QR code below to sign up.

Already a subscriber? Please accept a sincere thank you for being a fan of Black Rose Writing authors.

View other Black Rose Writing titles at
www.blackrosewriting.com/books and use promo code
PRINT to receive a **20% discount** when purchasing.